PENGUIN BOOKS

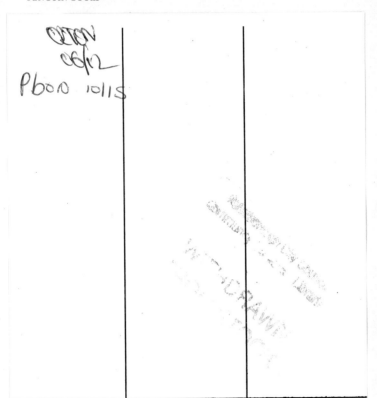

OTTON
06/12
Pb00 10/15

PETERBOROUGH LIBRARIES

This book is to be returned on or before the latest date shown above, but may be renewed up to three times if the book is not in demand. Ask at your local library for details.

Please note that charges are made on overdue books

Wild Abandon

JOE DUNTHORNE

PENGUIN BOOKS

PENGUIN BOOKS

Published by the Penguin Group
Penguin Books Ltd, 80 Strand, London WC2R ORL, England
Penguin Group (USA) Inc., 375 Hudson Street, New York, New York 10014, USA
Penguin Group (Canada), 90 Eglinton Avenue East, Suite 700, Toronto, Ontario, Canada M4P 2Y3
(a division of Pearson Penguin Canada Inc.)
Penguin Ireland, 25 St Stephen's Green, Dublin 2, Ireland (a division of Penguin Books Ltd)
Penguin Group (Australia), 250 Camberwell Road, Camberwell, Victoria 3124, Australia
(a division of Pearson Australia Group Pty Ltd)
Penguin Books India Pvt Ltd, 11 Community Centre, Panchsheel Park, New Delhi – 110 017, India
Penguin Group (NZ), 67 Apollo Drive, Rosedale, Auckland 0632, New Zealand
(a division of Pearson New Zealand Ltd)
Penguin Books (South Africa) (Pty) Ltd, Block D, Rosebank Office Park,
181 Jan Smuts Avenue, Parktown North, Gauteng 2193, South Africa

Penguin Books Ltd, Registered Offices: 80 Strand, London WC2R ORL, England

www.penguin.com

First published by Hamish Hamilton 2011
Published in Penguin Books 2012
001

Typeset by Jouve (UK), Milton Keynes
Printed in England by Clays Ltd, St Ives plc

B-format ISBN: 978-0-141-03395-2

www.greenpenguin.co.uk

MIX
Paper from
responsible sources
FSC   FSC™ C018179
www.fsc.org

ALWAYS LEARNING

For my sisters

I

'First off, the sky goes dark.'

'Of course it does.'

'Then they come out the ground and, if you're a certain type of person, drag you under, where your body is consumed.'

They got to the gate of the pen and Kate opened it, letting her brother through first.

'And I'm guessing you are that type of person,' he said.

She slid the bolt back across while he ran ahead, his boots squelching in the mud. Walking on, she watched him duck under the low roof, slapping the wooden joist with his free hand as he went inside the shelter. At eleven years old, her brother awoke every day buzzing. Everything he saw in these first few hours – the gravestones of pets, log piles, frost – deserved a high five.

'I'm gonna milk the face off you,' Albert told the goats. 'I'm going to milk you to death.'

He did resemble a trainee grim reaper, she thought, in his deep-hooded navy poncho, carrying a bucket to collect fresh souls. Following him into the shelter, she sat on a low stool next to Belona – her favourite goat, a four-year-old Alpine with white legs and a black comma-shaped beard – who was against the back wall with her neck tied. She stamped her hooves as she ate from her feed pan. Belona was notoriously difficult in the mornings; this was part of her and Kate's affinity.

Albert was talking as he milked. '. . . so she has this massive picture of what's at the centre of the universe and it's basically a pair of eyes – two huge evil eyes . . .'

Kate tried not to listen. She squeezed, tugged, closed her fingers from index to pinkie and focused on the noise of milk on metal; the sound slowly deadened as the bucket filled. She put her ear against

Belona's side and listened to the gurgling innards. The swell and slump of the goat's breathing.

'. . . and research shows, you'll have to wave bye-bye to gravity and time and university and . . .'

'*Albert.*'

He stopped talking but she knew his speech continued, unbroken, inside his head. She started to get a rhythm going, two-handed, fingers finally warming. Her brother, meanwhile, played his goat like an arcade machine.

'One nil,' he said, as he picked up his bucket and stool, and moved to the other side of the divider. He put a feed pan in front of Babette and she immediately dug in.

Belona started battling a little, her legs jerking, clanging against the bucket. With her knuckles, Kate stroked the tassels that hung from the goat's jaw and, leaning over, whispered to her.

'What are you saying?'

'Nothing.'

'Are you in love with Belona? That's okay if you are. Mum and Dad won't mind. They're totally easy with whatever. They just want you to be in a loving relationship.'

Belona kicked and the bucket tipped – spilling half the milk on to the mud and straw. Kate's jaw tightened.

Her brother, through years of collecting words from international visitors to the community, had compiled an armoury of exotic insults. He tutted and proceeded to call her something bad in Bengali.

It was just getting light. There was the smell of hay and shit. Hooves skittered on the stones. Outside the gloomy hut she could see the rain still coming down in the pen, filling the holes left by their boots.

Back at the yard, Albert poured his milk into a dented churn. Spots of mud and dirt camouflaged themselves among the freckles on his face. His right earhole, she noticed, held a cache of grit. She often tried to convince him that it was a duty, as someone brought up in a community, to battle stereotypes by maintaining, as she did, exceptional levels of hygiene. Albert wasn't interested. He longed to summon a bodily stench, regularly checking his armpits and foreskin – waiting for the big day – taking wafts from his fingertips like a sommelier testing a vintage.

She waited, then said 'tick', which was the signal. He looked at her, blinked – said 'tock' – then ran, letting the empty bucket clang on the brick.

They sprinted round the front of the house, skidding on gravel, in through the open double doors, up the wide stairs, side by side, a trail of mud across the landing, up more stairs and into the large shared bathroom. She was too old for this but without her she doubted he would ever get clean. They raced to undress.

Kate sat on the bench and yanked off her muddy boots, then peeled away her socks. Unbuttoning her jeans, she let them pool at her feet. Albert was kneeling, working determinedly at his laces, which he had finally learned to tie, but too well. Kate turned away from him and pulled her jumper and T-shirt off in one, uncovering three well-tended spots in the centre of her chest and, despite her posture that tried to hide them and a bra designed to downplay them, her breasts. Albert, seeing that his sister was already down to her underwear, became a frenzy of pushing and tugging, kicking at his boots, getting his hoodie stuck on his head, a line-caught trout, flapping on the tiles. She sat on the bench and pulled down her thermal long johns and knickers in a crouch. Kate's shoulder-length hair was the red colour of late-stage rust, though the box had called it 'vampiric'. She dyed her pubic hair too. Unclipping her bra, she stepped over Albert, who was just getting free of his boots, and slipped under the shower head, spun the tap-wheel to starboard. The applause of water rushing over her. Silt and mud and hay ran in clockwise swirls towards the plug.

'Go back to Velcro,' she said.

The creature responded in Malay.

Finally Albert yanked off his jumper and wriggled out of his trousers and pants. Kate blinked at his skinny, china-white body, full complement of visible ribs, hip bones sharp as flints, glowing knees, dick like a popped balloon.

'Cold, cold, cold,' he said and, getting to his feet, launched himself under the water. Kate, with a matador's grace, took a step back and raised her arms to avoid making contact with him. He hopped from foot to foot in the steam. His goosebumps sank. The water at their feet turned the colour of the liquid on top of Patrick's home-made yoghurt.

'Tick tock,' Albert said. 'How long have we got left?'

'A minute, maybe less.'

The community used a small, solar-powered, forty-litre water heater that gave up easily and now, in late April, would be overachieving if it got four people clean. When the shower 'turned' – channelling deep-chilled hill water – the screams of visiting backpackers could be heard from the bottom of the garden. Kate and Albert knew there was only time for pits and bits. No exfoliant, no conditioner.

'Not long left,' Kate said. 'You know what to do.'

Albert bowed his head. Squeezing out a palmful of egg yolk and oatmeal shampoo, she splatted it on his scalp, rubbed it around quickly then blasted him with the shower head.

'You're clear. Now me.' Kate doused her head under the water, then took a dollop of the grey shampoo and spread it on. 'We have a problem,' she said. 'No lather. Find the contraband.'

Hidden among the tall lotions and emollients huddled on a corner shelf at the back of the cubicle, Albert located a travel-size bottle of Pantene that one of the wwoofers had smuggled in.

The shampoo bloomed into froth on her scalp. Her brother watched the foam drift down her back, bum, legs. They started to feel the water temperature drop.

'How long?' he asked.

'Seconds.'

They began the countdown together.

'Five, four . . .'

Kate quickly dealt with her armpits.

'. . . three, two . . .'

They clambered out of the shower, soap-blind, feeling for the clothes rail, arms out like the undead, clamping towels around them just as the column of ice descended. Kate reached in and spun the tap off.

They sat breathing on the cork-topped bench, wrapped up, Kate's towel tucked above her breasts, their backs making wet patches on the floral wallpaper.

After a while, Albert spread his towel out in the middle of the bathroom floor.

'Albert, please don't do this.'

He crawled into a ball on the towel, his head between his knees. Goosebumps spread across his arms and legs.

She counted the teeth of his spinal column.

'What am I?'

'Too old for this.'

'What am I?'

'Annoying.'

He shivered a little.

'*No.* What am I?'

'A bomb?'

'Nope. Try again.'

For Kate, it was these moments *after* showering that were the real problem. He still behaved and looked like a child, but somehow she could sense puberty's greasy palm on his shoulder. She was damn sure she didn't want to be sharing a bathroom with her brother when it took hold. This would have to be the last time; she couldn't do it any more.

'A tumour?'

'Guess again.'

'A sack of bones?'

'No.'

'An empty shell?'

'No, sir.'

'A failed experiment?'

'Nuh-uh.'

Plus there was the thought of what the boys at her sixth-form college would say if they knew this happened. *You get soaped up with your brother? Is that how they do it in the commune? Dark . . .*

Fuck you, don't you dare judge me, she thought, making a mental note to carry that resentment into her morning classes. For the last seven months she had been studying at Gorseinon College, finishing her English, Politics, History and Sociology A-levels, since there were no adults in the community who she considered sufficiently 'specialist' to teach her. Prior to that, all her schooling had taken place in the community – with her brother – and, not unusually for home-educated children, they were substantially ahead of schedule, academically, compared to their state-educated peers. She had arrived at college with the expectation that it would be entirely populated by sexual predators and intelligence-hating dullards and, as a result of this, she had spoken to almost no one. Her first term had been characterized by walking fast between classes with a fearsome lean, bringing her own intimidatingly Tupperwared vegetarian lunches and working *really* hard. As a result, no one spoke to her either. By the start of her second term she had conditional offers from Cambridge and Edinburgh and an unconditional from Leeds, all of which confirmed her belief that she had been right not to make friends. The downside was that she had no one to whom she could actually say: *Fuck you, don't you dare judge me.*

'Oh no, hang on,' Kate said, pretending to puff on a pipe. 'Are you . . . a boulder?' He was always a boulder. He didn't say anything. He didn't like her to guess too quickly.

'Alright. Are you the last remaining human?'

'Not yet.'

'Or are you a boulder?'

'Yes!' he said, and he stood up, putting his hands in the air, his nipples like freckles. 'I'm a boulder!'

She picked his towel up and wrapped it round him.

'Great. Now get out.'

Albert pulled open the door and ran into the corridor. She put on her dressing gown and attacked her hair with the towel. There was a *thuk thuk thuk* sound coming from next door, her parents' bedroom. She knew what it meant: the community had recently held one of its open days to find new members. On these occasions, the farm was awash with all kinds of lost and cheery wayfarers as well as, quite often, an 'undercover' journalist pretending to be a primary school teacher. To become a full-time member you had to volunteer (and do shit jobs: cleaning tools, turning compost, infinite weeding) then have an initial short interview which, if approved, was followed by a minimum two-week stay (recommended six weeks), then a cooling-down break of at least one month, then another, more-involved interview to decide on full-time suitability. It was an undoubted power trip for the panel – particularly Kate's father, Don Riley, who, still stinging from a failed Oxford interview when he was eighteen, took great pleasure in devising questions.

Q: If there's a power cut and it's cold inside and out, how do you dry your clothes?

(A: Washing lines in the polytunnels.)

Q: If you were to cook a communal meal using seasonal ingredients, what would it be?

Arlo Mela was, famously, the only person who, having made elaborate culinary promises in interview, produced, as promised, a game-changing chocolate millefeuille.

'New members must have realistic expectations of us, and of themselves,' was how her father put it. 'Beware strangers promising *bouillabaisse*.'

The combination of a ruthless selection process and a high likelihood of mental illness among applicants had, over the years, produced some interesting correspondence. The community sent a primly bureaucratic template response to all abusive letters. *Thank you for your generous feedback . . .* Their father, however, was thin-skinned when it came to criticism of the community – he took everything as a personal attack – and liked to write replies, even though he never sent them. The typewriter allowed for maximum release of tension. *Thuk thuk.* In a similar way, everyone knew if Kate and Albert's mother was upset because a pile of newly chopped wood would appear in the barn.

The community had a guestbook and a detestbook, the latter containing choice quotes from twenty years of occasional hate mail. Highlights included a drawing of the barn in flames and a comprehensive list of unflattering anagrams of residents' names (only one of which stuck: Patrick Kinwood, a no-work dick-tip). Both books were on public display in the entrance hall to manage the expectations of new visitors.

But when Kate pushed into her parents' bedroom, she found that it was, in fact, her mother at the desk in the corner, fully dressed, writing at the beige Smith Corona. Her dark hair ran down to her armpits, parting over her shoulders. She was wearing a woollen jumper the colour of margarine. Kate watched her forefinger locate a letter on the keyboard, hover above, then drop. Noticing her daughter behind her, Freya stopped typing and rested her hands on the desk.

'What's going on?' Kate said, and massaged her mother's tightly upholstered shoulders. She read the letter, if it could be called that. There were just two words, *Dear* and *Don*.

Kate turned to look at her dad, who was in bed, sat up against the headboard. He always kept two pillows under his right foot because he said it needed 'to drain'. He had a thick castaway's beard – badly maintained – a trophy of unemployability. His children had no way of knowing whether he was strong- or weak-chinned.

'Dad, why aren't you up?'

'I *am* up,' he said, which was the same thing that Kate said when she wasn't up. He was in his pyjamas.

It was not unusual for her parents to fight; it *was* unusual for them to do it quietly. Even if Kate had somehow slept through the original row (not easy, given the thin shared wall between their bedrooms) then she would have expected her mother to come next door and wake her up, just to tell her about it. Ever since Kate had hit puberty, her mother spoke to her with total transparency – this extended both to her parents' relationship (*Mum, can you please not call it a relationship? You're supposed to be married*) and to the community at large. It was from her mother that Kate had learned that Patrick Kinwood, who she had always believed was penniless and possibly ex-homeless, was a former greetings-card franchise regional manager and, since the community had a pay-what-you-can system, he made by far the largest monthly contribution. Such disclosures were part of why Kate and Freya were actual friends. Being actual friends with her own mother only started to worry Kate after she saw other South Wales mothers and daughters walking ten paces apart through town.

'What's wrong with you two?' Kate said.

'Nothing's wrong,' Don said, speaking to the back of his wife's head.

Freya didn't turn round.

'Fine, I'm putting this in the repressed memories box.'

Kate went next door to her room and started getting dressed for college. She was wary of being labelled a hippy so avoided the obvious stigma-magnets: long dresses, cardigans, bangles – of which she, shamefully, had many. From the hallway, there was the scrape of something heavy being dragged along the floorboards.

She wore narrow blue jeans that didn't need cycle clips, black breathable trainers, a thermal vest under a lumberjack shirt that was warm but could easily be opened via poppered buttons when tackling the big hills, and a waxed yellow anorak with a peaked hood that her boyfriend liked because he said it tricked other boys into thinking she wasn't attractive. She opened her bedroom door and found a wall there, inexpertly built from shoeboxes, luggage and the wicker dressing-up box.

'Albert, I'm late.'

'This is not an exit,' the wall said.

'You know I don't like going, but I have to.'

'Apologies for the inconvenience.'

'I'm going to knock this over now, okay?'

As she pushed a load-bearing shoebox, the structure toppled into the hall. Albert was standing back, in his dressing gown, with the solemn look of a squatter watching the developers move in. She clambered over the rubble and made her way downstairs. Her brother climbed over the first-floor banister and hung from the handrail, his feet dangling. She stood beneath him, on the bottom step.

He said: 'If you go, I will end myself.'

'You wouldn't die. You probably wouldn't even break your legs.'

'I'll turn in mid-air so I land on my head.'

She saw that the bottom of his left foot still carried its foliage of verrucas. He'd promised her they'd gone. She reminded herself again: no more shared showers.

She walked across the hall, ignoring a Portuguese wwoofer who was sitting on the tiled floor, crying, with the house phone held to her ear.

'You have to tell me everything!' Albert yelled as his sister opened the front door. 'It's not fair for you to know things I don't know!'

As she walked outside, she heard her brother screaming that he was now in fact dead. His most ambitious attempt to stop her going to college had been a typewritten letter, purportedly from her principal, that began:

> *Dear Kate,*
> *I find you a real downer.*

She understood why it was hard for her brother. Now she wasn't around, there was only one other young person at the community whom he could have lessons with, and that was Isaac, who was six. It was a long way from when Kate was her brother's age and the community was awash with bright, multilingual children with dazzling names. (Stand up, Elisalex De Aalwis.) With classes of nearly a dozen young people of all different ages, subject matter had been pitched to the cleverest person, but with simpler alternatives. Their education had peaked with Arlo's now infamous class on cinquecento Italian architecture, which involved a high-level discussion of the villas of Palladio alongside an ambitious attempt to build 'La Rotonda' from Lego. Other popular lessons included Patrick's introduction to centrifugal force, with its reliance on fearless young volunteers with coins in their pockets. But since then, the numbers of young people at the community had dwindled, and nowadays it was unusual for lessons to consist of anything more than Albert and Isaac, at the dining table, quietly filling out workbooks.

As the first new young person in nearly two years, Isaac had been highly prized for how he tilted the community's age-profile. That was the main reason he and his mother had survived their trial week and got an interview; no one had particularly trusted her; her luggage included a Yeo Valley tote bag that contained the full back catalogue of a pamphlet series entitled *The Paradigm Won't Shift Itself*. Kate felt bad that her brother had no other friends, but she couldn't hold back her own life to keep him entertained.

Kate got her bike from the barn, the basket preloaded with books.

After breakfast, Albert and Isaac sat in the schoolroom, side by side on the Kirman rug, cross-legged, each with a notepad. Albert was practising trying to draw a perfect freehand circle. Isaac chewed his pencil like corn on the cob. He had a fringe halfway down his forehead and a few, ideally placed, freckles. With his startling white-blond hair, all the better for being badly cut, and a burlesque redness to his lips, adults were prone to falling silent in his presence.

Patrick went to stand in front of the TV to give his lesson. He was wearing a green fleece that, as it happened, for the first time in more than a decade, did not smell of bong water. Patrick was fifty-eight but seemed older, had a likeable, shapeless nose, watery eyes and big glowing ears that looked hot enough to dry socks on. After five clear-headed days, he was glad of the opportunity to share his intellectual energy. It was a rarity, nowadays, for the boys to be getting a formal lesson, so they were excited too.

'Okay, guys,' Patrick said. 'Have either of you ever seen an advert before?'

'Of course we have,' Albert said. 'We're not idiots.'

'I saw one about people who work in aeroplanes,' Isaac said.

'I saw one about this excellent soup,' Albert said.

Patrick held his palms out. 'So you haven't seen many?'

Isaac shook his head, the pencil clamped in his mouth.

'Good. And that's why our community is great. But the important thing to remember is that adverts are not bad, *per se*, you've just got to know how to handle them. We'll start with something easy.'

Patrick pressed play on the video recorder. There was a low-budget advert for a furniture warehouse in Pontypridd. It showed a couple in the showroom falling backwards on to a white leather three-seater, their legs kicking up in the air.

All this week, only this week, 50 per cent off everything.

It showed the sofa being lifted out of a van and then it cut to the couple snuggling on the same sofa – but this time in their home.

Come on down, we've gone soft in the head for sofas and beds!

Patrick paused the video, pulled across the Ad-Guard and muted the TV. Albert and Isaac stayed staring up at the bright shapes and colours behind the square of shower curtain.

'I'll let you think about it,' Patrick said.

They waited in silence.

'Okay, what do you think?'

Isaac looked at Albert, who said: 'I think that – if we needed some furniture – then now would be a good time to get it, because of the discount.'

'Very true. What do you think, Isaac?'

'I don't know. It was loud.'

'Good. Why was it loud?'

'So we can hear it.'

'Good. Why do they want us to hear it?'

Isaac winced and started working the tip of the pencil into the sole of his shoe.

'Okay, fine. Okay. Let's talk about sales language. "We've gone soft in the head for sofas and beds."'

Patrick said it in a game-show host voice and Albert laughed.

'Yeah, it's funny,' Isaac said.

'The advert shows this smiley couple, bleached teeth, glossy hair, picking up the sofa, being all contented' – Patrick mimed carrying one end of a sofa and then grinned, his teeth brown at the edges – 'and says that if you buy this soft furnishing you can be like them.'

'They are just an example,' Albert said. 'How could we be like them?'

'We can't,' Isaac said.

'*That's just it,*' Patrick said, putting one finger to the tip of his nose and, with the other hand, pointing at Isaac. '*Very* good. It's aspirational. People think they will be like them if they buy the sofa, but they can't be.'

'Who thinks that?' Albert said.

'Stupid people,' Patrick said.

'I don't believe you. Are you sure?'

'Absolutely.'

'Who are they?' Isaac said.

Patrick opened his mouth and then shut it. 'Let's try another one. This is a bit different.'

He pulled back the Ad-Guard, then picked up the remote control with both hands. Coming off the weed had had a strange impact on his relationships to children. He had discovered a desire to pass on knowledge from his own life. *Knowledge from his own life.* That was a new concept. He had spent two unstoned days preparing the video. He should have been helping to re-anchor the fences, but his shoulder, which was known to dislocate at the slightest encouragement – in the bath, reaching for the contraband shampoo, for example – kept him indoors. He recorded hours of adverts and tried to ignore the distant *dop-dop-dop* of the post rammer. It'd been twenty years since he and Don had sat down with a map of their farm's fifty acres – dividing it up with Biro. They had lifted tonnes of freestone into the back of their narrow Bedford van and driven it across the fields. Slowly, shirtlessly, they had dug trenches, stacked stones, Tetris-style, and said almost nothing to each other, except in the pure language of manual labour, coming home each day sunburnt and ennobled – and in truth, everyone else found them pretty irritating, with their tiredness-as-honour schtick, as though they could return to the big house after a full day's *real work* and just drop like, yes, stones, expecting admiration and exemption from washing up.

He pressed play on the remote. The screen went blank, then the Channel 4 ident appeared. 'Here we go.'

It was a long car advert – thirty seconds – with a soundtrack of intricate electro. It showed a man in a silver car disintegrating into atoms, then reforming as a toboggan team being led by the same man, then disintegrating again and reforming as a snow leopard climbing an impossibly steep slope, the man a glint in the animal's eye, then disintegrating and reforming as two ballet dancers, the man and a beautiful Eastern European-looking woman, spinning on a lake, performing a difficult lift, before turning back into the car in a Nordic landscape, with the man driving but, now, the ballet dancer in the passenger seat, smiling, brushing snow off his shoulders. The car was called the Avail.

Patrick paused the video. He hadn't noticed but Isaac and Albert were standing up.

'Motherfucker,' Albert said.

'Brilliant,' Isaac said.

They hugged.

'What you have to remember is that every advert wants you to think something; what does this one want you to think?'

'The car is an amazing car,' Albert said.

'What a car,' Isaac said, putting his arm round Albert's waist.

'You see what it's done to you?'

Don was watching from the doorway. He was wearing a jumper with the sleeves rolled up. He had stripes of mud on his forehead and cheeks. His beard had an actual twig in it, which seemed, to Patrick, a bit much.

'What's happening, Pat?' Don said, squinting at the frozen image on the screen.

'Media Studies.'

'It's amazing, Dad,' Albert said, and he ran to his father and lightly headbutted his stomach.

'Oh-kay,' Don said, squeezing his son's shoulder, 'and what are you learning about?'

In 2002, Don had invented the Ad-Guard after Kate, aged seven, had learned a dance to an advert for yoghurts. Pat remembered Don's speech at the meeting that evening, where he said he could whistle the tunes to, he estimated, nearly 200 adverts, and he sang ('Everyone's a fruit and nut case, it keeps you going when you toss the caber . . .'), delivered slogans with perfect intonation ('It looks *and tastes* as good as fresh meat') and then he said: 'Wouldn't it be better if our children could remember the words to poems, or songs, or stories? "Loveliest of trees, the cherry now / Is hung with bloom along the bough / And stands about the woodland ride / Wearing white for Eastertide."' This was in the days when his speeches really carried weight. He said he wasn't suggesting they get rid of the TV entirely and – to seal the deal – he revealed his

Ad-Guard, already made and ready to be glued on, cut from a square of shower curtain, attached to a rail, translucent enough to tell when adverts had finished, but misty enough to hide their content.

'I thought it'd be good to teach them how to understand adverts,' Patrick said, watching Don's eyes narrow, 'what they're trying to achieve – and, as a result, remove their power.'

Both men knew that Don, with dirt on his forearms, grit in his T-zones, had the authority. '*Whatever* experiences we have – no matter how we try to mediate them – affect us,' Don said, putting his hand on top of Albert's head, 'and particularly young minds in ways we *can't* comprehend.'

Isaac watched, looking back and forth as they spoke.

'But at some point they're going to have to face seeing adverts,' Patrick said. 'They should know how to deal with them.'

'That's just it, Pat – that's an assumption I'm not willing to make. Everything we see is a choice.'

A vein forced its way to the surface of Patrick's neck. There were still another six adverts on the tape. He had planned the lesson so that, at the end, there would be a couple of funnies to lighten things up: one about a talking sloth and another about an army of dancing bacteria.

Kate's first class was History. Leanne – they used tutors' first names – was a large lady who kept her grey hair in a neat plait and wore local artists' brooches in trapezium and rhomboid shapes. Her teaching style was to speak for the entire hour, with the implicit understanding that students were free to tune in and out, at will. Today, she was talking about Von Stauffenberg's failed assassination attempt on Hitler. When she talked about a briefcase with a bomb in it, she lifted up her own briefcase to help the class understand. When she read Nazi propaganda, she allowed herself an accent.

Kate's mind kept drifting, trying to puzzle out the memory of her mother at the typewriter, writing a letter to someone who was in the same room.

Later, at lunch, she realized she had left her packed lunch in the fridge. Blaming Albert, she wished him a painful, head-led landing on the bottom step. Knowing that her sandwiches, unclaimed for a whole morning, would now be under communal jurisdiction, she made her way to the canteen. That was where she had first met Geraint. On that occasion also, it had been her brother's fault: as part of his campaign to make her terminally late for college, he had hidden all Tupperware and cling film. It was a pleasing irony that her brother's attempts to sabotage her life had led to her meeting her boyfriend.

She remembered that day: it was not only her first time in the canteen, but her first time in *any* canteen. Her initial impressions of it had been largely as expected: blue trays and yellow food – chips, garlic bread, breaded turkey burger. The only hot vegetarian option had been cauliflower cheese, so she had picked that, with water-logged carrots. After paying, she looked for somewhere to sit, realizing that she knew this moment too – this awkward searching for a seat, peering around half-casually. There was something comforting about finally taking part in mainstream rituals. No one had invited her to join them. The only other person sitting on their own had been Kit Lintel, well known in college though not well liked; Kit practised parkour, or as he called it, *the art of movement*, around the blocky college car-park stairwells and could often be seen standing neatly on the corner of a high wall with his arms out like Christ the Redeemer. She sat at an empty table.

She had trouble cutting through the cauliflower's toupee of cheese. It looked bad but, once she got it in her mouth, there was no denying some talent at work. Was she imagining nutmeg? She made semiconscious *mmming* sounds. The cauliflower cheese's delicious-ness was the point at which the actual canteen had parted ways with the canteen of her imagination. And that's when she had found her boyfriend-to-be standing over her with a full plate: beef lasagne, chips, lettuce.

'You're in my sociology class,' he said, putting his tray down. 'I sometimes see you cycling in. I drive past you in my car. I'm Geraint.' A man of simple statements. His voice had the pitch-shifting quality of the Llanelli Welsh, like a slightly chewed cassette.

'Hi,' she said, holding her hand to cover her mouth, still chewing.

That was it. That was all he had needed. He began to eat. She had never thought of herself as a slow eater until that point. He poured the lasagne in. His teeth patted the food on the way past, as though encouraging a long-distance runner. She watched his throat pulse as he drank his squash. As a general rule, she despised carnivores, even those who only ate 'happy meat', but something about Geraint (did he even know lasagne contained beef?) made him different.

That day, they had got down to some logistically awkward heavy petting across the bucket seats of his Punto. They had known nothing about each other and this was ideal. From then on, once or twice a week, they would consume one another, and afterwards he would ask to drive her home, and she would say no. That was the pattern. She didn't want him to see where she lived, because she knew it would change his opinion of her. When he finally pushed for a reason, she said, 'Because my brother would try to kill you,' which wasn't a complete lie. Since Albert had spotted a slug-like love-bite on her neck, he had been making threats: 'Tell whoever is sucking your blood I will not stop till there's a stake through their heart.'

Patrick was sitting on the flat roof, legs hanging over the edge, with his back to the stand-alone bath that – for most of the year – was a velvety green pond, dense with frogspawn. A VHS labelled *Are Ads Bad?* lay next to him. A halo of aphids circled his head. He stayed out there for a long time, his hands growing numb in the cold, as he ran through the stages that had got him to this point.

Eight days ago, Don had taken him aside after dinner, sat him down by the fireplace and offered constructive feedback on the meal Patrick had just cooked. This in itself he could forgive because – according to Patrick's pet theory – Don only became condescending when something bad was happening in his personal life. Patrick had noted that, during times of marital strain, Don would aggressively encourage individuals to streamline their recycling process, for example. But since nobody had heard Don and Freya fighting this time, it was unclear what had been the catalyst. There were no other major issues: the community was financially secure (mainly thanks to Patrick, it ought to be said) and Don's implicit position as 'leader' had long ceased to be something worth questioning. So, when Don had put his hand on Patrick's shoulder and uttered the words 'I thought you might be interested in some feedback on your tagine', Patrick had responded by asking if there was anything that *he* wanted to talk about and Don had frowned as though not understanding.

After that feedback session, in which Don suggested that perhaps Patrick's tastebuds were being damaged by how much weed he smoked, Patrick, throbbing with a pure kind of humiliation that only Don seemed capable of provoking, had walked across the yard, past the workshop, through the market garden and back to his geodesic dome, which, with its many panels, had suddenly seemed to Patrick to have the melancholy look of a partly deflated football, kicked to a corner and forgotten. Once inside, Patrick sat on the sofa and worked his one-hitter until it was too hot to hold without gloves, which was his usual way to de-stress.

Next morning, with his eyes not visibly open, he went to the airing cupboard beneath the staircase where he dried his soggy, mellow home-grown and discovered there wasn't any. That was okay because he was expecting a visit from Karl Orland that lunchtime. Karl was a singer-songwriter and steel-guitar man who funded his lifestyle by selling baggies of bush weed. But Karl Orland didn't turn up. Patrick had hoped one of the wwoofers or day volunteers would have an eighth he could buy. He went round, asking, making sure only to approach people in enclosed, private spaces because he didn't want Don to see him 'talking to new people' and think it was the result of one of his improving suggestions. But the whole farm was dry, there wasn't even any resin.

That night, Patrick had cleared out the carved wooden smoking box and found enough leftovers for a spliff. The next morning he smoked the dog-ends in his CN Tower-replica stand-up ashtray. That night he scraped out the cone of his ice-bong and chewed on the tarry gak. Then there was nothing left. *Fine*, he thought, *I'll stop smoking for a few days. Either that or Karl will come.*

For two days he had done well, enjoying renewed energy, hand-eye coordination and inklings of short-term memory. He continued to steer clear of Don who, he feared, would sense his straightness and come and give him a big encouraging hug.

On the morning of the third day, strip lights had batted on in Patrick's mind's attic. Junked memories. Cardboard boxes, one labelled *my version of events* and another, *knowledge to pass on*. He decided that, for too long, Don had made him feel that he had nothing of value to teach the children. So he made lesson plans. 'Introduction to the Political Spectrum'. 'Ideas of Class in Modern Britain'. 'The Invention of the Teenager'. 'Are Ads Bad?'

On the morning of the fourth day, he had woken up angry. He had not been angry in years. He found young people – by which he meant wwoofers, people in their twenties – awful.

On the morning of the fifth day, there emerged – the worst of all his symptoms – the first gnawings of sexual desire. He had walked out of the dome in his green fleece and wellies and, as he passed the seedbeds, saw Janet, wearing a wartime work shirt and fingerless gloves, her hair pinned with chopsticks, surrounded by a group of keen-looking young volunteers. She had on one of her own necklaces.

Janet was one of the community's founding members and ran a successful mail-order business – Accessories to Murder – making and selling one-off pieces of proto-Gothic recycled jewellery: earrings of diary keys, necklaces made from shattered windscreen glass, antique lockets that opened on to photos of keyhole surgery in the small intestine. Her work sold internationally. Fashion magazines loved that she spent half of each year in a commune and – as Patrick saw whenever he periodically looked her up online – *Elle* magazine wrote: 'From horticulture to haute couture, both her lifestyles are controlled by the seasons.' In more than one interview, she had said that the community 'kept her sane'. Every now and then a groupie would visit, just to spend a few days cleaning the tool shed under her modish command. For the past decade, she had been spending April–September at the community and October–March in Bristol, where her studio was. Half her earnings, for the half of the year she wasn't in Bristol, came back to the community. Don had given Patrick a copy of *The Waste Land* with the first few lines highlighted, since every April she cruelly swept back in, creative and healthy, with her perfect work-life balance, handing out gifts of last season's stock. This last time she had returned with a boyfriend. After years of failed relationships with handy, politically switched-on men, there was Stephan, who lived in Clifton and represented – and was proud to represent – the victory of market forces. This was Patrick's pet theory, anyway. He hated himself for needing a pet theory. The six months Janet spent away each year were never quite enough time to forget her. Even with the dampened libido that his bong helped maintain, he still found green shoots of sexual desire each springtime. It didn't help that she made him presents – this year, a signet ring with a cattle brand instead of a family crest.

As he walked passed her, this morning, he had heard her lecturing the wwoofers: 'A frost this late will murder tomato transplants, aubergines, sweet peas, and put onions, broccoli and kale on suicide watch . . .' Cloches, blankets, unclaimed jackets, rugs and tarpaulins were piled up in the yard, ready to insulate the vegetables. He watched her hot breath clouding as she sent the young people to work.

It was helpful then to have the distraction of teaching Albert and Isaac an important lesson about advertising – that was until Don had stepped in to flex his ideology, at which point Patrick had come up to the flat roof to cool off. That was some hours ago. His hands were now so cold that he couldn't close them properly.

He didn't hear Don, presently, climbing out of the window. Instead, he felt a hand on his shoulder as Don lowered himself down and sat next to him on the edge of the bitumen roof.

'Wondered where you'd gone. I'm *really* sorry if I embarrassed you earlier, Pat – I didn't mean to, if I did – but I just think sometimes it's better for the children to be innocent of that stuff.'

Patrick stared out at the farm. He didn't want Don to see his unbloodshot eyes. It was vital not to give him the satisfaction. So, in mimic of his old self, Patrick got out his pipe, a brass one-hitter, and turned his body away from Don. Patrick still carried all the paraphernalia with him. With his half-numb hands, he managed to open a small plastic bag that was now filled with cherry tobacco. He tore off a bit and tamped it down into the cone.

'I noticed that one of those things was a car advert,' Don said. 'An executive Saab. The same car as the one that Janet's new fella drives.' Don made an elaborate *hmmm* sound, then put his hand on Patrick's thigh and tried a little warmly mocking laugh but didn't quite nail it, the warm part. Everyone in the community knew when Janet's boyfriend came up the drive because his car, as Don had observed, sounded like the MGM lion. The geodesic dome was right beside the lane and the engine noise, as it passed, vibrated Patrick's book-case.

'Yes,' Patrick said, staring straight ahead. 'It's the same car.'

'It Has Been Noted,' Don said in his *Big Brother* voice, making his eyes go wide. 'So many other women here, Pat. I'll say it again: take a break from the grass. Rediscover that crazy libido. Unleash some famous PK charm.'

'It's not famous,' Patrick said, then took a deep breath, pushing his shoulders back to open his lungs.

'Some of these *wwoof*ers coming through,' Don said, pointing down towards a volunteer in three-quarter-length jeans who was selecting unconventionally shaped cucumbers. 'Woof.'

'You're off the mark.'

'Still hung up on Janet after how long? If you stopped smoking so much green, you'd realize.'

To Patrick, there were few things more galling than Don being right about a thing.

'Not so.'

'Well, you *should* be hung up on her, Pat. She's tremendous.'

'That was a long time ago.'

'Isn't there a saying about love not knowing what time it is, or some such?'

Patrick patted his chest for the shape of a lighter in his shirt pocket. He hooked it out with his forefinger. Shielding the pipe with one hand, he lit it and sucked the whole lot through in one, in the style of a hit, his lungs burning.

'I get the feeling it's not easy for you to see Janet with someone like that,' Don said. 'Do you see a little of your old self in him?'

Patrick's chest pulsed – he held on for a few seconds longer – then let the smoke out in a megaphone shape, blowing it away from Don.

'I guess it's easier to talk about an advert for her boyfriend's car than it is to talk about her.'

'I'm going to go now,' Patrick said, and he tapped the pipe on the edge of the roof, pocketed it, then stood up, wavering slightly with the head rush. He was easily high enough above the patio, if he were to fall, to crack open his nearly hairless skull. Behind them, the sound of a car over-revving as it pulled into the yard.

Don reached up and held Pat's hand.

'Got you.'

After her canteen lunch with Geraint, who once again showed off the charisma of his appetite, they both went to Sociology. Somehow, their tutor had discovered that Kate was from an unusual upbringing. This was not good news. They were reading Emile Durkheim, who viewed society as a collective consciousness. Durkheim said that collectively agreed morality was maintained by people performing deviant or unconventional acts, and that without people testing the boundaries of behaviour, society would collapse, and how could there be a nuclear family without the opposite, and did Kate have anything she'd like to add?

'I think people like to know that somewhere, someone is testing out a different way of living,' Kate said, 'so they don't have to.'

'Any examples from your own home life?'

She felt Geraint's gaze on the back of her neck.

When she went to the bike shed after class, it was raining hard. Geraint pulled up in his white Fiat Punto with red four-point seat belts. He'd had it cleaned. The wet poured off the peak of her anorak. He got out of the car and, with rain darkening the shoulders of his powder-blue MILK IS DELICIOUS T-shirt, he said: 'You've got no choice. I'm driving you home.'

He helped her take the front wheel off her bike. Putting the seats down, he did not say a word as a slash of chain grease marked one of the headrests as they wedged the bike in. He was drenched by the time they sat back in the car. He pulled a CD wallet out of the glovebox and handed it to her.

They drove off and she looked through his music collection, judging him, but then feeling bad for judging him – blaming her parents for making her judgemental – and then putting Sean Paul on. Geraint did a fairly lame gangster's click with his fingers and was possibly adorable. A line of inflamed pores ran round his neck like a choker. His face was shiny from the wet. He drove, she felt, in a wealthy way, with his hands sitting softly on the part-leather thick-stemmed steering wheel – hands not gripping but resting flat, except for the tops of his fingers, which were bent, as you might rest your hands on a stranger's shoulders during an organized cha-cha.

'What was that question about, in Sociology?'

There was no point hiding it any more. If she was going to tell him, she might as well be bold: 'I grew up in a commune. I never went to school.'

She was hoping for a bigger reaction; he somehow kept the car on the road.

No one in the community ever used the word *commune*, they used the word *community*. The word *commune* had a special and dangerous power, and with great power came great responsibility. Geraint straightened up in his seat and tried to be nonchalant. They passed Gower's tiny airport as a biplane took off. The roadside sheep looked grey.

'I drove to a free party once in a commune in Brecon,' he said. '*Proper* mental. A bloke set himself on fire. Bet you get some right nutters?'

As he drove, she described Blaen-y-Llyn with the broad, lazy strokes she had been raised to avoid – the clichés that were expected from local journalists (or, at least, the ones who did their research online): *yes*, synthetic drugs; *yes*, boundary-testing sex; *yes*, chanting and nudity and nameless individuals waking in their vegetable garden. The latter had once actually happened, but Kate told the story as if most days they found gentlemen visitors asleep in a cloche. It felt good, watching Geraint's increasing alertness as she told him these things. By the time she was done, he was nailing it, breaking the speed limit through Gowerton.

'So wait . . . you live in The Rave House?'

'Yes. The Rave House.'

The term had been coined after Kate's fifteenth birthday when she had asked that her usually wholesome birthday tradition (a day at Three Cliffs bay, swimming, eating and playing an all-community game of rounders) be scrapped in favour of hiring a decent outdoor sound system. It was all pretty low-key – playing tunes from a box of old records they'd found in the attic – until the noise had attracted a group of teenagers from Hill End campsite. The teenagers made some calls to their older brothers and sisters. About two in the morning, a convoy of souped-up cars came up the lane, chained together by their headlights. Kate was excited to have her birthday sanctified by the presence of older boys and girls. She made a deal with her parents that if the party moved into the barn, they could keep it going. There followed nearly twelve hours of unfashionable but undeniably hea*vee* drum and bass while the adults remained besieged in the big house. She went with one of those older boys to the flattened grass in a clearing behind the barn. The boy's erection, softened by drugs, made for a kind of beginner's erection. Plus, she suspected that the vibrations from the subs helped. That she enjoyed losing her virginity, she had since discovered, made her rare. By lunchtime the next day, the ravers had fallen asleep: in polytunnels, in Don and Freya's bed, among the baby leaf salads, and next to the bonfire, their hair too hot to touch. Over the following weeks, tales began to emerge online of relentless debauchery, of parental absenteeism, of meatless barbecues at . . . *The Rave House*.

Without Kate noticing, Geraint had taken them on a detour through Three Crosses. He pulled up in front of a link-detached house, set back from the road, with vines climbing the front.

'So guess where I live,' he said sombrely.

She examined the house. Again, she was annoyed with herself – with her upbringing – for her disapproval of the heptagonal plastic conservatory, so she said, 'I *really* like your conservatory.' The house had a garage, which was open, and inside there was an old-style Jeep that looked almost military.

'My dad's into vintage four by fours,' he said.

While she was still wondering how to respond, he drove onwards to the community. Fifteen minutes later, as they got near, Geraint slowed at the top of the lane to observe the wonkily wood-cut sign, BLAEN-Y-LLYN, and the American-style mailbox.

'Why did you say your brother wanted to kill me?'

'Ask him yourself.'

Geraint went slowly up the narrow tree-lined lane, showing a total lack of judgement regarding which potholes were worth avoiding and which you had to attack. Between the trees on the left-hand side Kate pointed out the geodesic dome, on its own at the back of the market garden.

'That's Patrick's place. He's kind of like my uncle, I guess. My deputy father.'

Geraint said nothing. They passed the wind turbine, which stood at the top of the tiered permaculture garden. They passed three dead cars, left behind by guests too poor to get them repaired or too lazy to sell them, now rusted beyond saving, warning totems for those men foolish enough to venture this far.

Geraint dropped to first as the driveway took a short, steep incline before opening on to the gravelled yard. In the past, when there had been enough young people to make it feasible, this space had been the ideal size and shape for games of rounders or base-ball. The batter stood at the big house's double front doors, which still bore the marks of a few wild back swings and, when the batter ran, they passed the apple tree at first base and went from second to third along the length of the workshop before skidding home in front of the windows of the kitchen, where a victory dance would have its largest audience. It was agreed that if you hit as far as the barn or the pottery shed, set way back behind first and second base respectively, then that was a boundary. If a ball ever reached

Patrick's geodesic dome, at the furthest end of the garden beyond third – which never happened – then the hitter automatically won everything.

But there weren't really days like that any more. In the market garden, two wwoofers, boys, were grimly laying out blue and grey blankets. They did it as though covering the dead. Janet, who could usually be relied on to bring glamour, was sweatily weeding the beds that ran along the front of the house, pompoms of green in each hand. Kate's father was sitting on the flat roof, partly obscured by the stand-alone bath, holding hands with Patrick, who was standing beside him.

Kate tried to imagine Geraint's thoughts. It struck her that the big house didn't even look that big. The lumpy whitewashed walls, patches of psoriatic flakiness here and there, windowsills made from large unpainted slabs, moss on the roof tiles: it was basically a cottage. A cottage that had been known to sleep forty-two. She watched his expression change as his expectations met reality.

'The term *Rave House* might have been a bit misleading,' she said.

'So you live with these people?'

'Some of them are only visiting. But yes.'

'Which room's yours?'

She pointed to her first-floor bedroom, through the window of which her *Meat is Murder* poster was just visible.

His eyes widened. 'And who's in that window?'

She looked. Albert was standing in his bedroom window, arms by his side, staring at Geraint with the death-eyes, which was something he'd been practising.

'My brother. He's seen you. You'd better go.'

'How old is he?'

'Eleven. But surprisingly strong.'

Geraint laughed, looked at Kate and by the time he turned back to the window, Albert was gone.

'You should probably pop the boot,' she said.

As she got out and went round the back of the car she heard, through the open front door, Albert's footsteps clumping down the stairs. Geraint started the engine. She yanked her bike out just as

Albert came outside. He was holding a purple water pistol, a Glock, held upright in both hands in the manner of the televised FBI.

'Go, go, go! He'll kill you!' Kate said, and much to her pleasure Geraint did go, slightly for the show of it, but also, she thought, slightly for real – wheel-spinning, gravel pinging against Kate's ankles as he showed off his Punto's nippy turning radius with his boot still wide open. Albert started to run, in his socks, holding the gun out in front of him. He didn't quite have the commitment to fire – either that or it wasn't loaded – but in a moment of what looked like confusion, of a need to do something, anything, of running faster than the car was moving, Albert kind of dived, barrel-rolled, into the open boot of the car. It was not a high-risk stunt, in the broad scheme of things, but Kate was impressed. His feet hung over the bumper as the car disappeared down the incline and out of sight, the sound of its raised boot door clattering against branches as it went. She heard the engine idle, then stop. There were no more sounds after that.

Eventually, Albert walked back up the lane without his gun. He came up into the yard and stopped in front of her.

'Sorry, but I had to kill him.'

'I'll get over it.'

'I didn't enjoy it, but he's dead now so.'

'What happened to your gun?'

'I left it with the body.'

She admired her brother, heard the sound of Geraint's car moving off again, then picked up her bike frame and front wheel, turned and carried them towards the barn.

'You lied to me,' he said. 'You said all your friends were mutants. That one had a face.'

'Did he?'

'He is a proper *assho*'. Tell him I want my Glock back.'

They heard the phone ringing in the entrance hall. The phone was always ringing. Albert's mouth twitched. He was the only person in the community who actively wanted to answer. He was much admired for his phone manner. *Good afternoon, you are through to Albert Riley, whom can I help you reach?* He was always willing to broach wind and rain to track down a volunteer, even if they were waist deep in water trying to clear the filter on the hydroelectric pump.

'It must be someone important,' she said, raising her eyebrows. 'Only important people call in the mid-afternoon.'

He rubbed the end of his nose with his palm, then said: 'Marina says the things you learn in college will be of no use in the next world.'

'It's for you-hoo,' she said, dropping her bike down in the barn and starting back to the big house.

'Tell me what you learned today,' he said, glancing over towards the front door, the phone now on its eighth ring.

'People with prizes to give away often ring around siesta time.'

'Did you learn about self-defence, survival or weaponry?'

'Actually, there was a little on bombs.'

'Tell me.'

Albert was hopping from foot to foot now. The phone was his domain, his contact with the outside, and he defended it fiercely. He could often be seen sprinting across the yard in his socks, skidding into the hallway, grabbing the newel post to alter his trajectory – skating the tiles – then plucking the handset from its cradle, hardly out of breath as he delivered one of his lines: *Good morning, Blaen-y-Llyn, if you speak to one of us, you speak to us all.* Or sometimes just breathing heavily down the line.

'It could be an international call,' she said. 'It's morning in Montreal.'

He swallowed.

'Oh well, looks like nobody's in,' Kate said, holding her phone-shaped hand to her ear. 'Guess I'll give this free helicopter to somebody else.'

He started to jog backwards. 'This is not over.'

Albert turned to run, kicking up gravel. He disappeared inside and grabbed the receiver halfway through its sixteenth ring.

'Hello please!'

Kate came in and sat halfway up the stairs to watch him at work. He trapped the handset between his ear and shoulder.

'I'm afraid he's busy. Maybe I can help. I'm his eleven-year-old son.'

He was known for taking word-perfect phone messages and his intimate knowledge of guests past and present. He knew who was back living with Granny, who had fallen in love and gone to Suriname, who was studying paediatrics. It was his responsibility.

'There're around twenty of us usually: seven big, three small, and ten wwoofers – which stands for World Wide Opportunities on Organic Farms – and they sleep in the attic dorm.'

He was very adept at deflecting TV researchers and journalists. Part of the reason they received so many calls was that Blaen-y-Llyn was first, alphabetically, on a website listing communities of Wales. Pinned to the cork board above the phone was a printout of answers to Frequently Asked Questions. Albert had learned that most people could be discouraged with a few uninspiring details. He listened, then leaned forward to read off the sheet, speaking with the singsong voice that people get when they have said something many times.

'Blaen-y-Llyn is a community and farm where we grow our own food and run a small-scale veg-box scheme for North Gower. The money from the boxes helps pay for luxury items like . . .' he looked at his sister '. . . body armour. We keep hens, goats and did have plough-horses until they were replaced by machines. We sometimes kill animals and eat them. My mother is a one-woman abattoir.'

Albert looked at his sister and licked his lips. Their mother, Freya, a self-taught but industrious butcher, was in charge of all slaughter on the farm. She could wring a chicken's neck with the coolness of someone opening a jam jar. She kept up to date on the latest fashions in humane abattage. When Kate became a vegetarian, her mother, perhaps out of guilt, confided in her that she had never *chosen* her role as executioner-in-chief. Don had pushed her into it, she said. He had invented the phrase: 'one-woman abattoir'.

'Fifty acres in total, divided between fruit, vegetables, crops, livestock, pasture and our famous orchard.'

The orchard was one apple tree, planted on the day of their parents' marriage. Kate looked behind her and saw Patrick coming slowly downstairs, looking unsteady. She smiled at him.

'The community was formed during the early nineties recession. More details on our website.'

Patrick went to the bathroom under the stairs. She smelt smoke on him as he passed. She saw, beneath her, in the cracks between boards, the light click on. This toilet had a low ceiling, so boys had to sit down to wee.

'Yes, we have broadband internet, advert-free television and some really bad DVDs that my dad likes. The TV is small and in a corner and all the furniture is arranged so that it does not dominate the room.'

Patrick came back out. There was no roar. The community only flushed for solids.

'My favourite film?' Albert said, looking worried.

Patrick took the notepad next to the phone, wrote something down and held it up.

'*Eat Drink Man Woman*. Anything else you'd like to ask?'

Kate noticed there were little damp spots down Patrick's inside trouser leg. Part of her relationship with Patrick involved him telling her about the terrible ways in which his body was changing, and that it was coming for her, and soon.

'You alright, Pat?' Kate said.

'There is a membership application form, available to download. The final decision is made by the entire community based on' – again Albert squinted at the FAQ – 'entirely subjective criteria.'

Pat nodded, then grabbed the communal Volvo's car keys that hung above the phone.

'My tutors graduated from high-ranking universities.'

As the one-man switchboard, Albert was given special allowances, like being allowed to get up from dinner without excusing himself.

'My favourite subject is Home Economics.'

One of Janet's old boyfriends, an allergist, once told Albert that in the modern world it was important to have an elegant phone manner, and he clung to this belief and sometimes could be heard repeating it back to the people who phoned: 'It's important to have an elegant phone manner in the modern world.'

'Our policy is no access for video cameras. Photos are not well liked either.'

Albert twirled the cord round his finger in the manner of a girlfriend talking to another girlfriend. Patrick nodded to Kate and slipped out through the front door.

'It sounds like a very interesting project, but my father says your industry is inherently evil.'

There was a long wait.

'Really? He is one of my favourite presenters. In that case, you can have Dad's mobile telephone number.'

It was useful for Albert, when fending off aggressive producers, to be able to give out one of the two community pay-as-you-go numbers. These mobile phones were for emergency-only use and, as such, were almost never switched on.

'Awesome!' he said. Then he read out the community's address.

Over the years, he had received a number of autographed A5 photo-portraits.

Patrick drove the communal Volvo through light rain. He had the heater on full; a biscuity smell came from the vents. He put on his favourite swing jazz mix tape, 90 per cent Benny Goodman, but even that seemed shallow and toneless. He had not been stoned for five and a half days.

In Parkmill, he stopped in the bus bay outside Shepherd's Ice Cream. It was late afternoon. He looked up and down the road but couldn't see anyone. His skin tightened as the air recycled. Ejecting the tape, he flicked between radio stations. Classic rock, popular, classical, choral, local unsigned. *All music is bullshit*, he thought, though he didn't mean it. Patrick knew only one person who did not like music: Don, who said he found it manipulative. Among the sorts of people who frequented the community, not liking music was up there with not liking foreigners or homosexuals. It had always pleased Patrick to know Don's secret shame.

As it started to get dark, he saw them riding their BMXs through the car park. He flashed his headlights twice and wound down his window.

'Boys!' he shouted, with his famous lungs. 'Boys!'

They skidded to a halt, then cycled over to the window. All three of them had their hoods up and scarves over their mouths and noses, Zapatista-style.

'Alright, gramps,' one of them said.

'Alright, lads. You want to run your old man an errand?'

'I ain't giving you a blowie.'

With their scarves, Patrick couldn't see their mouths move. Their eyes glistened in the cold. He handed over a twenty and watched as they cycled off, bums raised in the air, bike seats ticking back and forth like metronomes.

In the schoolroom, Isaac plucked at the exposed strings through the open base of the stand-up piano. He was half listening as Kate explained to her brother what she'd learned at college that day. She and Albert were sitting opposite each other, cross-legged on the rug, and Kate had some of her primary sources out: reproduction pamphlets of the White Rose movement, photos of key members, one who looked like a Morrissey fan.

'The first thing to know is that not everyone in Germany during the war was on the Nazis' side,' Kate said.

'That's bullsheeet,' Albert said.

'Bullsheeet,' Isaac said. He had a power ball that, when dragged down the piano's bass strings, created a noise like whale song.

'The White Rose movement were a group who stood up *against* the established views in German society, even at the risk to their own well-being.'

'They sound like Mum and Dad,' Albert said.

'They're nothing like that.'

'Mum and Dad reject the norms and values of our society,' Albert said.

'*Norms and values?*' Kate said.

'Ask Marina,' Albert said.

Isaac climbed through the wooden loom that was standing in the opposite corner to the piano. He liked to get himself tangled in the threads and then, imagining it was a combine harvester about to be switched on, challenge himself to escape.

'Our community changes people all the time,' Albert said. 'We have that power, though our time is running out.'

'Shut up, moron. Who told you that?'

'When people come here they realize that it is possible,' Albert said, sounding like he was quoting someone, 'that they too can change the way they live.'

'*Seriously*. You shouldn't listen to everything people tell you.' She hadn't noticed that Isaac had escaped the loom and was standing behind her, listening.

'Real education doesn't happen in classrooms.'

'Listen, Albert, before you switch off all independent thought,' she lowered her voice to a whisper, 'you should realize that communities like ours *maintain* the status quo. Ever wondered why Patrick lives on his own in the dome? He's depressed; they put him in there as quarantine.' She was discovering how she felt by speaking. 'And all the *volunteers*, they're just tourists. And Marina, my God, do you remember why they let her join?' She started to point and chop for emphasis, unaware that these were her father's rhetorical tics. It felt good to say all this stuff. 'She was touring communities – a perpetual tour – never working or paying rent. Mum and Dad don't even like her! That's why they put her in the workshop! It might as well be a council house . . .'

Kate trailed off. Albert was staring. There was something behind her. Turning, she saw Isaac standing on the piano stool with a look of vertigo on his face. She got up and stood in front of him.

'Hey, little dude,' she said.

Isaac waved at her even though they were only arm's length apart.

'We are like the White Rose movement, aren't we?' Albert said.

Kate kept looking at Isaac: 'Yes, brother and sister, rising up against society, and Isaac is the professor, aren't you, Isaac?'

Isaac looked like he was thinking of something. He peered down at the floor.

'What do you mean about my mum?'

'Nothing. I didn't say anything about your mum.'

'You said no one likes her.'

'I didn't say that. Isaac, I think we should play a game, don't you?'

'Why don't you like her?' Albert said. 'She's the best.'

'*I* like your parents,' Isaac said.

Kate took hold of Isaac's hands and tried to think of a cliché. 'Everybody here is your parents.'

'Are you?'

'Sure.'

'Okay, let me try,' Albert said. '*Go to your room, Isaac.*'

'Ha ha!' Isaac laughed, holding his ribs.

'*I've had just about enough of you, young man,*' Albert said to Isaac, wagging his finger.

'Ha ha!' He creased up at the waist.

'Albert,' Kate said.

He started shaking his fist at Isaac. '*I don't want to hear another peep out of you. I ought to fetch my slipper.*'

'Albert, where do you get this?'

'The *Beano Annual*,' he said, standing up. He pointed at Isaac. '*You ungrateful little shit. I wish you'd never been born.*'

'Okay, that's enough,' Kate said.

Isaac rubbed the top of his head with his hand.

She turned her back to him and offered him a piggyback. He jumped on.

She said: 'Where would you like to go?'

It was half a year ago that Isaac and Marina had been interviewed for full-time membership. They had been staying with the community on a trial basis for the previous six weeks and normally, at that point, there'd be a month-long cooling-off break before a final evaluation. But just before they were due to leave, Marina started making loud enquiries on the house phone into whether the nearby campsite did a discount for a four-week stay, which rather suggested they had nowhere to go to cool off. Typically, if an applicant admitted they didn't have anyone who was willing to take them in, then that was its own kind of bad signal. But on this occasion the community agreed to forgo procedure, largely because of Isaac who, with his youth, and his kinship with Albert, seemed to represent the beginning of a new generation of young people at the community.

Seated at one side of the round dining table in the centre of the kitchen was the core team who led the interview: Freya, Arlo and Don, in that order. Marina was opposite them. The table had been known to seat twenty, so it looked bare. The other vote-casting members, she and Patrick, were watching but not contributing, sitting on the blue sofa against the back wall. Janet was away in Bristol, working on a new collection. From where Kate was sitting, she could also see Isaac and Albert underneath the table, crawling in circles, counting everyone's toes.

'So, I'd be interested to know what your plans are for the future?' Freya had said. 'What your aims are, in the long term?'

'Well, I'm really most focused on what's best for Isaac,' Marina had said, and her son made a *woof-woof* noise on hearing his name. 'The great thing about Blaen-y-Llyn . . .' Don's eyes tightened as he assessed her pronunciation '. . . is that it's a fantastic, open place where he can learn and make friends.'

Marina had a round face, with grey wavy curtains, her cheeks like apples that, to those who fantasized about such things, would have been the best bits, if she were to be cooked. She was big but robust – the term is *jolly* – and was wearing a body warmer.

'And how long would you like to stay with us?' Freya said.

'Well, as long as I can. I mean, I think we'll all be reassessing things by the end of the year, so it's probably not good to have anything set in stone . . .' she smiled and laughed in a way that indicated she hoped her interviewers were on the same astrological page, but found two hard expressions and Arlo, distracted by his nails.

'Why so?' Don said.

'I just think we'll see some big changes by the end of 2012,' Marina said, changing position in her seat, 'in both the physical and spiritual spheres. Around that time.'

Don was nodding now and steepling his fingers.

'Is this about the Mayan calendar?' Freya said.

'I know it can sound loopy. I completely understand. But it's not really about the Mayans, though people find it fun to think so. There's a strong scientific backing.'

'I'm interested,' Don said, leaning forward.

Kate was highly attuned to sarcasm in her father's voice.

'Well, basically, if you imagine this table is the Milky Way, our galaxy,' Marina said, putting her hands out on to the wood, 'then it's fairly standard stuff to say that at the centre is what they call a super-massive black hole. Ours is known as Sagittarius A-star. It's incredibly dense . . .' Kate noticed her father smile at this. '. . . it's three million times as heavy as the sun, but invisible to us – its gravitational pull is so powerful that even light can't escape. Scientists know it's there because of the way everything around it is drawn in.' There was a hole in the middle of the table from when it had accommodated a sun umbrella, and Marina made a show of peering down into it. 'Because this black hole is, as they say, "starving". It has a *hungry* gravitational pull – sucking things in and swallowing them . . .'

Don decided to start enjoying himself.

Marina stood up off her stool. 'Imagine that this pepper mill is the earth and this' – she lifted a *Merry Christmas* mug – 'is our sun. We all know it takes a year for the earth to orbit the sun, but the problem is that the earth's path is not a perfect circle, it's eccentric' – she showed the pepper mill doing ellipses around the mug – 'and it takes 26,000 years of orbits before we come back to our exact start point, right?'

Freya was listening hard.

'Abso*lute*ly,' Don said.

Arlo, it was clear, hadn't been paying attention and was just now trying to catch up.

'Which of course the Mayans knew all about, along with loads of other cultures, the Sufis for one. Then eventually . . .'

Marina swung the pepper mill round the mug as she took steps round the curved edge of the table towards Freya. Don's expression was now one of having happened across something really cute, like a cat standing on a cow.

'. . . eventually, 26,000 years eventually . . .'

Kate could see Isaac and Albert examining and discussing something they'd found on a table leg; from her own years as a small person, she knew about the carpenter's hieroglyphics on the table's underside.

'. . . there will be an eclipse. But it's a particular kind of eclipse.' Marina put the pepper mill down and then, with gravitas, put the Christmas mug – the sun – between the mill and the black hole at the centre of the table. 'We all know about lunar and solar eclipses, but next year, at the end of this 26,000-year cycle, we'll have a galactic eclipse. And that's when the sun comes between us and this monster, Sagittarius A-star, at the centre of the galaxy. And when that happens, well, no one's totally sure – there's a lot of conjecture – but when the most powerful force in the galaxy is blocked out, and remember, it's millions of times more powerful than the sun, there's going to be some major changes, it's fair to say.'

Don was grinning now, absolutely loving it, not wanting the performance to end. 'But you must have a theory on what *you're* expecting?'

She looked at him. He had his mouth open, waiting.

'I'm genuinely intrigued,' he said, and just about managed to hold it together.

'Well,' she said finally, seeming a little awkward now that she was standing, trying to make her way back to her seat, 'nobody knows for sure, but I'm anticipating a shift in gravity – and I mean gravity in the widest possible sense – gravity of the mind, the soul, relationships, moral and spiritual gravity. An untethering. A topsy-turvy world. Some people think the world will stop spinning, others expect South Wales to get the Mediterranean climate it deserves.' Arlo liked that. 'All I believe is that something major is going to happen, and those who are ready to adapt will have to make the world new. It's going to be a test. A *real* test. Because what's a test if you can't fail?'

Don clapped enthusiastically. He was known for his loud clap. Freya rubbed her eyelids. Beneath the table, Albert and Isaac were shaking hands.

'Brilliant,' Don said. 'Absolutely brilliant.'

His wife wouldn't look at him. Marina, still standing, shifted back to her stool.

'A really enigmatic iteration,' Don said, looking around. 'People can be terribly drab with that sort of stuff, but I think you gave it real oomph. And the scientific data too. Is that your own, Marina, or can I look it up online?'

She looked at him, then down at the table, then she reached under it and said: 'Come on, Isaac, we're going.'

Taking her son by the hand, she marched upstairs to Janet's room, where they were staying. Through the ceiling, they heard the sounds of first a door slamming, then Marina noisily packing their stuff. Don held up his hands in apology.

It was then perhaps partly to show his humane side that her father went on to argue that they should be allowed to stay because Marina was 'harmless enough' and Isaac 'was key to the development of the community'. Patrick said it wasn't right to invite someone to be a full-time resident just because they matched certain criteria. Arlo, in his usual, instinctive way, said he thought they were nice and should be asked to stay. Freya said it was obvious they were only at the community while they looked for something better. While this discussion went on, Kate could see Albert, with both arms round a table leg, listening earnestly to the sounds from upstairs. He cast his half-vote in support of Isaac.

With two and a half for and two against, it came down to Kate to decide. Her brother had not spoken to her since she started college and, if she voted against him, she knew he would probably never speak to her again. While she deliberated, he knelt and, with ceremony, laid his head on the bench, with his eyes closed, in the manner of someone waiting to be beheaded.

It was dark by the time the Zapatistas reappeared, their breath evaporating against his driver's side window. Patrick wound down the glass. One of the boys reached into his pocket and pulled out a small plastic bag, held theatrically between his index and middle fingers.

'High-grade hydro,' he said, his voice muffled by his scarf. 'It cost twenny-five, naw twenny.'

Patrick blinked. 'I admire your entrepreneurial verve.'

He had always suffered from low-level paranoia, and one of the best things about smoking cannabis was that it gave him something to blame his paranoia on.

'I'm naw lying. You owe us a fiver.'

The other two boys were on lookout, watching the road ahead and behind.

'You think you can do one over on me,' Patrick said as he scooped five quid of someone else's money from the ashtray and handed it across.

They passed him the bag and he took a long sniff – it reeked – then dropped it in his lap. Driving back, he imagined everyone, especially Janet, wondering where he had gone with the car while they were in the cold, insulating the vulnerable vegetables. He thought about her wartime navy work shirt, sleeves rolled up, tangible biceps.

Turning into the community's driveway, he switched off the headlights, hoping not to alert anyone to his return. He put the car in neutral to let it silently roll along the lane, parking just before the upslope that led to the yard. Maybe they had needed the car to get some vital bag of charity shop blankets and because of him there would be no asparagus this summer. Getting out of the car, he saw, parked parallel to him across the path, the moon reflecting its expensively undulating surfaces, the Avail. He imagined Janet's boyfriend arriving to a hero's welcome, the back seat of his car clouded with old duvets.

Walking a back route to the dome, he passed brassicas and endives covered by rugby coats and sheepskin rugs. Once inside, Patrick held the bag up to his bedside lamp. The bud was compact, bristling with tiny orange hairs and covered in crystals like it had been dipped in sugar. He didn't like the way cannabis culture had become somehow macho: muscle-bound super-skunk. The great thing about Karl Orland, his usual dealer, was that he appreciated the pleasures of pale grass, twiggy and mild. Still, he would have to make do.

Normally he saved bhang lassis for the solstice, but since he'd been straight for about 200 hours, he thought it only right to mix a catch-up dose. Emptying the lot into a mortar, he ground it with some brown sugar. It would save him time to mix a big portion now and ration it out over the next few days. He took his camping gas stove and heated the mixture outside, so it wouldn't stink out his dome. At one point, someone walked past; he couldn't make out who in the dark, only knew it was a woman when she said: '*Someone's having a party.*'

Marina was sitting on a bench in the shed, with the pottery wheel between her legs. She sometimes let Albert control the speed of it, but mostly he just watched, as now, sitting beside her. Isaac had already been put to bed. The room was lit by a strip light that hung from two chains; it was pitch black outside. She wet her hands from a bowl beside her and thokked a blob of clay on to the wheel. As she pressed the foot pedal, the wheel spun. She centred the clay, then, shaping her hands into a broken circle, raised it up. Albert sometimes laughed at the rude shapes the clay made but he was never really sure why he was laughing.

One of the most impressive things about Marina was that she could throw a teapot and talk at the same time. It gave her the air of a magician, the hands doing the trick, clay-charming, while she talked to Albert about the future.

'What are you making?'

'A present for you.'

'Yes! Is it a helmet?'

'No.'

'Is it body armour of any kind?'

'Not really.'

Along the middle shelf on the wall opposite were the unclaimed workshop pieces: mugs, butter dishes, scenes from the Nativity, a four-piece band. Albert had seen the pleasure that Marina took in her quarterly cull – the catharsis of visitors' crappy vases, misshapen animals and bad likenesses of friends shattering into a masonry-strength bin bag. On the shelf above that were her own elegant milk jugs and bowls.

All full-time members were asked to put in eighteen hours a week of work that contributed to the functioning of the community. Most of the friction around this idea arose not from people working too few hours, but from a shifting definition of what was a worthwhile contribution. Marina included her hours in the pottery shed as part of her quota because on the one hand she was teaching Albert and Isaac a useful skill, and on the other, as the community averaged a minimum of three pieces of broken crockery a week, she was helping replace stock.

Albert stood up off the bench and leaned over the spinning wheel, peering down on top of it, trying to hypnotize himself as the shape dilated.

'By the way, my sister thinks you're a liar,' he said, still staring down into the revolving portal.

'That's not very nice,' Marina said, concentrating.

'You should show her the truth. Is it a bowl? It looks like a bowl. I don't really need a bowl.'

'It's not a bowl.'

Her hands moved steadily. The tips of her fingers were grey. Some clay splatted on Albert's trousers.

'Bowls are okay but not great.'

It was more conical than a bowl, and taller. She took her foot off the pedal and the wheel stopped. She looked at Albert's mouth for a moment, then took a wire and cut the clay at its base. Lifting the cone up, she showed him it had holes at both ends. She rested the shape on a tray by her side.

'What is it?' he said.

'Guess.'

He chewed his lip. 'A silencer?'

'Here's a clue: I'm going to paint it with red and white stripes. It's to help you get your voice heard.'

He started to look scared.

'It's a megaphone, Albert.'

'Oh sweet!'

'It will be ornamental though, really. A *symbol* of your right to be listened to.'

'I've always wanted a megaphone,' he said.

Once he'd made the bhang, Patrick added pistachio and blitzed it in with the plain lassi. Little clumps of weed and nut whizzed past like fence posts in a hurricane. He watched the yoghurt take on a green, ill-looking tint.

It was late now, gone midnight, and although he was tired, he didn't want to sleep until he was stoned. He drank a third of the lassi and went for a walk around the garden. It was a brutally cold, clear night, and after thirty minutes he felt his mind rearrange itself in a familiar formation. Certain memories receded. Lights clicked off in his internal attic. He stretched his back and felt the blood slosh round his brain.

Getting back inside, he wound up the radio to full capacity and set it playing on Radio 3. Music was good again. He sat down in his overstuffed armchair. After a while, the radio died and he found he was incapable of winding it back up. Pinned to his seat, he felt his mind over-revving while he stared at the heptagonal skylight.

He thought about the dome, which had been built as a present for him. When they had first moved to Gower, Patrick used to stay in what was now Kate's room, sharing a thin wall with Don and Freya. As an infant, Kate had a cot at the end of her parents' bed, which is where she did her sleeping and, more to the point, her not sleeping. Patrick had little choice but to synchronize, napping in the one- or two-hour bursts of silence, a tasting menu of sleep.

On Kate's first birthday, Don had made a speech in which he said: 'I don't think it's fair Patrick should have to put up with our clatter and Kate's air-raid siren, and it's his birthday coming up, so I thought – I know he's interested – we could get to work on a dome.'

There is no perceptible difference between something made with love and something made with spite, except spite works to a schedule. Six months later, they moved him in with his books and his spices and Don bought him a bag of weed to say thanks for keeping the big house smoke-free for Kate, and that was when he properly started smoking again. With resurgent paranoia, he began to wonder whether the dome had, in actual fact, been built as a way to get him out of the big house.

Patrick made the biggest monthly contribution to the community's finances and, as such, was prone to believing that they only put up with him because of his money. He was also acutely conscious that if Don ever heard Patrick imply his wealth entitled him to better treatment than anyone else then Don would absolutely pounce, ideologically. Which meant Patrick had never – not once in twenty years – suggested that his position as financial load-bearer entitled him to not feel alienated.

His best attempt at expressing his discontent had been just a few weeks ago. Cider-drunk on spring equinox, during those fearful few days before Janet's most recent return, while sitting round the fire with most of the community, he had suggested that the geodesic dome, in its isolated position beyond the tubers at the top of the garden, and given people's generally withering, lightly nostalgic attitude towards it ('Well, it must have looked like the future when it was built'), was an analogue for how people viewed him personally. He had thought the statement might come out as light-hearted, and that they would make jokes in response – 'Yeah, Pat, we put you out there as, like, quarantine' – but his audience's reaction was the kind of stonewall denial – '*How* can you say that?' – that people adopt when someone has absolutely nailed a thing.

He began to harbour a strong belief that people talked about him behind his back. You could always hear people talking somewhere, and he often heard double plosives that sounded like his name and, depending on that day's psychological lean, he would provide the context. In a good frame of mind: 'Patrick seriously delivered with the kedgeree this a.m.' In a bad one: 'Is it me or was Patrick's kedgeree pre-chewed?'

When he felt this way, he turned to music and art for comfort, and this presented another problem. It was not possible to hang art in the dome, all the walls being curved and omnitriangulate. When

Patrick had moved out of the big house all those years ago, he had donated to baby Kate, in her new bedroom, a smoggy, oil-acrylic seascape and eight wildly imprecise line-drawings: *Studies for Any Female Nude I–VIII* by Marcel Le Lionnais. On the day before Kate's third birthday, Don returned them to Patrick, carrying them under both arms to the dome, saying they were 'a bit much, for Kate, at this stage in her development'.

Since Patrick couldn't hang the art, he had decided to make use of one of the awkward spaces that existed behind every piece of non-dome-specific furniture. Rectangular sofas, rectangular book-cases, rectangular wardrobes: anything not designed to back on to a spherical wall created dead space. So Patrick, in a fit of innovation, took the pictures out of their frames and put them into cardboard-backed plastic sleeves. He then stood the images on a cradle-style print browser that he'd bought from an art shop in Mumbles. It fit-ted behind the futon-sofa, thus utilizing, albeit awkwardly, the dead space. If he knelt on the sofa, facing the wall, he could then peruse the images at his leisure. This soon became one thing that made Patrick feel truly wretched and alone: the eight line-drawings now a kind of flick-book, creating the impression of a naked woman exploding, limbs distending, tearing at herself, followed by the undeniably bleak and featureless grey-black-blue seascape. This final image captured Patrick's feelings whenever he tried to enjoy his modest collection of original art.

The only wall decorations were Patrick's string instruments. When they had built the dome, Don installed wall-mounted brack-ets for Patrick's guitar and banjo. It was a small act of genuine thoughtfulness. Over the years, the community had bought Patrick a number of stringed instruments, each one smaller, *quieter*, than the last. Two Christmases ago it was the samisen, a three-stringed Japanese guitar.

The acoustics in the dome were unsettling. If Patrick sat on a stool in the middle of the room with his Spanish guitar, it added an unwanted 1980s-type reverb to his fingerpicking, making his compo-sitions sound like restaurant music. He could never achieve a lo-fi, stripped-back sound. Also, much of his record collection became unlistenable and overproduced within these walls, which Patrick blamed Don for as well.

Through Kate's mid-teens, Patrick had happily transcribed and played her favourite emotional indie rock so she could practise singing. He was one of the only people she would allow to hear her voice, plus she actually preferred how she sounded with the dome's built-in reverb. The other advantage was that Patrick had no neighbours who could overhear them. He felt privileged to be, as far as he knew, the only person she talked to about her new boyfriend.

Now, as Patrick stared up at the raised recessed bed at the top of the dome, he found himself thinking about the night that he and Janet had spent there. Not long after Albert's birth there had been a party; Janet had gifted her own bed to two friends who were visiting, and the schoolroom floor was dominoed with people top-and-tailing, so Patrick – in an honest-to-goodness unsleazy way – said there was spare room in the dome. It was freezing and raining when they ran across the yard, still drunk. They set the wood-burner going, and climbed into bed fully clothed and hugging. The way the heavily insulated dome worked was that heat rose and kept the top a lot hotter than the bottom. There was a window above the mezzanine bed for ventilation, but if it was raining, as it was that night, it had to stay shut or the rain came in.

In the morning, with the sun shining through the skylight, they woke up in a tropical weather system. Drenched in sweat, drymouthed, brains loose in their skulls, steam particles in the slanted sunlight, condensation on the rolling hills of duvet – reminiscent of North Gower at dawn – they stripped off their jumpers, gasping for air, laughing, coughing, throwing their clothes down from the mezzanine bed, until it would have just seemed unnecessarily prudish, given their night together and the genuinely sauna-like conditions, not to take all their clothes off and lie on top of the covers, breathing.

Their matted hair, bodies shining with sweat, chests rising and falling. Patrick opened the window and let the light elliptical rain fall through on to them. It felt – in every way but one – post-coital. So, without self-consciousness, they kissed and hugged and fell back to sleep.

Something about this experience, Patrick felt, had sealed off the possibility of them getting together. They had achieved all the awkwardness and shy chatter of good friends who have slept together, but without ever having crossed that threshold. It would have seemed oddly regressive to suggest they start any kind of courting ritual, but equally he didn't feel able to take the bolder route and talk to her about the thing that had almost happened and whether it could actually happen. As time passed, it seemed impossible to talk to Janet about that morning. He began to suspect she wouldn't even remember.

Patrick managed to heave himself out of his chair and get to the kitchen cupboard. Among the other herbs, he had a jar of dried magic mushrooms that he'd picked last autumn. He needed something to try and turn his evening round and he thought they might open a few internal windows. Sitting back down, he chewed on three tiny caps, washed them down with the rest of the lassi, which he'd forgotten he was planning to keep, and tried to think of something positive.

That was when he heard the roar of a very large animal.

Upstairs, in the big house, Freya and Don were in bed, each sitting up with a book and their own lamp. She had her hair tied in a side ponytail so that she could rest back against the headboard. He was re-reading *Ways of Seeing* and occasionally laughing with his mouth closed, which Freya felt as a series of vibrations in the mattress. He had two pillows under his right foot for drainage.

Closing the book, he watched his wife, then silently leaned across and kissed her on the cheek. 'Silently' because eighteen years into their marriage, two years ago, Don had started to make an involuntary kiss-kiss noise (the noise didn't sound like kisses; it sounded like a small sealed bag being opened) every time he was seeking, or was about to give her, affection. It just started one day. In the dark of the bedroom, she would hear the two quick vacuum-sealed, slightly wet noises and know that he was shortly to make contact. At the breakfast table, before his lips were on her neck, she would hear the pursed schlupping. The noise was similar to the one people make to attract the attention of a cat. She had never found his kisses repellent before, but something about the self-announcing quality of these noises – a comedian offstage, doing his own intro – really got to her. She had thought it only fair to let him know: 'That thing you do, before you kiss me' – she wasn't able to impersonate, so made a kind of chewing noise – 'it's awful, can you stop?' His small eyes widened. He had not been aware he was doing it.

Of course he would stop, he said. From that point, whenever he made the sound he'd halt and curse. He battled his auto-self. Eventually, after weeks of struggle, Don was able to kiss and receive kisses without making pre-emptive smoochies.

Except something of it remained: a ghost of the sound, the impulse but without its audible counterpart. She became attuned to Don's repression of the noise and, lying in bed in the dark, knew with just as much clarity when she was about to feel his lips and the swish of his beard against her. In many ways, this was more distressing than the original kiss-kiss noise. The sound was gone but the idea lived on, made bigger, more upsettingly complex; a process between them.

She read the same line in her poem again and again. The line was: 'That is the way with amputations.' Recently, she'd been finding that if Don got to sleep before her, then she stayed awake, preoccupied by the light pan-pipe moods that whistled from his nostrils. She used to say how much she liked the chords his sinuses played, but not now that they kept her awake. When she was not sleeping she worried about her son.

More and more, she was seeing Albert skulk off to the workshop or pottery shed, both of which were far enough away to make it difficult for Freya to casually pop by – to check on him – without having some genuine reason for doing so. It had been Don's idea to take Marina and Isaac out of the big house (since Janet was shortly to reclaim her room) and put them into the workshop's spare room. Publicly, he said it would give them independence – 'You can be your own family unit' – while remaining within the communal fold. In truth, he wanted to keep Marina at a distance. Don complained she was 'too intense', but what felt like over-intensity to an adult, felt to a child like that person was actually listening.

Although it was tempting to casually dismiss, as Don had, all her talk of a galactic eclipse, Freya preferred to understand the idea first and then be able to reject it definitively. A *know your enemy* sort of thing. Her online research showed that supermassive black holes did exist and that our spiral galaxy did indeed have one at its centre: Sagittarius A*. It was invisible; dramatic photos from the Chandra satellite observatory showed where it wasn't. An article on the NASA blog, written with, she assumed, pre-teen astronomers in mind, said the 'SMBH' was 'hungry' and 'gobbling up all-comers' and that 'beasts of its kind' had the power to 'bend the space-time continuum'. NASA didn't go as far as mentioning the end of days, but Freya wouldn't have been totally surprised if they had. This was science trying to compete for the attention of the young imagination. But when she searched for 'galactic eclipse', that's when the real nutters emerged: gaiamind.org and prophetsmanual.com.

The communal desktop computer was in the attic and had a button next to it that allowed thirty minutes of access to the internet at a time. For Albert, this meant that he took his access seriously, going up there with a list: *solar flares (12 mins), galactic equator (10 mins), knife-vest (8 mins)*. Freya's concern was not just that he believed in the same things as Marina but that her beliefs were gateway beliefs into the vast, unquenchable fruitiness of cyberspace.

All this had come together to convince Freya that she ought to remove Albert from the community for a time. That she also needed a break from Don was just a lucky symmetry. The simplest and cheapest solution was to go to the roundhouse, a twenty-minute walk away through the woods; not much of a holiday destination, but it would give him (them) a little breathing space. The roundhouse was made of cob, which was, put simply, mud. It had originally been built as an educational tool: a group of visiting undergraduates on a Sustainable Built Environment degree had assembled it over four days, spent two nights in it, then tried to take it apart again. It was a testament to the hardiness of cob housing that destroying it was more hassle than building it; the students gave up, and left the structure mostly intact. After that it became the community's overflow sleeping area, though it had not been used in a long time.

It didn't seem like a big thing to be asking Don: a fortnight's time out, for her and for Albert. A month maybe. After all, they both agreed that something needed to be done. Yet she found herself unable to broach the subject. All of which went some way to explain why, this morning, after a night of maddening sleeplessness, she had decided it would be a good idea to type him a letter about it. She got as far as *Dear Don*, then her daughter came in, and that was the point that Freya realized she was behaving like an unstable, sleepless person, not a wife communicating to her husband about a shared concern.

Freya let her poetry book drop to the duvet. Her reading glasses fell off her nose and hung round her neck. She turned to her husband, but he started speaking before she could.

'I told Patrick he needs to finally forget Janet,' Don said. 'Don't be the victim. Stop moping. Quit the demon weed. He was still puffing on that pipe – some potent concoction.' There was a tone in his voice, and an angle of his chin in delivery, that let her know he was saying something he'd already practised in the well-attended auditorium of his mind. He spoke up towards the curtain rail. Sometimes he would premiere a statement with Freya, then over the next few days she would hear him say the same thing to other communards, perhaps editing a word or two, depending on the audience. A good strong utterance might see nine or ten outings before being archived. 'You live in a community with a constant flow of young, attractive left-leaning men and women. Get stuck in, Pat, I said. Sixty's not too old. All these tremendous women spending time here, intelligent, free-thinking, body-confident. Get out there. It feels good to make other people feel good. Be active. Sweat out your problems. Let's re-anchor the fences. But I think he's worried about dislocating his shoulder. It's his *mind* dislocating that I'm worried about.'

'Don.'

He turned to look at her. He had the sheen of an uncollected sneeze in his moustache hair. He saw something in her expression and closed his book, let it drop to the duvet and patted the back cover. 'Yes,' he said.

'I'm worried about Albert. I don't think it's good for him to be spending so much time with Marina.'

'I'm with you, Frey. You know that.'

'I was thinking he and I could go to the roundhouse for a while. A fortnight, maybe. A kind of holiday.'

Don blinked twice. She felt the mattress shift as he sat more upright. 'But the roundhouse is half built.'

'I thought that could be part of it. I'll show him how to finish the cobbing. It'll be educational.'

He looked around the room. 'When did you think of this?'

'I've been thinking about it for a while.'

'You're saying you want to move out of the house, you and Albert?' The volume of his voice spiked.

'I thought we could talk about it.'

'All this because of Marina? Let's not go crazy. Why doesn't one of us just speak to Albert? Education, not prohibition, we could . . .' she saw the hairs on his neck ripple as his Adam's apple bounced '. . . dig out the Personal Instrument?'

'You're kidding.'

'I honestly think it might help.'

'I'm sure you do.'

'Why are you being like this?'

They stayed in silence for a while. The Personal Instrument was a learning tool that, according to her husband, helped 'encourage young people to make active choices between right and wrong'. He had built it himself. Every young person, shortly after their thirteenth birthday, got to wander the farm wearing the device. Don liked to say the experience was equivalent to the vision quest in Native American cultures. It was frightening to glimpse the gap between Don as he viewed himself, and the reality. She pulled back her side of the duvet and swung her legs out. He watched her get dressed and take a blanket out of the bottom drawer of the dresser. He listened to her go down the corridor and knock on their daughter's door.

★

Patrick was standing in the middle of the geodesic dome in shapeless boxer shorts, holding a table leg with both hands, in a baseball stance.

It had been little comfort for him to realize that the growling, animal noise, which had got so loud that he felt vibrations in the soft flesh along his jawline, was not the sound of a beast, awoken after thousands of years, come to wreak vengeance on this earth, but a Saab Avail, announcing Janet's boyfriend's exit, presumably with her purring in the passenger seat. After that, when he felt the second half of the lassi start working, he climbed up the wooden staircase into bed and, lying beneath two duvets and a blanket, started to feel nervous. Soon, nervousness became twitching paranoia and, not long after that, twitching paranoia blossomed into a higher state of pure understanding: his fellow communards were not his friends, they were planning his removal.

It would be so easy. There were no locks on the doors. So Patrick got out of bed, took the loose leg off the table and barred the double doors by feeding it through the two coat hooks. He tried to go to sleep again. It didn't work. He listened to the ash tree outside groaning like a man slowly dying. He heard the distant sound of laughter that might well have come after a vicious but finely judged joke regarding his personal odour. He heard an unknown dog barking with a hoarse mindlessness, starved and bloodthirsty. He got out of bed again, took the table leg off the door and stood with it in his hands like a bat, which is where he was now, waiting for them to burst in.

Listening to the noises outside his room, Patrick constructed a narrative: for years, Don had been looking for a way to get rid of him, had been telling everyone about his creepy, masturbatory, weirdo-in-the-dome obsession with Janet. Don had been saying that Patrick was a hermit, a recluse. He'd told them he was no longer useful, he was spent, a drain on resources, but by dint of Patrick's financial liquidity, he was difficult to expel.

Firstly, they had paid off his dealer, Karl Orland, then they had waited for Patrick's stash to run dry. Secondly, they had made bets on how long it would be before his mental collapse. Thirdly, at a secret brunch-time meeting, they had planned in exquisite detail his final hours, discussing every contingency: disposal, legal matters, a bonfire of his guitars, and through their commitment to putting Patrick in the ground there would bloom a new communal solidarity, as though he were the finest possible compost.

Fourthly, this very afternoon, when Patrick had taken the car without asking, and hadn't helped with the cloches, and hadn't returned the car key, they all knew he was going to the bus bay outside Shepherd's, so they made the decision to act. Later, when one of their spies came past and said, 'Someone's having a party,' she reported back that he was brewing a strong dose and would shortly enter a state of reduced motor function.

Albert – who was good at climbing – was in the ash tree above the geodesic dome, with his hands on a high branch and his feet on a lower one, stretching and bending his legs, making the tree creak loudly, knowing the fearful sleeplessness this would bestow.

Marina had brought out her four-octave Korg keyboard with the surround-sound speakers and set them up in a circle around the dome. With total disregard for electricity consumption, she was using 'Set 665: Unnerving Sound Effects', working 'Fearful Wind' with one hand and with the other, 'Laughter at Your Expense', and occasionally 'Growling Dog in Blood Lust'.

This was all in aid of getting Patrick into a state of terrified paralysis so that when Arlo, Marina, Freya, Don, and a number of masked, ambitious wwoofers who wanted to show their commitment to the community, came into his room, chanting his name and wearing robes with deep hoods, come to take him at last, Patrick would stay still, shaking in his bed and, given his family history, in addition to previous addictions, perhaps suffer a fatal embolism. If his heart held they would simply lower the rainbow-coloured pillow on to his face, pin his arms and legs down and continue chanting until his body stopped moving. Then they'd lay his arms across his chest in an X and in the morning, they would say: 'So peaceful, he must have known it was his time.'

They would dispose of his body in the compost, and he would be replaced, for there were tens and tens of people who'd take his position, and they were younger and supple and spoke more than one language.

His only option was action. He could not stand still waiting for them. He would have to duck through the low double doors, step out of the porch and into the moonlight, swinging his blunt implement, smashing the keyboard first, which was something he'd been wanting to do anyway, then targeting Freya, who was more dangerous than her husband, then cracking Arlo's skull like the top of an egg, on and on, one after the other, notches on the table leg, though even in Patrick's wildest delusions, Kate was not involved.

Last of all would be Don. Patrick would drag his unconscious body to the deep part of the river where he would wait for him to wake up, then, as though absolving himself of every wrong, washing away every bitterness, skimming off his misery, Patrick would baptize Don, again and again, under many different names.

Breathing hard through his mouth, Patrick kicked out the double doors. As he stepped outside into moonlight, the cold landed the first punch, smacking him in the nose. He couldn't see the keyboard. He couldn't see the hooded figures. There was a bonfire smell. The market garden was still covered with a patchwork of coats, tarps, rugs.

As he stepped along the slate path that led towards the yard, the cold ran up through his feet, his ankles, rattled past his knees and settled in his stomach. He tried to be positive: in just his underwear, he would be that much nimbler while they, in their ungainly robes, would be like sacks of steak to tenderize. He thought of punching Don again, this time with the ring that was a present from Janet, and leaving a cattle brand on his temple. He looked back at the dome, checked the roof. Nothing. He looked up into the bare ash tree; it creaked of its own accord. But then, at last, there was laughter. A knowing, hollow laugh.

As he made his way across the yard, the sharp gravel made him wince. Keeping close to the south wall of the big house, he stayed out of the patches of moonlight. He was shivering. Mud clotted the thick hairs on his calves. As he walked down the stepped woodchip path, he saw there were some people around a small fire at the bottom of the garden, which was not unusual for a Friday night.

His mind swiftly reordered the previously stated narrative to make sense of the new information. They would tell him he was paranoid. They would put a flammable blanket round him. They would ask him whether he should consider laying off the green lassis. Then they would tip him on the fire and beat him, burn him, dance and raise a glass to his great sacrifice and, by morning, his bones would be nothing more than ash, sprinkled over the beetroot patch and returned to the earth.

Who will come looking for me?

Nobody. They'll keep signing for your pension, so that even after your death, you will still fund the community.

It was Janet, Freya and Kate sat on three kitchen chairs, with Freya in the middle and one big blanket around all their shoulders, each with a mug. They were leaning in to each other. There was a bladder of wine at their feet. The reason Janet had sent her boyfriend away, Patrick now decided, was because she didn't want him to witness this ruthless act of housekeeping.

He could hear them as he got close.

'. . . you haven't met him because he's a doofus,' Kate said.

'You call your boyfriend a doofus?' Janet said. She held her mug in both hands, keeping it close to her mouth as though it was tea. She had her hair tied back but a sweep of fringe across her forehead.

'You wouldn't like him,' Kate said.

'I would,' Freya said. 'I'm into doofuses. Is he ugly? I like ugly men.'

Janet picked up the foil bag and, squeezing one end, topped up their mugs. Her face was puffy. She had two red wine stains, shaped like devil horns, at the corners of her mouth.

'He's not ugly,' Kate said.

'I knew it. He's beautiful,' Janet said. 'You have to let us meet him.'

'Never going to happen.'

Freya said: 'I'll put on some make-up and pretend not to be your mother.'

'I don't want to see that.'

'Patrick?' Janet said.

He was standing on the other side of the fire, the table leg down at his side, and he was shivering so fast he could have turned to gas. In the firelight they saw the skin on his shoulders, sun-aged and slack. His chest hair was not at all dense, but it was evenly spread.

'Come on then,' he said. 'I'm ready.'

'Pat, what's happened?' Freya said. 'You must be freezing.'

They stood up together, the blanket falling from their shoulders.

'I suppose you're the lure. The sirens. Kate, I've got to say I'm disappointed in you.'

'Tell us what's wrong,' Janet said. 'You're shivering.'

'Yeah, that's it, offer to warm me up. *You won't get fucking near me.*'

Kate spoke slowly: 'What are you talking about?'

He shouted into the woods. 'Come out!' His giant lungs flapping. 'Come out! I'm ready for you!'

There was the noise of disgruntled birds. Leaves shuffling. Albert, in his room, in a hammock, opened his eyes. Don was already at the window. He had been watching his wife.

'Sweetheart, let me put this round you,' Janet said, coming towards him with the blanket held up, matador-style. Patrick raised the table leg.

'I'm not gonna hurt you, Patrick. I'm Janet – you know me. We're friends.'

'I know perfectly well who you are, you patronising cow. I should've known all along.'

Kate came round the other side of the fire, followed by Freya.

'Put down the table leg,' Kate said.

'Pat, what happened?' Janet said. 'Should I call an ambulance?'

'That's it. Pack me off!'

Janet took a step closer and raised the blanket up. Her eyes were red. They were closing in on both sides.

'You're cold,' Janet said.

'*You're* cold,' he said, raising the weapon.

Kate and Freya were treading slowly towards him.

'Back off!'

And then, dropping the table leg, he turned for the fire, ran towards it, his shivering body, his loose skin purple in patches, and leaped over the heat, the knee-high flames, his feet passing through them. He landed on the other side with a grunt, and was away, running. They watched him disappear, brief seams of flame in the pale hairs on the backs of his calves, like lit brandy on a Christmas cake, the skinny legs clattering off into the woods.

Everyone was awake, standing round the last of the fire at the bottom of the garden. They were pale-faced, interrupted dreams just beginning to fade. Arlo was in his professional rugby coat, thigh-length, black, some shine from the polyester. There were four wwoofers (unprepared for the cold, wearing fashionable jackets) holding out their hands to the last of the fire. Isaac and Albert wore waterproof ponchos over jumpers over pyjamas. In their hoods they did not look unlike the death-bringers that Patrick envisioned.

Don, in an act of deliberate melodrama, was out there in his blue casual kimono (which he wore around the house instead of a dressing gown) over pyjamas, as well as a woollen hat and walking boots. He thought of himself as useful in an emergency.

They passed the table leg from person to person, each trying to gauge Patrick's mindset by moving their hand along its corniced midsection. The moon was bright, and if there was a night for finding a pale potbellied man running through undergrowth, this was it.

Janet was pacing. 'Let's just go,' she said.

Don pulled his kimono tight and tried not to be distracted by his wife, red-eyed and swaying slightly, holding her mug of wine.

'Janet's right. We have to act fast. Freya, Arlo, Gabriella and her friend, follow the river. Janet, Kate, you saw which direction he went, try to find his trail. You two,' he said, pointing to the Belarusian lads, 'check the barn, workshop, shed, polytunnels. Marina and Isaac, you man the headquarters. Stay inside. Albert and I will take the lane.'

This was a rare chance for a display of leaderly navigation. With the air of a sergeant letting his squadron know that they would not all come back alive, he said: 'And I'm turning the mobile phones on.'

A torch for each group. They moved away from the fire, clutching their faces as the cold hit. Making their way into the dark, they were able to mark Don and Freya's progress by the distant sound of months of text messages and voicemail finally coming home. This was the phones' first genuine emergency. The needlessly loud message-received tone that nobody had ever learned how to change, like some strange birdcall, echoed back and forth through the woods.

The frozen puddles on the lane blinked in Don and Albert's torchlight. Albert was worried and excited and full of the pleasures of a well-defined objective. His father seemed youthful, tying a knot in his obi.

'Dad, is this the beginning of end times?'

'No, Albert. Sometimes bad things just happen.'

They were now on the road and walking at pace. Albert had to jog every few steps to keep up.

'Marina says we'll start to notice more and more bad things as we get closer.'

'Look for yellow cars and you see yellow cars. We call that "confirmation bias". I'll teach you about it someday.'

'Okay, I'll start looking for good things.'

'That's better.'

'Do you think Patrick's dead?'

'He's not dead.'

'How do you know?'

'It's an educated guess.'

'I want to make an educated guess. Is that something I'll learn from the Soviet Hat?'

'Funnily enough, me and your mother were talking about that.'

Albert watched his father with wide eyes. 'Oh my God, really?'

Don lifted his eyebrows and picked up the pace again.

'If you're *really* good, then we might let you have a certain lesson *before* your thirteenth birthday.'

'Yes!' Albert said, and started conscientiously swinging his torch-light into the bushes at the side of the road.

From the woods they heard yelled reassurances: 'We're not out to get you!' 'We love you, Patrick!' 'We're your friends!' This was just like the sort of hippy trust game that Don had always retreated from – that Blaen-y-Llyn was definitively against – but now, occurring naturally in a dramatic situation, it filled Don with pride and adrenalin. Under torchlight, standing water showed the sudden April frost: shattered geometric sheets of ice. Along the bank, the saplings glittered.

Following the river were Freya, Arlo and Gabby Orles – a Catalonian and regular visitor to Blaen-y-Llyn, this time returning with her new partner, Patricia, who looked beautiful when suddenly woken, and they held hands as they shushed through the semi-frozen undergrowth.

'Patrick! Listen to your heart!' Arlo shouted.

Kate and Janet tried to locate and follow Patrick's track, which began as a dark path scratched through the wet ground but soon faded to nothing. Janet was way out in front, climbing over fallen trees and pushing, without complaint, through waist-high nettles.

As light started to seep in above the horizon, so the edges softened on Patrick's paranoia. He was clinging to the branch of a low oak tree, his feet wedged in a Y-shaped split in the trunk. The one thing he was absolutely certain of – that his friends were out to kill him – was becoming unconvincing.

The difficulty was he didn't want to be wrong. What if there was no fundamental problem and he should just be a bit more outward-looking and cut down on the weed a bit and try to help other people and practise a few new recipes, and that would be enough? He prayed to any God that this was not the solution. That *moderation* was not what he needed. That these people really were coming to shake him down, to tell him some home truths. That they came with a bolt gun and a panel saw.

In the cold, his body was shrinking. He had no toes; they had disappeared an hour ago. He had no feet. He had no hands, no nose. His ears were missing. His eyes made insectile clicks each time he blinked; they would freeze over if he gave them a chance. He was losing all the senses except for his tongue.

'Ahhhh!'

Even if he had wanted to call the names of the people he cared about, the cold would not let him pronounce them. Only vowel sounds remained. He heard voices coming from different sides.

'Ahh!'

He had no wrists, no elbows. And although he now knew, deep down, that they were not out to kill him, he would do anything to delay their sympathy, their thoughtfulness, their forgiving.

He let himself fall from the tree he had climbed. There was a dry, cracking sound. Everyone heard it.

He had no ankle to shatter.

Dragging himself onwards, he stumbled, making small animal noises, with splinters of bone beneath his skin, while three parties closed in and Janet yelled: 'Patrick! We're coming!'

At the edge of the forest, where the National Trust boundary ended, there was a Taylor Wimpey homes development: a single cul-de-sac built on the edge of Llanmadoc, with views of the woods beyond. It had just been completed and no one had moved in yet.

Patrick crawled into the street. The windows were blank, no curtains, no trinkets, no cars in the drives, just ten subtly non-identical detached homes, pine doors, tapered drives leading to one-car garages. In a curious and isolated nod towards a made-up past, there were replica Victorian street lamps. A road shaped like a thermometer – a turning circle at one end.

In the lamplight, Patrick noticed that his ankle was grossly swollen, nearly the same size as his skull. He lugged himself to the centre of the cul-de-sac's bulb and flopped on the even concrete. His body shook. The street light was steady. He was the same colour as the moon.

It was Janet who first spotted him and started running down the street, followed by Kate and, not far behind, Don, Albert and the rest. A cloud of them, steam coming off their scalps. Patrick was curled up, but with his left leg stuck out in an attempt to keep it numb. The ankle had ballooned, the shape of his foot lost to the swelling. He made the low gurgling noise of a radiator filling. Janet unbuttoned her coat as she ran, and behind her, the others followed suit. His thin boxer shorts were torn and stained, a purple testicle like a limpet against his thigh. They took off their clothes as they descended on him – just as he had feared – and smothered him in coats and jumpers, laying out everything they could and swaddling him until it was just his head at one end and, at the other, his broken ankle, a half-deflated football, a geodesic dome, the skin dying, turning grey and dusty at the edges, and the impossible angle of his foot.

While Janet efficiently tucked the clothes in around him, Don – who couldn't look at the injury – made a display of knowledge, standing, speaking towards the mock-Victorian lamps.

'The predator here is the cold. Patrick is at risk of going hypothermic. He's stopped shivering – that's not good. It won't be enough to simply cover him in coats. He needs body contact. Patrick, I am going to give you a hug.'

And with that, he retightened his robe, dropped to his knees, fell to his side on the Tarmac and spooned in behind. Patrick's slack expression didn't change. Don had a man's-gotta-do-what-a-man's-gotta-do tough-guy look, resting his jaw on to Patrick's shoulder. Freya rearranged the coats over both of them. Two heads peeking out, old friends, bonded by labour and a shared vision. Patrick's eyes bulged a little as though trying to leap free.

Waiting for the ambulance, they took it in turns, snuggling in under the pile of jackets, passing on their body heat through his pale, blueish back, the milk-white notches of his spinal column. Everyone was part of it. Patrick had decided to be silent, to not give them anything more. Even when feeling Janet's small breasts and tangible nipples against his back, he kept schtum. She gripped him and put her warm lips against his neck. Now that it was her turn, she wouldn't let anyone else take over. Patrick wondered how, when his body was under such extreme pressure, it still found time to siphon blood to appease his groin. Strangers put their hands on Patrick's shoulder and squeezed mechanically, as though testing his pressure. After a while, Marina, Isaac and the Belarusians turned up with Thermoses. Isaac ran in loops round the turning circle, blowing his breath, pretending to be a train.

No one but the newest of the wwoofers took notice of Don sitting on the pavement, wiping his eyes. He cried, on average, once per quarter. He liked the release. He was good at it. This sometimes involved a kind of play-blubbing, his mouth opening and closing before the real crying could begin.

They shivered by the roadside as the ambulance drove into the cul-de-sac. They felt like a cult then – in a good way – standing in a neat line with bed-heads as the flashing lights reflected off the white lilac bushes. The empty lounges and unfurnished bedrooms filled with blue light. Pulling into an empty drive, the ambulance reversed to where Patrick was lying. Freya knelt next to him, trying to keep him awake by asking why Miles Davis was overrated. They stood aside as two paramedics appeared from the back doors carrying plastic green briefcases.

'What's his name?' the woman asked.

They replied in chorus.

Some of the group hoped the paramedics' first reaction would be 'Woah, weird, what are you people even doing here? It's five in the morning', but it was as if the paramedics couldn't see them. Don was in a *casual kimono*. There were *Spanish lesbians* here, for God's sake. But there was no comment, no look. The paramedics just peeled away the layers of clothing until they found Patrick and Janet's embalmed bodies at the centre.

'Hello, Patrick? I'm Helen. How long have you been outside?'

He couldn't speak though he was still conscious.

'About two and a half hours, we think,' Janet said, and she unclamped herself from behind him.

'Okay. Patrick, I'm going to give you some oxygen now?'

The other paramedic, a guy, brought a gas tank out of the ambulance, set it down with a clank and put the respirator over Patrick's face. There was a noise like automatic doors.

'Patrick, nod if you've taken any drugs or alcohol?'

He just stared. Freya said: 'Only cannabis, as far as we know.'

'We're going to give you something for the pain, okay?'

She looked for veins in his arms but couldn't find any, so she injected the morphine into his bicep. Don stood next to his wife and put his arm around her. He still couldn't look at the injury. They wrapped Patrick in silver and lifted him on to a cloth stretcher.

'Okay,' the paramedic said, 'I need an adult to come with us.'

They were all standing there listening to the engine, and in that moment they realized, having ridden a wave of collective love for this hard-to-love older man, having all felt unified by their support for him – in spite of his laziness, his depression – that they were each expecting someone else to jump at the chance to ride in the ambulance, that there was surely someone – they each thought – who was the right person to go, one among them for whom it was clearly *best*, and no one wished to push in and say *me* because that one *right* person should be allowed to accompany Patrick at this important and high-octane time.

Nobody spoke.

And the blue light scrolled across their faces, which were sad and solemn and some defiantly smiling, until at last the right person gave in, and she said: 'Okay.'

2   A Partial History

1989

It was a warm September morning, her second day on campus, and Freya was on a bench outside Norwich University's flagship Olympic pool, wearing a jumper with two wet patches on the chest. This was when Don first saw her. A week later he had taken up swimming and was half a length behind her in the medium lane. He had goggles and, underwater, saw her body magnified. She was so lithe as to be, Don later claimed, 'indistinguishable from the water she passed through'. During his seventh length, he stroked her arm as she went by. In his eighteenth length, she kicked him in the thigh with a painted toenail, almost drawing blood, though she has no recollection of this.

He waited at the shallow end, expecting her to apologize. She did ten lengths, swimming clockwise, tapping the edge of the pool next to where Don was standing. She changed to butterfly and did five more. He used his locker key and, underwater, sawed at the cut on his leg a little, to make it look worse. Then he stood in the middle of the lane, his back to the shallow-end wall, so she wouldn't be able to turn. She was doing the breaststroke towards him, and he watched her head repeatedly pop out of the water, 'the dripping oval of her mouth,' as he told it, 'dark and inhabitable'.

She slowed as she came near, a look of recognition, or swallowed water, on her face. Without goggles she couldn't have seen much through the chlorine. Then she slid under the tricolour floats, into the fast lane, tuck-turned and slithered away.

Freya first met Janet when they lived opposite each other in the same halls. They were a year older than the rest of their corridor, so felt superior and wise, the same way a nine-and-a-half-year-old feels about a nine-year-old. They could think of nothing more pleasurable than sitting at the edge of the Union Square, backs to the Student Advice Centre, judging their peers. The square was shaped a bit like an amphitheatre: stepped seating on three sides, and a lower area in the middle that was, in effect, a stage. Janet and Freya observed the way freshers' postures changed as they approached the limelight as though getting into character; the un-casual casualness of onstage Frisbee and Hacky Sack; the theory that people semiconsciously positioned themselves according to their looks: munters on the mouldy paving near the dining-hall exhaust vent versus hotties having their literal time in the sun, smouldering away in the suntrap south-east quadrant.

Although Don had always felt that it was his unique powers of underwater seduction that had won Freya over, the truth was that she and Janet had been watching him. Don was in the year above them. He had a very part-time job (Wednesday afternoons, fortnightly) delivering the student newspaper, *Off Beat*. There were four newspaper dispensers in the corners of the square. On a number of occasions, Freya and Janet sat with cups of tea and a slice of banana bread watching the gloveless machismo with which he tore off the plastic ties on each stack. He was chubbier then, pre-beard, with thick, soft arms and a shallow quiff that dangled three fishing lines into the centre of his forehead. The student population was genuinely excited by the prospect of a new issue of *Off Beat* – it had won awards – so as soon as he filled a dispenser, nearby first-years would scurry across to grab a fresh one, giving Don the air, which he clearly enjoyed, of a zookeeper at feeding time. He used a six-wheeled sack trolley and deliberately, they decided, carried way more at one time than seemed practical, even when going up steps. He used a red Ford van, one of the few vehicles allowed on to pedestrianized areas of campus, which he drove with an arm resting on the unwound window, parking, they again observed, in deliberately provocative positions, on cross-hatched markings, in front of fire exits, all to signal his maverick approach.

Although he was ridiculous, there was also something likeable about him, and Janet knew Freya was keen when she described his bum as looking 'like an alarm bell'. Janet encouraged her to make the first move.

On a day that felt, to Don, no different from any other since he was unaware of the mechanisms at work, Freya waited for him outside the changing rooms. She asked him if he'd like to sit with her and, in the café that overlooked the climbing wall, they shared chips with cheap mayonnaise. He admired her chlorine-burnt eyes.

'I like how hungry I feel after swimming,' she said.

'We have such agency when we're hungry,' he said.

There was the sound of a free-climber hitting the crash-mat.

'Before we eat,' he said, raising one fist into the sky, 'we are revolutionaries. Afterwards, bureaucrats.'

She picked up a chip and dunked it in the gunge.

The next time he saw her in the pool she was wearing goggles. Underwater, she could see the reason he always let her get out of the pool first: his hydrodynamic spoiler, an inverted fin, bulging from his shorts. When she went to the changing rooms, he stayed in the pool to swim it off, which took two and a half lengths. She was waiting for him in the intermediary foot-washing room with indentations on her forehead from where the goggles had been too tight. The smell of chlorine would always remind them of their first kiss.

After a fortnight, they consummated their relationship in the family changing room. In recent renditions of the story, Don toyed with an awkward joke about how the family changing room should be renamed the 'changing the family' room because it marked the reinvention of established ideas of family, but he hadn't worked out quite how to make it funny yet.

By the end of the second term, Freya and Don spent most of their time in her bedroom enjoying the fact that, almost by accident, they had swimmers' physiques. The remaining time was spent with Janet, who was ruthless on enforcing a ban on canoodling in her company and, if she caught them at it, was known to clap loudly and say *hey* in the manner of someone shooing a dog away from a picnic.

1989 was a good, or at least action-packed year, to be at a left-leaning university. In one corner of the Union Square there was a well-meaning but badly made Tiananmen Square memorial: a life-size sculpture of the 'Unknown Rebel', the man who, with shopping bags in each hand, halted a column of Type 59 tanks. That the memorial was never made to wear a traffic cone showed the seriousness among the student body. In other news, Thatcher was starting to look unhinged; Black Monday revealed the vulnerability of the stock markets; the Happy Mondays revealed the quality of drugs from the continent. It was at a One Berlin-themed squat party in a derelict nursing home that they first discussed the idea of communal living. Along the corridor they could hear the sound of two adjacent bedrooms, east and west, being 'unified' with the blunt end of a fire extinguisher. In the hallway there were wreckheads jousting in NHS wheelchairs in the name of anti-capitalism.

After the party they went back to Janet's and sat on her mattress drinking West Country cider. Freya said something about how, in their halls of residence, with the tiny shared kitchen, the two unisex shower cubicles, the papery walls, weren't they already a kind of commune? And was it just a rumour that the design of the hall was based on a low-security Swedish prison? And the way all students wore the same clothes! They were a cult! Don was not yet known for his charismatic public speaking, but with a skinful of opaque cider he started to build a reputation. Janet and Freya sat on the bed either side of him, feeling the mattress shift as he gestured and worked up a rhythm.

'All that hippy bullshit,' Don said, starting boldly, though giving the impression that he was not sure how the sentence would proceed, 'just about ruined the project, just about sabotaged the whole idea, so they could spend a few years getting *idealism* out of their *systems*, then go succeed in their start-up businesses, running fucking plant nurseries and art supplies shops, and referring back to the wild years they spent trying to reinvent society, *man* [he made the peace sign, then flipped it round to a V] – telling their friends and children "imagine our naiveté" and "*if* me-then could see me-now" – and the truth is, they were never going to get it right first time, they were never going to just *think up* a new way of living, a new basis for society, *and* carry it out successfully, no chance, so you can't call the hippy movement a failure – you can call them *weaklings* – but we should never forget it was just the first attempt, and it *was* decent, they should have kept going but the whole thing got dismissed as a fad, as educated druggies patting themselves on the back, as part of fashion, part of the sixties, because – and this is the real fuck-up – they let it get smeared with the *sexual* revolution, which has nothing to do with *new structures for living*.'

'You're *that* bloke,' Janet had said, sipping from her plastic cup. 'My brother warned me you'd be at university.'

Freya remembered noticing that after Don had said his bit he kept nodding, as though his sentence continued on, unheard, in his head. He strongly agreed with himself.

In their second year, all three of them moved off campus into a mid-terrace place on Maud Street, of which Patrick Kinwood was the private landlord. Janet was only willing to live with a couple on the agreement that they avoid all but the most cursory demonstrations of physical affections within her sight or earshot, saving it for the campus darkroom and swimming-pool changing rooms. This was perhaps one reason why Janet welcomed their landlord dropping by: he punctured the atmosphere of covert groping.

With his rental properties, tinted glasses, coke problem and loneliness, Patrick reinforced all they hoped was true about someone made wealthy by the greetings card industry. 'He signals the impending collapse of consumerism,' Don said, and nicknamed him 'the canary in the coalmine'. Patrick supported Norwich City Football Club, the Canaries, who played in yellow and green, and sometimes, when drunk, he was known to shout 'I'm canary till I die' and this pleased Don. It was obvious when Patrick had enjoyed an excessive weekend because he would turn up on their doorstep on Monday holding a toolbox, ready to work through his self-loathing with DIY. Their house had a lot of work done that summer.

Don, meanwhile, was the tenant who told his landlord: 'Property is theft.' It helped that Patrick was, at that time, mostly in love with Janet and would stop mid-sentence if she walked across the lounge in her towel. After a couple of months of getting to know Patrick, Don stopped calling him 'the canary'. It had become difficult to see him as merely a representation of a particular world view. Eventually, there came a point when they were not freaked out to find their landlord – without the statutory twenty-four hours' notice – waiting on their sofa for them to get back from seminars. It helped that the house was falling apart so there were always new reasons for him to turn up in grimy joggers. Being fifteen years their elder, but thinking of himself as broadly part of their generation, he made a point of not commenting on the state of the flat, red wine on the walls, a webbed crack in the skylight, two missing banisters.

When Janet asked if she could redecorate her room – three walls white, one aubergine – Patrick said he would help her. He paid for paint, rollers, brushes, dust sheets, and they spent days together in a poorly ventilated room, giddy from vapour. Patrick's oft-proclaimed love for women in work clothes stemmed from Janet in a paint-spattered Radio 1 Roadshow T-shirt. Don enjoyed reminding Patrick of this: 'You thought it was chemical attraction; she thought it was paint fumes.' Don and Patrick built their relationship on warmly assassinating each other's characters. 'God bless you, Don, safety valve of Middle England's discontent.' It was only much later, while building the community, that he and Don, keeping their style of direct communication, slowly lost the buffer of goodwill.

After graduating, Freya, Don and Janet moved to London, where the early 1990s recession had bedded in. Although residential rent was still high in central London, they'd been advised to look into office space. Don bought a second-hand suit and met the estate agent – Ash – a broad Australian with a sun-ripened face and almost no lips, to look at a dirt-cheap block in North Lambeth. They shook hands and kept shaking as they walked. The entranceway was entirely mirrored, so that in all directions Don saw himself multiplied: an army of smartly dressed versions of himself shaking hands with an army of estate agents *for ever*. Don sometimes said it was the horror of this image from which the community was born.

The agent opened two locks and pushed through into a lightless space, unfastening and throwing up the industrial metal shutters which covered each window. The shutters made a sound like a train passing. Also, trains passed. The space was a huge, single white room, the floor covered with the thinnest blue office carpet, dusty windows running the length of two sides. They were overlooked all around by other offices, which were empty. The flat tar roof, a four-storey climb up a New York-style fire escape, had a view as far as Crystal Palace in the south-east, and to the north they could make out a lack of buildings that, it took them some time to realize, was the river.

Once they'd moved in, they discovered that, each morning, the smell of burnt bacon fat pumped out of a nearby ventilation pipe and that huge rats patrolled the bins in the quadrangles between the surrounding buildings.

They built their own walls using office partitions and shelving, piles of books, shoeboxes, wardrobes, dressers and breeze blocks from a skip down the road. Janet hung curtains and pashminas as doorways. Sound travelled. She invested in musician's earplugs rather than listen to her housemates' idea of *silent* sex. The corner by the fire exit became the kitchen, with knee-high gas canisters and a two-ring camping stove on a school desk. They found a still-functioning industrial contact grill (one ribbed surface, one flat) out the back of the café opposite. It produced an unsettling plastic smell but was otherwise perfect.

Don managed to get a job that related to his film studies degree, working at the twenty-four-screen Elephant and Castle UCI. He squeezed out bags of nacho cheese, grease-sprayed the hot-dogs and, best of all, emptied bladders of salsa that looked like liposuction fat. Popcorn dust clogged his sinuses.

Each screening had to be checked every half an hour to make sure nobody was smoking or having full intercourse in the deluxe seats. He never saw whole films, just glimpses as he moved from screen to screen: a man being tortured with a vice, a boy hugging a dog, animated clocks dancing, a male nurse talking about love, a series of massive explosions, snow on a lake, blood on bed sheets, a gondola trip . . . and so on, for twenty-four screens. His dissertation had been called 'Collage and Sleep in Late European Cinema' and it was in this essay that Don had first put forward the idea that it was valuable to think of life as a film. Not that the individual was the star and there were cameras watching, but that our eyes and ears were a camera that was always recording. We had to make decisions about what our lives – a live broadcast, one-shot, un-editable film – were going to be about. In Don's life-film, there was no soundtrack. He preferred the ambiguity of silence, he said. This was just one justification, of many, for why Don could not enjoy music.

He became irritatingly discerning, saying he would not consume toxic food or toxic culture, saying that nacho sauce, *Lethal Weapon 3* and Margaret Thatcher all spawned from the same toothless maw. The UCI radicalized him. He knew by heart the trailers for *A Few Good Men*, *Batman Returns*, *Basic Instinct* and *Aladdin*. He knew the taglines from numerous high-end adverts: Tanqueray, Omega, Bosch. When he was made redundant, he said this to his boss:

'Your mind – it is the centre of your life. Everything you see and hear and feel. How would you know if someone stole your mind?'

It was from the trailer to *Total Recall*.

Freya worked in the admissions department of the School of Oriental and African Studies. Her two colleagues were married to each other and the office sometimes felt like an extension of their bedroom, with pet names and passive-aggressive whispering. The man was an alcoholic; five or six times a day they'd hear the conspicuous hiss of a can of Holsten Pils spitting froth on to the underside of his desk. It was never mentioned, though at the end of each work day he had the cans lined up by his feet. As far as Freya could tell, it had got to the point in their marriage when it was easier for his wife to pretend that the regular *kerrrr-chisss* sound was a normal part of the administrative bustle: keystrokes, photocopying, continental lager. As a way to feel better about her job, Freya stole and cycled home so much good quality stationery that she started to get backache. The notepads and rollerball pens would become key tools in planning the community.

Meanwhile, Janet worked in a vintage clothes warehouse. Campaigners used to come in and slash the furs. Addicts used to steal novelty ties from the one-pound bin. The clothes arrived in huge, tightly wrapped bales which, once cut, flopped out, trebling in size: marshes of dead people's dirty glad-rags. There was no heating because heating was pointless in a space that size, so Janet had a permanent dust cough and sniffles and was eventually diagnosed with bronchitis.

This said, the three of them were reasonably happy: Freya and Janet bonded by jobs they despised while Don, newly jobless, was the stay-at-home housewife, cleaning and cooking. Then Patrick arrived. The recession had hit the rental market and he'd had to sell off a property. They didn't find out until later that the one he sold was the one he had been living in. He was homeless. They thought he would only stay for the weekend, but on Monday evening Janet and Freya came home from work to find he had laid out a bribe: two dozen oysters and a bottle of champagne. Since he'd quit cocaine, he had taken up eating. As Janet frowned and prodded at one of the frilled, quasi-testicular sacs, Patrick realized that oysters were no guarantee of seduction. Don, on the other hand, dove right in.

During those first two weeks, Patrick made himself indispensable, doing practical things like building plasterboard walls, which – Don claimed – were mainly motivated by his desire to achieve privacy with Janet. Then Freya got made redundant too and Patrick offered to cover the shortfall in rent, at which point he became permanent. While Janet went to work, the three of them explored free London: morning swims in Hampstead mixed pond, lunch from the Hare Krishnas, museums in the afternoon. Each night, when Janet was at her most tired and susceptible, Patrick would show her his leather-bound notebook full of primitive sums proving that, with a mixture of mild benefit fraud and some extra flatmates to lower costs, Janet could quit her job and join them in enjoying *the summer of the slump*. One glorious evening, when she could feel a new chest infection brewing, Janet caved.

They brought in an old university friend, Li, who was clever, lonely and had a nose-bridge so slight she had to tie on her glasses. Don suggested they invite Ash – the estate agent – by handwritten letter because, as Don wrote, 'I thought I saw something in you that was longing for the other,' but they got no reply. They brought in Perry, a skinny would-be scriptwriter who built himself an actual garden shed in one corner of the room for live/work. There was Chris, who was repetitive but useful, an eco-carpenter in the days when eco-*something* didn't just mean he had once climbed a tree. There was Alana, who 'disliked bread' and brought with her a hypoallergenic kitten. There was Arlo Mela, a young Welsh-Sardinian sous-chef who worked so many hours at Le Gavroche that they were never sure if he slept in his bed or just muddled the duvet for effect. With each new recruit, they rearranged the walls to make new bedrooms. The rent dropped. They shared food. Sunday lunches were gourmet – oysters not unusual – with above-the-rooftop views.

By the end of the summer, the recession began to subside. On the roof of a neighbouring office, a crane appeared. Drunk, one Sunday, watched by all his housemates, Don decided to leap across the small gap between the roofs and climb it. At the top, by the driver's seat, he found bottles of Celtic Spring mineral water, filled with piss in different shades of dehydration. He wanted to yell, 'The heart of the capitalist dream,' but didn't. Instead he 'noticed his desire' to. At that time, he was into noticing his emotions.

By autumn, the surrounding office blocks were nearly full: ergonomic shoemakers, licensed taxis and a life-science industry magazine called *Research? Research!* They had grown too used to feeling that the building was their own, and their neighbours, people with real jobs, didn't like walking past on a lunch break and seeing shutters rattle up on a tableau of dropouts in towelling robes. One morning, Ash turned up with two big blokes from the council.

After they got served their month's notice, Don made one of his speeches. Except at that point he didn't make speeches, so it just seemed impromptu and genuine. He said they had two choices: either return to the familiar, piss-drinking drudge of city life or run with the summer's energy, the shared skills, the collective joblessness, their youngness, and try a different life, in the countryside. That's all he called it. The countryside. 'The city will still be here, waiting to eat us up, the moment we want to come back.'

This speech was not a surprise to Freya. She and Don had already talked at length about it – had even discussed how best to pitch it to their housemates and how best to hide it from Alana, who no one liked. But Freya played along, pretending to be struck, right then, by the idea's ripeness.

'I'm ready,' she said, standing up. 'Who else is with us?'

Out of seven of them, only Arlo stayed seated. A few weeks later, they heard he'd won a scholarship to work as a *patissier* in New York. Not only that but it was with his culinary hero, a legendary Austrian chef with an empire of restaurants and his own range of implements, including a signature veal mallet.

They spent the next couple of weeks doing road trips in two cars – one Chris's, the other Li's – searching for an appropriate property. They went to Yorkshire, Northumberland, Dumfriesshire, Mid Wales, North Wales, South Wales – anywhere that was cheap. In North Gower they found a building that was previously a parish school, a single classroom its best feature, and a rundown cottage attached. It sat on unpromising-looking farmland on the gloomy west side of The Bulwark with an almost-fantastic view of Rhossili beach if it weren't for the downs in the way. But it was undeniably cheap, and the farmer who was selling it, in a charming reverse of their other experiences, did not hide his desperation to get rid. He said: 'I'm desperate to get rid.' He had tremendous visible capillaries in his nose. His only attempt at estate-agent spin was when he referred to the Gower peninsula's 'microclimate'.

After showing them the house, he walked with them to the top of The Bulwark, which rose up behind the farm. From there, they could see north, the Loughor Estuary; west, Worm's Head pointing out to the Irish Sea; south, the Bristol Channel and the cliffs of Devon beyond. To the east was Swansea and industry and that which they were trying to escape. For Don, to whom such things were important, a peninsula had the right implications: something that pushed out from the mainland, making an *insular* path into the unknown.

Patrick – now at the peak of his love for Janet – paid the deposit. They got a joint mortgage that named Patrick, Freya, Janet, Li, Perry,

Chris and Don as tenants-in-common, dividing up proportions of ownership, and therefore of repayment, according to what each person could afford. At the same time, Patrick had a solicitor draw up a Declaration of Trust that, in an act of clear distrust, committed each person to pay a little each month, beyond their share of the mortgage, to reimburse his deposit. He was happy to see his experience as a landowner coming in useful and he set up a sink fund and bought comprehensive insurance. In October, they moved in, when the only space with a fully functioning roof was the schoolroom, so that's where they slept. It was lucky that London had got them used to living in close quarters. They brought their gas stoves and favoured slow-cooked stews and curries because they radiated more heat into the room. They had not expected snow on the beach by Christmas.

During that first winter, they worked on pinning down the project's details, from breeds of unusual vegetable the microclimate would support – breadnut, gumbo, black salsify – to the stepped permaculture garden, the badminton green, an Aylesbury drake and six ducks, the yurt village, a Gloucester Old Spot, radicchio, garbanzo, cowpea, their right to a lobster pot at Broughton and fully off-grid power: hydro, solar, wind, and car batteries concealed in beehives.

By spring, they'd lost two members: Li, who said the damp was making her ill, and Perry the scriptwriter, who'd gone to live with his parents and write a feature-length script about life in a commune. With seven people living in one room, privacy was hard to find. Everyone knew how Patrick felt about Janet and they watched to see if she would capitulate. With no TV, they became the soap opera.

Their numbers swelled as the weather got better, and under Chris's supervision they got to work on repairing the house and outbuildings. The stairs were rotted in a slapstick way and they used a wood-fired steam-powered log saw, Chris's pride and joy, to cut planks. The gas-fed Rayburn oven, which they had assumed was ruined, awoke from hibernation, a roar of flames in its stomach. The house and gardens were in such a state that hour by hour the impact was dramatic. After a day with scythes and machetes, clearing brush, nettles, brambles and weeds, they could celebrate around a victory bonfire. The whole first year, in fact, was characterized by this sensation of making big steps.

Official meetings were, and remained, on Thursday mornings, at first weekly and later fortnightly. They were chaired by a different member each time until they realized it was easier to allow Don to be permanent chair than it was to try and control his contributions. One of his earliest suggestions was to change the name of the farm to Welsh. Don expressed his support of the Meibion Glyndwr movement – a then still-active group who had been firebombing English-owned holiday homes on Anglesey and the Llyn peninsula. He said the anglophone destruction of Welsh culture was unforgivable. To watch Don pronounce *Meibion Glyndwr* was to see a man battle his own genetics.

'Good on 'em, I say,' said Don, whose family was English, but who had a dram of Scots blood somewhere way back in his ancestry.

'I'm sure they're relieved to have your support,' said Patrick, who was, with his Welsh mother, the only one among them who could claim to be returning to the motherland.

They bought an English–Welsh dictionary and set about trying to mash together the two words that best captured their geographical location, since Welsh house names tended to be purely descriptive: 'house on triangular piece of land', for instance. There followed a fortnight of gruelling discussion, longlists, shortlists, blind voting and, each day, the sound of people absently repeating different combinations of words – *Ty Nant*, *Cwm Mawr*, *Trem Coed*, *Treffoel*, *Dolclogwyn* – to gauge how they felt in the mouth.

Blaen meant 'extremity' and 'beginning', both of which, Don felt, said something about their reasons for being there. It also referred to a place at the head of a valley. They were at the side of an almost-valley. And *Llyn*, meaning 'lake' or 'pool', referenced the swimmable section of river in the woods. All that first winter they had talked about how they would bathe and picnic there, in much the same way that people buying more suburban homes visualize barbecues they will never have. Don liked the name for its challenging consonant and forbidding stand-alone extra vowel. Blaen-y-Llyn was a mark of their early commitment to the language and would subsequently be a reminder that some of the grown-ups never moved beyond a toddler's conversational Welsh.

The first animal they bought was a Gloucester Old Spot called Hog. They gave him that name to avoid too strong an emotional attachment, since they planned to fatten and kill him. Hog had different ideas, making himself indispensable by becoming the community's premiere cultivator of previously unworkable scrubland; pretty much the entirety of what was now the market garden was first dug up, and shat on, by him. Only when there was no more uncultivated land left for Herzog (as Don took to calling him), did they decide to eat him. Don picked the short straw to see who would wield the .22 rifle they'd borrowed from a neighbouring farm.

The night before the slaughter, while julienning spring onions, he took the lid off his trigger finger. Much bleeding and, some people felt, affected swearing followed. Hamming it up, appropriately. He said he was gutted but it compromised his marksmanship, though he was still happy to supervise. Another round of straws was pulled.

Werner was eating scraps from a bucket when Freya shot him in the brain. Don, trying to help, fell to his knees and pinned the pig on its side, wrestling style, while she cut the artery in its neck. Then, as research had said it would, the pig appeared to come back to life, a nerve response causing the body to buck and the legs to kick. Werner was big, bigger than the man pinning him down, and as Don scrabbled to get up, he took a hoof to the ribs.

For six days, Don walked slowly up and down steps and made elongated sighing noises when getting in and out of chairs. He also took any opportunity to mythologize his wife's role: her calm manner, perfect aim but underlying humanity. As a result, it was suggested that Freya be the first person in the community to apply for a firearms licence, and once she had that, her fate was sealed. She was the executioner. Don was never asked to help again, but still, he ate bacon with an air of moral immunity.

After two years, Arlo came back. So the story goes, the legendary Austrian chef had visited the kitchen to decide who of the trainees to keep on full-time. He had complimented Arlo who, at the end of a long shift, held back tears of awed happiness, flushed red from head to toe and felt his skin grow clammy. They shook hands. The next day the message was passed back that Arlo 'did not have the palms' for pastry.

Nobody has ever found out where Arlo went for the intervening years. He arrived on New Year's Day, walking up the frozen lane with a roll of Japanese knives under his arm instead of a sleeping bag. By then, he had the kind of beard that was unacceptable in a professional kitchen. He had no gloves and his hands were blue.

When the big house was finally habitable, they had a grand opening party. Don chose this day to announce that Freya was twelve weeks pregnant. This boosted morale, and kickstarted new projects. Don, Patrick and Janet set to work on building the workshop. Chris, Arlo and Freya oversaw the creation of a market garden and finally bought books on permaculture.

Twenty-six weeks later, Freya staggered into the schoolroom, sumo-stance, hair tied back, breathing like a weightlifter, trailed by a midwife and her trainee in squared-off navy pinafores. Kate Bronwyn Riley (or Bronwyn Kate Riley, as she would have been called, had Don got his way) was twelve days early. When Don had left that morning – to collect a boot-load of baby clothes, books, toys and a cot from a like-minded community in Somerset – he kissed Freya and whispered into her bellybutton: 'Don't even think about it.'

He was lucky that the news got through to him at all. In Somerset, the phone rang in the Mongolian-style meeting house and, by chance, he was nearby. Speeding back through narrow lanes, he beeped his horn at blind bends, biting his tongue, on to the motorway, dominating the fast lane, his aura of necessity, sweeping cars aside with a flash of his headlights. A part of him was relieved that his role in the birth was so clearly defined. *All you have to do is go as fast as you can.* And he secretly hoped to hear the newborn wail of a police siren behind him, to be pulled over, to speak to the officer in candid terms, share a desperate play on words – 'I'm sorry I broke the speed limit, but my wife's waters just broke' – and be back on the road with the officer's best wishes, having crashed through the fourth wall between government and citizen. In truth, the race was all but over by the time he crossed the Severn bridge, but they had no way of letting him know, so he powered onwards, kept the split-screen narrative going, drawing parallels between the engine's straining, pushing, sweating beneath the bonnet, and his wife – as he visualized her – screaming: 'Where the fuck is Don? I need him here now!'

When his car came skidding into the yard it was dark, and entering the hall he knew by Patrick's hair, which was swept across unevenly in the manner of someone who has been involved in something major, that he had missed it. Freya and Kate were both asleep and Don had to accept that his biggest role in proceedings would be to feed the placenta to the goats. He listened to them chew.

Patrick had been in the right/wrong place at the right/wrong time and had tried his best to help Freya, even – in a moment of uncharacteristic boldness – nodding when she asked him if he wanted to cut the umbilical cord. He can remember its gristly texture, the resistance first, then the give. If he had moments of feeling unsure about his place in the community, of whether he was there for the right reasons, it was then that he felt tied in.

3   Treatment

Saturday

'Dad, time to arise.'
　'Mmm.'
　'Open your eyes.'
　'What time is it?'
　'Late. Terribly late.'
　'What time exactly?'
　'Nearly double figures.'
　'Albert, your father's tired.'
　'Your wife has been awake for hours.'
　'Okay.'
　'You said you'd let me try on the Soviet Hat.'
　'Did I?'
　'Last night while we were in the woods, you promised.'
　'I think we're going to see Uncle Patrick in hospital today. Why don't you write him a nice get-well card?'

Kate was in the waiting room. Her father had given her one of the community's two mobile phones. *36 unread messages and 60 missed calls.* The calls dated back to the previous summer. The messages were mostly from unknown numbers trying to contact people who had left months ago.

Friends, this is Nova – the 'Finn with the Grin'! Now in Mumbai – working for an NGO. If you want to visit, my floor's comfortable! ;-) Miss you!

Don't know if Jake's still there – but if he is: PENBLWYDD HAPUS I TI, CARIAD! Dan x

Frey, hope you're feeling better. Sorry to hear things have been difficult. If you want to talk – I'm here. Be brave. xx

Solstice Approacheth! Swiss Andy here. Best wishes from La Senda, intentional community in Santiago de la Compostela, Spain. Thinking of you all, and of Arlo's paella (better than here!!) Ax

The message that had just come in read:

Morning K, we all very eager to visit PAT. Call me as soon as you can. V proud of you. Love DAD

They had erected a bear-hugger around Patrick – a kind of paper duvet – into which they blew hot air with a fan. They fed him warm fluids, injected directly through the stomach wall and with two IVs, one in each arm. He was given oxygen while student doctors watched. He could not remember the last time he felt so cared for. The focus of years of study! Monitored by four machines!

'What makes Patrick a priority?' the doctor asked.

One of the students, a small girl with dedicated eyebrows, stepped forward.

'Here,' she said, pointing. 'The skin over his ankle is dying.'

When he woke again, in the ward, hours later, he had metal scaffolding built around his ankle with struts that joined on to plates in his bones. His foot was bandaged and raised above the bed, held in a blue sling. The TV hovered in the air above him, held by a metal arm. He looked around confused, then, recognizing Kate sitting beside him, relaxed a little. She took his hand and squeezed it.

It didn't take long for a nurse to arrive with a tray: a glass of lemonade, a straw and a plate covered with a plastic dome. 'Luncheon, sire,' she said, and pulled the lid off with a flourish. Patrick watched the cloud of steam rise up and spread out across the low ceiling. Cod in parsley sauce, mash, peas. She bowed and walked out. He stared at the colourful food for a while, then tried the lemonade.

'Patrick, I'm so sorry. Do you remember what happened?'

His voice was muted and coming from his throat. 'Some.'

'I came with you in the ambulance. The others will be here soon.'

He sucked the straw until it rasped. 'When?' he said, treble return-ing to his voice, looking more awake now. His leg shifted in its sling.

'They'll visit this afternoon.'

'*When?*' He tried to sit up but couldn't. He looked around for a clock.

'It's one-fifteen now. They'll be here about three.'

'No,' he said, louder. His hands pushed against the sheets, but he couldn't prop himself up. He made a low growl as he struggled.

'What's wrong? Don't get agitated.'

'*Tell* them *not* to come,' he said, gripping the bed's metal safety bars, his head turning this way and that, his voice spiking, mucus rattling in his chest.

'They're your friends, Patrick. They're worried about you.'

He clawed at the tubes on his wrist, trying to peel off the surgical tape.

'I'll get someone.' Kate stood up.

'Hoh,' he yelled, sounding like a tennis umpire, his slung leg swinging as he knocked the tray of food off his bed, the plastic plate clattering, the bladeless knife and a snot of mushy peas on the lino-leum, the cod fillet sliding into the gangway.

'You have reached the forefront of human development.'

This was one of the new ways that her brother answered the phone.

'Hi, can you get Dad please.'

'Where are you? With your boyfriend, I bet.'

'You know where I am. I'm at the hospital.'

'Tell your boyfriend I am a terrific marksman.'

'Fine, Al, I'm calling you from the boudoir. Get Dad please.'

'As I suspected.'

'You need to get that grip I was suggesting you get. *Get* Dad.'

She listened to him put the phone down and disappear.

'Hello?'

'Hi, Dad.'

'Kate! I've been trying to call. So good to hear you. How is he?'

'He's okay. Been to theatre. The operation went well.'

'Good – we're getting a convoy ready. The hamper to end all hampers. Sherry onions.'

'He's awake now and he's asked that nobody visits him.'

'Arlo's made fresh wild garlic pesto. Albert made a card.'

'He went schiz. He doesn't want you to visit. The nurse asked if you could wait a day or so.'

She could hear her father breathing elaborately into the handset. The same noise that had come from the hall after the post had arrived and they'd not got planning permission for the yurt village.

'Righty,' he said.

'Sorry, Dad.'

'Not your fault.'

In the background, she heard her brother saying something about the Soviet Hat and then the sound of him running upstairs.

There was a syringe full of morphine hanging up next to his bed and a rubbery grey button, shaped like a tiny mushroom, that he could press with his thumb when he wanted a dose. The button was on a plastic box, designed to sit comfortably in the hand. It allowed him one shot every half an hour.

They let Kate stay at his bedside, beyond normal visiting hours, because of his erratic behaviour. They were on an eight-bed ward with blue curtains that kept everyone segregated. The man in the bed opposite was having his dressing changed. Half his head had been shaved and there was a long, scimitar-shaped scar on his scalp, ridged with dense scabs. Kate could hear the sound of someone's iron lung wheezing in and out, which reminded her of her father's breathing at the end of the line.

Patrick woke for a rerun of *Who Wants to Be a Millionaire?* He used his grey morphine dispenser button to buzz in every time he knew the answer. Eventually, the syringe hissed. He passed out again as the credits rolled.

'Everything that goes in, stays in.'

Don and Albert were standing in the yard in thin sunlight. They had coats and scarves on and could see their own breath. Don was wearing his Personal Instrument and explaining that he had built the device based on a 1985 design by the Polish artist Krzysztof Wodiczko. When Don was eighteen years old, before he met Freya and Janet, he was travelling through Eastern Europe and reading Kafka's *The Castle* when he came across Wodiczko's Cold War art-technology and decided to make his own replica. Now, many years later, it was an infamous part of the community's curriculum. Kate had been through it, and so had two dozen or so young people over the years; he typically approached someone after their thirteenth birthday, but for Albert, he made an exception.

'Life is about avoiding bad information and amplifying the good.'

If his son could only develop the critical faculty to help him *choose* not to be influenced by Marina, there would be no need to take him away to the roundhouse. Don called this lesson 'The Human Filter', but it was more was commonly known as 'The Soviet Hat'.

Freya was round the side of the house, chopping wood with a regular *thok*. Marina and Isaac were out in the pottery shed. Janet was sitting on a bench in front of the schoolroom, wearing finger-less gloves, writing Patrick a letter on a spiral-bound notepad.

'The idea is to help develop your innately discerning intellect,' he said, speaking loudly enough for his wife to hear. 'What should we listen to and what should we ignore?'

It was an especially pertinent question, since Patrick's accident had stemmed, in Don's opinion, from an inability to weed out, pun intended, certain untrustworthy internal voices. Don wore a pair of large, on-ear headphones, a red beanie and black gloves, all of which were connected by wires. There was a small directional microphone on the front of the hat.

'Firstly, I decide what I want to hear by looking at it. The micro-phone will only pick up noises coming from that direction. Now if I *choose* to, I can hear your mother chopping wood,' he said, and he looked to the side of the house.

'I can already hear her,' Albert said.

Don aimed his forehead towards Albert's mouth. 'Say that again?'

'I said I can hear her.'

'Okay, and if I want to hear you, I look at you.'

Janet looked up, frowned, flexed her notepad and kept on writing.

'Secondly, I get to decide whether I want to hear high- or low-pitched sounds. If I open this hand,' Don said, waving his right hand, 'I can hear birdsong and whistling. If I open my left, I can hear bassy sounds like car engines. And if I open both, everything. It's all controlled by light sensors in the palms of the gloves.'

'What it's for?' Albert said, his voice coming to his dad clipped and thin.

The chopping sound slowed.

'It's an example of how we sometimes take for granted the way in which the world influences us. Everything we see, hear, read, taste, *smell* even, affects us in ways we can't fully comprehend.' The chopping stopped. 'Some things are worth listening to, some things not. Think of all these *inputs* as *ingredients in* the recipe that will go to make you – Albert Riley – the delicious fluffy man-cake that we all hope you will rise to.'

The chopping started again, faster now. Don moved his hands around, opening and closing his palms as though practising t'ai chi. Janet got up and went inside.

''Kay, Dad. Can I have a go now?'

Don gave the helmet and headphones to Albert, who slipped them on to his small head. Then he put on the gloves.

'Now, tell me what happens when you have both hands shut?' Don said.

'I go deaf.'

Albert looked up at the sky and across at the workshop and down at the floor. Then he looked at his father, whose mouth was silently moving, so Albert opened both palms.

'. . . be careful with it, Alb, it's valuable.'

'You said you made it yourself.'

'You don't have to pay money for something for it to be valuable.'

Albert walked round the side of the house, choosing only to hear low frequencies as he passed his mother. Holding the axe in two hands, she turned to watch them go down the shallow, woodchipped steps through the kitchen garden. They passed the polytunnels and went into the woods, Don trailing him all the while, saying 'Be delicate', which Albert was selecting not to hear.

Down by the river, the high pitch was the wind through the trees and the low pitch was the trunks aching. Then, later, the high was a chaffinch and the low was his father: 'Before you choose something, you have to ask yourself: Do I trust this source of information? How intelligent is it? What are its motives and history?'

They walked on, in stops and starts, Albert led by his ears. There was a rumbling sound. Don could hear it without the Personal Instrument on. He tapped Albert on the shoulder and pointed to where it was coming from: uphill, towards The Bulwark. Albert turned and held his hands up, open, as though at gunpoint. He made directly for the sound, ignoring the path and clambering over brambles that snagged his jeans. The snarl of something up on the hill. Albert felt like Superman hearing danger. Tracked by his father, he hiked up to the crumbly, moss-blotched stone wall at the edge of the woods. Picking a spot where the stones had tumbled, he climbed over into the long grass at the base of Llanmadoc hill. They heard the gurning of a generator or a fleet of zeppelins.

'It's come early, Dad. End times. Marina said the date was moveable.'

They picked a route through the heather, on a steady incline that led to The Bulwark: the remains of an old Iron Age fort, one of the the highest points in Gower, dotted with scraggy sheep. They saw, just at the lip of the hill, a head popping into view then dropping down. It happened again. A head appeared, disappeared. And again, along with the sound of motors rising and falling.

'Chainsaws,' Albert said, and he carried on up the slope.

'We shouldn't go too far. Most important life decisions are domestic.'

Albert kept the microphone aimed at the sound. 'Combine harvesters. Modified for battle.'

Just then, three quad bikes popped up over the lip of the hill and pegged it down across the rough ground, kicking dirt behind them. They were driven by three men, their bums lifted into the air and their knees bent. Sheep turned to run. The bikes' exhausts produced sheep-shaped puffs. Albert had his right hand, his bass hand, open and held in the air, a high five awaiting completion as he walked towards them through bracken, the noise in his headphones like the grinding of tectonic plates.

The three quads weaved in and out of each other as they moved down the track of flattened grass. As they got closer, it became clear that they were boys, not men, and only a couple of years older than Albert. The quad bikes were three-quarter size. They stopped in front of Albert and Don, skidding as though they'd been practising it. Albert held up both hands to hear everything, but resembled someone surrendering.

One of the boys pointed at Albert and said something that couldn't be heard over the motor noise. The boy had a kiss-curl pasted flat against his forehead. His hair was stiff with gel and shiny like an exoskeleton. He was wearing a fresh-looking green hoodie and cartoony skate trainers tied with fluffy bows, but everything was spotted with mud. The impression was of a countryside tough kid undermined by his own affluence. The other two boys had styled themselves on him, but each with a key marker of individuality. One had a Jacksonville Jaguars American football jacket, the other a rash of badges across his chest. None of them wore helmets.

'What's that?' the boy said again, yelling this time.

'Soviet technology,' Albert said.

'Can I have a go?'

'Yes,' Albert said.

'No, it's very valuable,' Don said.

'You can try Quadzilla,' the boy said, and he hopped off his bike.

'The thing is, it's antique,' Don said.

'Go on,' the boy said, stepping towards Albert with his palm out. 'Giss a go.'

Don turned his back to the boys and spoke directly, quietly, into the microphone on Albert's forehead: 'Now remember what I said about choosing inputs to follow and those to reject.'

He had his bass hand closed so his father's voice sounded unimpressive. Albert took the hat and gloves off. He stepped forward and handed over the Personal Instrument.

'There's a few things you have to understand before you try it. Hold on a minute,' Don said.

The boy started putting on the gear, snapping on the gloves dramatically then doing the *Saturday Night Fever* dance. Don winced as the boy slid the red hat over his slick reflective hair. Finally, the boy squeezed on the headphones. Don felt that he recognized these lads, somehow.

'Sweet!' the boy said. 'What does it do?'

'Be very careful,' Don said.

Albert stepped up to Quadzilla. He climbed on and could reach the footrests.

'Albert, step down from there right now,' Don said.

'What are these for?' the boy said, clapping his hands together. 'Is it a metal detector?'

As Don moved to stop the boy damaging the light sensors in the gloves, Albert revved the quad and jerked forward, laughing. Don turned to see his son twist the throttle again and slowly move downhill.

'Okay, that's far enough!'

Albert practised cornering left and right. He came back up the field and did a wide loop around where his father was standing. Don turned to the boy, who was not listening, and said: 'It's an art piece about how you experience the world.'

The boy turned to his friends, still on their quads, and did an impression of a scratch DJ.

'It's about choosing what to take in,' Don said, 'rather than just being passive, absorbing whatever comes your way.'

'I can't hear you,' the boy said, his eyes closed, raving, reaching for lasers, his mates cracking up.

Albert started picking up speed, bouncing across the meadow, leaving a dark trail of flattened flowers. Birds abandoned a phone line.

'Do you live in The Rave House?' one of the boy's friends asked.

'We're from the community.'

The boy wearing the Personal Instrument pointed his head towards Albert in the distance, opened his right hand, his treble hand, and could make out, above the engine noise, a long *Hoooooooo!* They watched Albert disappear over the brow of the hill, up to The Bulwark.

They waited for Albert to reappear. The sheep relaxed.

The boy mimed clay pigeon shooting. After a while, he took off the hat and gloves.

Don was sitting on the back of the quad, one hand around the boy's waist and the other holding the Personal Instrument to his chest. The boy was bony beneath the hoodie, and when Don gripped on tight, he could feel his ribs. They chugged across open ground, spraying mud behind them in long arcs, taking a straight line towards the brow of the hill. Two to each quad, four of them tracking his son across the meadow.

Don smelt the gel and examined the boy's pale scalp between the swipes of hair. The quad struggled under Don's weight and he kept slipping off the back of the seat so he had to half stand, his knees bent.

Albert's track ran in a winding sine wave, occasionally scuffed to mud where he'd turned too sharply. The boys yelled directions at each other. 'Take the gap road!' 'Cut him off!' They were excited.

The land rose and fell in concentric circles. When Don walked here he liked to acknowledge each peak and trough of the original Iron Age fort: escarpment, moat, ramparts, ward, inner wall, inner courtyard and finally the principal stronghold: the donjon. They passed a National Trust sign that Don had read many times: *Off-road vehicles are causing damage to these ancient earthworks.*

Clinging to the back of the quad bike, the engine over-revving as the wheels came off the ground, Don did not consider the donjon. He had only the image of his son's broken body, the wheels of an overturned off-road vehicle spinning in sunlight. He thought of these three lads saying he'd got what he deserved and the phrase *be active, Albert, make choices* rotating in his head.

There were many more tracks along The Bulwark and it became difficult to tell which one was his son's. They came to a stop on the donjon. A pile of stones marked the highest point. It was a clear day and they could see the Worm's Head rearing in the west and a jig-saw of wetland to the north. They waited. The sun started to dip behind Rhossili Downs. They felt the air get colder.

'What's his mobile number?'

'He doesn't have one. We use a landline.'

Just then, there was the sound from somewhere of Albert's horn bleating and getting replies from the sheep. They revved and started off, following a walkers' path that cut across the side of the hill. They found Albert on a steep camber, driving carefully over the knots of molehills and heather. He glanced back at them, then accelerated.

'*Albert Riley!*' Don yelled.

'It's okay,' the boy said.

They kept following. When they got out on to open ground, Albert started winding back and forth across the field. The other quads caught up and plaited in and out as well. Albert was a natural.

'Stop right now, Albert!'

The boy with the hair slowed to a stop. 'You're too heavy,' he said, and waited for Don to step off.

Don watched them disappear out of sight and a few minutes later come back round, having swapped drivers. Albert was now rid-ing on the back, his arms round the boy's Cougars jacket. Don watched as they did long loops.

He listened for the sound of his son's screams. He thought about putting the Personal Instrument back on, but didn't. Eventually, when the quads were going back up the incline for the fifth time, one of them ran out of petrol and rolled to a stop. They stepped off the bikes and stood in a circle, talking. Albert was in the middle. Only then did Don recall once being in the car with Patrick, stop-ping off in Parkmill to score weed: these lads were the delivery boys.

He started running.

'What is it like living in The Rave House?'

'Pretty amazing.'

'What stuff have you seen?'

'Like what?'

'Like clusterfucks,' the boy in the Cougars jacket said.

'And space docking,' the boy with the badges said.

'Um, I once saw a cow giving birth. There was a man with his arm in a cow, up to the shoulder. When the calf came out it couldn't walk and it kept falling over like a *goddamn* drunk.'

They laughed for a bit, their breath making clouds. Albert felt glad. He looked across at his dad, who was small and out of breath, burrs attached to his trousers, stomping uphill towards them.

'Okay. What else?'

'Sometimes people walk around with tops off, even women,' Albert said.

'Alright.'

'What are they like?'

'The tits?'

'Yeah.'

'They're like . . . um . . . they're like when a balloon has been behind the sofa for a few weeks.'

'Yug!' the main boy said, and clutched his throat.

The other two boys laughed. They really liked that.

'What about hypnosis?'

'Oh yeah – that happens. Last night a man lost his mind so we chased him.'

'What about the parties?'

'And have you seen people shagging?'

'Yeah, there was a couple doing it in my bed.'

'Were you in it?'

'*Oui.*'

'Man!'

'Holy! Did you do her?'

'I just watched.'

'Holy shit.'

'Fucking,' said Badges.

'What school are you in?' Albert asked.

'Bishopston.'

Albert took note. Then he said: 'I can also kill goats. It's easy. My mum taught me. If you come round to mine, you can try it.'

'To The Rave House? I won't be allowed,' Cougars said.

'Your dad said you 'aven't got your own phone?'

'I know,' Albert said. 'Lame.'

'Oh man.'

'What's your number?' Albert said. 'I'll remember it. I've got a good memory.'

'Really?'

'Yup.'

'Okay. Oh Seven Eight Six Oh. Five two three. Six two three.'

'Right. Oh Seven Eight Six Oh. Five two three. Six two three. Got it.'

'Good.'

Albert mouthed the number again, but with his eyes closed. Don arrived, huffing.

Don said: 'You're destroying ancient earthworks.' They just looked at him. He grabbed his son by the wrist and walked him back down the slope. Looking behind, Albert saw the boys squinting after him. They watched Albert go and, after a while, started to walk their quads home.

Albert was too busy repeating the phone number under his breath to be angry with his father.

'Dad, I want you to remember something, okay?'

Don was distracted, toying with the Personal Instrument, wiping little bits of hair gel off the inside of the beanie. Albert tugged on his sleeve.

'You have to listen to me,' Albert said.

'I'm listening.'

'I need you to remember five numbers.'

'Okay, what are they?'

'Remember oh seven eight six oh.'

'Oh seven eight six oh.'

'Got it?'

'Got it.'

Walking back to the big house, Albert chanted 'Five two three six two three' to the melody from 'The Twelve Days of Christmas'. Albert felt that, although the Soviet Hat itself, after the years he had spent jealously watching others use it and anticipating its powers, had been a bit of a let-down, the day's experiences overall had been unparalleled. He had mud all over his clothes and face, which was excellent. He jumped on molehills as he went along – hopscotch-style – and instead of five gold rings it was 'Five! Two! Three!'

Don had taken his coat off and had a heart-shaped sweat patch on the back of his shirt. Checking his mobile, he saw two missed calls from Kate and a message.

Pat is improving but still not ready for visitors. I will get bus home. Kxx.

Albert sang all the way back to the house. Skipping into the porch, he grabbed the notepad from the wall beneath the phone and ran back to find his father, who was on the bench outside, writing a text message with his index finger.

'Alright, Dad. What is it?'

'What's what?'

'The number.'

'Oh.'

Albert wrote down a zero. 'Then what?'

It was dark when Kate got off the bus at Llanmadoc, so she walked using the phone as a torch. As she came up through the bottom of the garden, she could see the kitchen light on. She was tired and the last thing she wanted was to have people listen attentively to her. She took her shoes off before walking on the gravel and pushed carefully through the front door. The hall was empty but she heard adult voices, restrained and intent, in the kitchen. She stepped on the edges of the stairs where they didn't creak, then slipped down the corridor and into her room, quietly closing the door. Leaving the lights off, she sat on her bed in silence. She hadn't slept since the night before last.

That's when a voice spoke to her.

'I've been waiting for you.'

It came from under the bed.

She clicked on her bedside lamp, sat back on the mattress and rubbed her eyes with her palms. The voice spoke again.

'Bad things happen when you go away.'

'Albert, I need to sleep. How long have you been under there?'

'It's hard to tell.'

There was a light feline scratching sound at the bed frame's wooden slats.

'Dad says that Patrick's sick, mentally. *Mentally sick, dude!* Marina says his accident was the sort of thing we should come to expect as we get closer. I heard he'll have metal in his legs, which is way better than bone. By the way, I smell in*sane*.' His index finger appeared from underneath the bed, smudged with grey and black. 'Try my belly gunk.'

'Stop, Albert.'

'Try it,' he said, the finger waggling. 'Yum.'

'I'm serious.'

'Tummy fudge.'

'Go and have a shower then.'

'Not without you, dear sister.'

'Albert, please, leave me alone. What's wrong with you?'

'I've *missed* you. Tell me you won't go away again.'

He slid out from under the bed and sat with his back well-postured against the fireplace grate. He had spots of mud on his face and a string of cobwebby dust in his hair, like a streak of grey; it scared Kate to think of her brother not young.

'Check this,' he said, and he pulled up the sleeves of his jumper. He rubbed his right hand quickly up and down his left forearm. Little balls of condensed dirt and mud and dead skin formed like the residue when rubbing out pencil marks. 'It's the same all over my body.'

Her brother seemed wired somehow. She wondered if he'd gained access to some black-market jelly sweets.

'Why are you covered in mud?'

He seemed to think for a while.

'I did it deliberately because I wanted to have a reason to spend time with you.'

'Oh good God, I hope that's not true.'

'The more time you spend away, the worse I get, so they say.'

'Fuck off, Al. Seriously.'

'Tick,' he said, and he stood up.

'Albert, look, I'm not being mean but we can't have showers together any more.'

'*Ya wee radge!*' he said, twirling a full circle on his heels. 'I'm completely innocent. Tock.'

She wiped her forehead with her sleeve. 'It's not your fault. I'm just changing and I'm older and I don't think it's appropriate.'

'*Appropriate.* My God, who are you?'

'It's my fault.'

'You have a boyfriend and he's a complete *ass*hole,' he said, clapping.

She put her head in her hands. He came towards her and, while smelling her scalp, said: 'I'm getting the fragrance of hospitals and old age. If you don't have a shower with me then I'm *never* going to wash.'

'Come on, Al. I'm tired.'

Looking up, she pulled the grey out of his hair, taking years off him.

'Will you at least watch me shower?'

She hesitated.

'Will you at least be in the same room?'

Kate sat on the bench-cum-cupboard that ran along the back wall of the bathroom with her legs pulled up underneath her and her left palm raised to shield her vision.

'What's happened to you?' Albert said.

'Please hurry up.'

'It's your boyfriend's fault you've turned like this. I would like to destroy him.'

Albert pulled off his clothes and hummed what he thought of as stripper music – 'New York, New York' – throwing his T-shirt at Kate, yanking off both trainers, wafting the rich, stewed cabbage smell towards her. He pushed down his boxers and kicked them at the wall.

'Ta-da,' he said, standing there naked, his hands in the air.

She examined the join between the sheets of floral wallpaper.

'Darn you, spatchcock. Just talk to me, okay? You don't have to watch.'

She heard water hit porcelain, then the shower curtain pulled across.

'So, sister. I've been learning some new things.'

She turned round and watched the ghost of his shape move behind the curtain, occasionally glimpsing a pink hand above the shower rail.

'Although I told you that the twenty-first of December is the most likely end date, Marina said it's not as simple as that. It could come early or late – we have to stay vigilant.'

Kate listened to his voice change pitch and volume as he moved in and out of the water.

'You're an idiot.'

'It won't be the end for all of us – just the ones who aren't on the high-score table, which is most people. Some get selected and some rejected.'

She heard him jump as he said *rejected* and his feet slapped on the porcelain.

'You should probably try to get a grip,' she said. 'I'm not saying a whole grip – just a thumb and forefinger.'

'I am guided by my own powers, but doubled,' he said, and she could see that behind the curtain he was lifting up his biceps, making a Mr Universe pose.

'Where were Mum and Dad while you were being brainwashed?'

'I wash my own brain.'

She watched the grey blob morph and bulge behind the curtain. There was a fizz of particles above the rail, like when you add water to soluble aspirin. She liked to imagine him dissolving.

'I think it's gonna be like snow,' he said. 'It'll look just like normal snow, falling on everything, making everything white, but then when it melts, there'll only be me and you and Mum and Dad and Marina and Isaac and maybe Janet and Arlo left, and everyone else will have gone, washed down the drain, and it doesn't matter if they try to ride away on quad bikes because they will never escape.'

Kate frowned. She heard him scrubbing at something. The air around her was starting to white out. The room was warming. The water stopped and she watched Albert's shape behind the curtain, a freak-show specimen waiting to be revealed.

'You know,' she said, 'every few years someone predicts the world's end. In medieval times they thought it would end, but it didn't. At college, we studied a cult who killed themselves because they thought that would help them survive the apocalypse, but they just died, thirty of them, all in single beds with their arms across their chests.'

'You promised to teach me everything you learn.' Then he called her something in Catalan.

He was standing still. She could see his fuzzy silhouette.

'You'll be a teenager soon, Alb, and you shouldn't have to waste time listening to idiots like Marina when you should be having fun. Patrick escaped for a reason.' She hadn't thought about what she was going to say. 'And things are changing with Mum and Dad. Something is happening, has happened. Albert? You should be out there having fun. You need to make some new friends. Meet people your own age.'

She saw the shape halve, folding in on itself. A grey round shape at the bottom of the shower.

'I don't have anything in common with people my own age,' he said.

She tried laughing. It sounded stagy in the bathroom's acoustics. She stepped up to the curtain and, listening, could only hear the shower head dribbling, the gap between each drip getting bigger and bigger until it stopped.

'But you get along with everyone,' she said.

She pulled back the curtain.

He was folded up on the floor of the shower, his skin shiny, shampoo still in his hair, his forehead touching the plughole, a boulder, the teeth of his spine sticking out through his back. The soles of his feet, she saw, still dirty, a bouquet of verrucas on his right heel. He stayed there, unmoving, starting to shiver.

'Albert, I didn't mean to upset you.'

'I'm not upset. Why do you spoil everything?'

'Albert, don't say that. I haven't slept.'

She felt tightness at the back of her throat.

'Are you crying?' he said, still balled up, his voice muffled. 'You'd better not be crying.'

She folded her arms across her chest.

'No way,' he said, and he unfolded from the boulder position and stood up. 'That's not right.'

With her on the bathroom floor and him raised in the shower cubicle, they were the same height. Water ran off the tips of his fingers. He was completely hairless. A tear hung off the end of her chin. Albert put his hand underneath to catch it.

'It's me that should be crying. I'm younger than you.'

He caught the tear and rubbed it under his armpit.

'Why wouldn't you have a shower with me? Why are you so stupid?'

He caught another tear and wiped it on his hair.

He caught another and ate it.

Sunday

In the car on the way to dropping her at the hospital, her father seemed small-eyed and drawn, his cheeks loose.

'I want you to tell Patrick that we miss him,' Don said.

'Okay.'

He was wearing navy jogging bottoms and his 'driving socks', which had rubber grips on the soles.

'Tell him it's not the same now he's gone.'

Kate flicked the direction tabs on the dashboard heater. Don changed lanes twice along Mumbles road, though there were no other cars.

'His energy, his ideas, the discussions we used to have, even the fights, I miss having someone to fight with.'

'Are you okay, Dad?'

'I'm tired.' Don checked all three mirrors but didn't change lanes.

'What's going on with you and Mum?'

'She and Albert are going to spend a couple of weeks down at the roundhouse, we've decided. Give Albert some space from Marina.'

'Why don't you just do something about her?'

Kate examined her father's profile while he kept his eyes on the road. He had a small nodule of grey – she hoped it was porridge – trapped behind the bars of his moustache.

'It's more important that Albert learn to understand his own mind, rather than have us force our beliefs on him.'

'But he's eleven.'

'We think a fortnight's holiday at the roundhouse will help.'

'You think or Mum thinks?'

'We do. It's an experiment.'

The workshop contained a disc sander, bandsaw, two wooden work-tops and a shadow-board with half the tools missing. A storage room at the far end had become Marina and Isaac's bedroom, and when Freya knocked and went in, she found them, with Albert, playing cards on a single bed.

'This is a nice surprise!' Marina said.

They were playing cheat. Freya said hello and sat at the end of the mattress to watch.

'We're discovering that your son is an exquisite liar,' Marina said.

'Here's the face I use,' Albert said, and he showed his mother his honest face.

The concrete floor had, at its centre, a rug the colour of bandages. Light came through a single high window. They played a hand and Isaac yelled 'You're lying!' at his mother, but she was telling the truth.

Above Marina's bed there was an image in a clip-frame, a panoramic photo of deep space that had what looked like two phosphorescent eyes at its centre. A thin handwritten label ran the length of the frame: *Chandra Telescope 2001, The Centre of the Milky Way: Sagittarius A*. What do you see?* The two eyes glared at the opposite wall, which was decorated with Polaroids of Isaac.

'Cheat!' Albert said. 'Massive cheat!'

Isaac looked down, made a face, then picked up the deck.

'Do you want to play, Mum? I bet you're terrible.'

'I was actually popping in just to update you on Patrick,' Freya said. 'The good news is he's on the mend, but the bad news is the doctors don't think he's quite ready for visitors.'

'But Kate's been to see him,' Albert said.

'Well, they don't want him to be overwhelmed.'

'But she is overwhelming.'

'Maybe he just needs a few days to get his bearings,' Marina said, speaking quietly to Albert, holding his shoulder. 'He must be feeling confused.'

Albert conceded with a frown.

'But I thought of something fun we could do instead, since it's sunny,' Freya said. 'How would you guys like to build a house out of mud?'

The syringe hissed. Kate watched the fluid snake towards his arm. Eventually, his fingers went slack and uncurled. The plastic box stayed in his palm, tipping on its keel. He came in and out like this, fading to unconsciousness then eventually drifting back in. Half an hour later, his eyes opened and he rolled his head towards her on his pillow.

'Ah Katie,' he said. 'How's your boyfriend?'

'He's okay. We have fun.'

'At your age, you should be single. Where's Janet?' he said. His lips were dry and ill-defined, seeming to fade in to his skin.

'At home. Why do you ask?'

'You should leave Blaen-y-Llyn and do something with your life. Meet men. Have sex. How old are you?'

His voice sounded croaky.

'Seventeen,' she said.

'I thought you were older,' he said. 'You have to leave as soon as you can. Don't lose your entire life.'

His thumb continued pressing the grey morphine dispenser button, like someone absently clicking the lid of a pen.

'I think my parents are breaking up.'

She saw his Adam's apple nod. 'Well, that's for the best. Your mother could do better.'

Kate concentrated on remembering when Patrick had been likeable. She remembered the dawning of her vegetarianism when she was ten. It had been dark and raining – everyone was outside in the garden, with many different kinds of scissors, committing genocide on the slug population. She had learned that slugs could climb trees – *that they could bungee down on lengths of mucus* – and it was unacceptable to her to kill a creature who had that kind of ambition. When Patrick found her she was standing in the rain, crying, arms out like a scarecrow, a slug moving surprisingly fast up her forearm. Patrick had dimmed his head torch, knelt in front of her, plucked the slug off, attached it to his upper lip and spoken with a French accent: 'Come with me, mademoiselle. En Fronce we treat zee mollusc with respect.' He carried her away from the sound of the scissors, down to the edge of the woods. She managed to both sob and laugh. Plucking his moustache off, she set it free by a nettle patch. They stayed to watch its long slither to freedom.

When the nurse came to look at his morphine intake, the machine told her he'd pressed the button 115 times since his last dose.

'Go easy on this stuff, sir,' she said. 'It'll bung you up.'

Patrick didn't say anything, he just thumbed the grey button a couple of times, confrontationally.

'Unless you want me digging around in your rear end?' she said, and she wiggled her pinkie in the air.

He started grinning and pressing the button as fast as he could.

A little while later, the syringe hissed again. Kate waited for it to take effect then she broached the subject.

'Don says everyone's really missing you at home. Maybe they could visit, now you're settled in?'

There was a wait and Patrick's eyes lost focus.

'Not a chance,' he said, smiling. He looked around the ward, rolling his head back and forth on the pillow. 'So long, geodesic dome – praise be, four walls.'

She told herself it was the morphine speaking.

His lunch arrived: minced lamb with creamy mash and finely cut carrots and courgettes. All the stomach's work done in advance.

'Bellissimo!' he said, and blew a kiss for the nurse. 'Dinner!'

'*Lunch*,' the nurse said. 'It's one o'clock, light outside.'

As she walked away, he pointed at her with his knife: 'Attractive, not beautiful.'

Kate watched him put more minced lamb in his mouth, a sheen

of watery gravy around his lips. She didn't want to be at the hospital any more but neither did she want to go home. Patrick's left hand held his fork, digging around in the vegetables, while with his right he rhythmically thumbed the grey button. After he'd finished his lunch, the syringe hissed once more. Once it had taken hold, she got out her mobile and dialled the number. She'd had enough of being responsible.

The person who answered was not Albert, which was unusual. A Germanic wwoofer said: 'Ha-llo.'

'It's Kate. Can you get Don please?'

She wondered if Albert was already at the roundhouse. If her brother was not around, it made her feel a little less bad about what she was about to do. Patrick rubbed the crown of his head on the pillow.

'Dad, it's me.'

Patrick turned to look at her. His hands closed; the IV in his arm strained against the surgical tape.

Don was glad to be the chosen emissary. He drove above the speed limit for most of the way. Within an hour, he was stepping out of the car with a bunch of wildflowers in one hand and a reusable shopping bag of clothes in the other. Kate had said she needed a change of outfit, and he hadn't asked why. In his trouser pocket, he had a letter from Janet that she had asked him to pass on. This letter, as with all her business letters, was sealed with pink wax that had been stamped so that it looked like a male nipple. Janet was right to assume that, otherwise, Don would have read it. Walking through the hospital, he passed the smell of vats of watery mashed potato and admired the murals on the walls: waves crashing on Viking ships, a cloud city. He considered the word *ward* and its connotations of medieval boroughs, administrative districts, dominion, bureaucracy.

Kate was waiting for him outside the double, plastic-lined doors to Patrick's ward.

'Hey, Pops,' she said, and she kissed him on his cheek and took the bag of clothes. 'I'll let you two have time alone.'

When Don pushed through the double doors he put the hugest

smile on – like it had been rigged from behind, like it should have had a credit list: lighting, set design, cinematography, technical support.

Watching Don approach, Patrick felt the cords in his neck tauten. He let go of the ergonomically designed morphine dispenser, which slid off the bed and swung in the air just above the linoleum.

Don said hello to all the nurses.

'Hi, I'm Don. Here for Pat.'

They eyed his beard as a possible source of infection.

It was just gone two in the afternoon. The linoleum was patterned with stripes of colour – Don walked across blue, yellow, green – then Patrick, with a yell like a weightlifter in the clean-and-jerk, whirled his right arm round, gripping the night bag, the big plastic sack of honey-coloured piss and little wisps of smoky blood that he had worked on all through the quiet hours, one and a half litres, and he swung it over his own broken ankle and let go, sending it up in the air, and Don – who had decided, above all else, that when he saw Patrick, he must present a positive and hopeful outlook – thought for just a second that maybe it was some kind of welcome, a conciliatory balloon perhaps, and this expression – *a golden balloon, for me?* – was the one he had on when it hit.

The only thing stopping the roundhouse from being entirely round or, as far as amenities went, a house, were the walls. The Sustainable Built Environment students had left them unfinished, with various potholes and, on the east side, a V-shaped wedge missing, probably a failed window.

The boys had helped stomp-mix the cob (earth, straw, sand and water), which was now rolled into sticky, grapefruit-sized balls, ready to be slapped into the gaps. Albert's style was to apply it meticulously, smoothing down each patch in turn. Isaac liked to make a series of well-padded, breast-shaped mounds.

Marina and Freya worked in uneasy silence on the big hole in the east wall. Through the gap, they could see the inside of the roundhouse, about the size and shape of a sumo ring, with a wood-burner made from a milk churn in the middle. A cantilevered bench was built into the far side, beneath a pattern of green and blue glass bottles plugged in the walls to let in light.

'So what made you think to come down here?' Marina said.

There were two answers, one of which was: *Because I don't want my son to be near you.* She decided to give the other one.

'It's been a bit of a rough time, me and Don.'

This didn't seem to take Marina by surprise, and she carried on working her patch of wall. 'Well, it's good to be sensitive to that. A bit of headspace makes all the difference. I had noticed you two not quite connecting.'

This claim at intuition irritated Freya, but she let it go. Marina continued shaping the walls, her skills as a potter coming in useful.

'How long will you spend down here?' Marina said.

'A fortnight, I think. Don and I are calling it a holiday. A fortnight's holiday.'

'Costa del Mud-hut.'

Freya laughed more than the joke deserved. Albert appeared round the edge of the house.

'Mum, are we going to stay here?'

'Well, I thought it might be a fun place for us to come for a while.'

'How can it be fun?'

'Just for a few days. Me and you versus the wilderness.'

'But I've got my own bedroom.'

Freya opened her mouth but didn't know what to say. She had been planning to present the idea to Albert in an exciting way. Marina's voice came from behind her. 'If you think about it, Albert,' she said, 'being able to build and survive in your own sustainable housing is likely to be a key skill for whatever lies ahead.'

Freya's eyes tightened but she stayed silent.

There was a pause while Albert looked at the house. Two layers of extra-heavy draft curtain stood for a doorway. A washing-machine window was a porthole. On the turf roof, meadow grasses had grown as tall as the stovepipe.

'Okay then.'

Freya turned to Marina and mouthed the words *thank you*. Marina nodded and said, 'Any time.'

'Can Eyes stay as well?' Albert said.

Isaac was creating a D cup on the south-facing side.

'Of course he can!' Marina said. 'But you must both come and spend some time with me too, so I don't get lonely.'

'Oh thank you!' Albert said, and he threw his arms round Marina's waist. She looked at Freya while running her hands through his hair.

Walking back up to the big house, the boys were far quicker than their mothers. So it was that Albert came into the yard first, to find his father shedding his power with a pair of kitchen scissors. Don was sitting on a log in the last of the sunshine, shirtless, with a towel round his shoulders. Latvian wwoofers were cross-legged on the gravel beside him, angling an oval mirror up.

Albert stood in front of him and watched the clumps of black, grey and white tumbleweed blowing across the ground. Don offered his son the scissors and Albert just stared. During their upbringing, the beard had been a place of infinite possibility, allowing his father to effortlessly portray wizards, gods, samurais, lions and the Sun. All the role models. When Albert felt shy, he used to sit on his father's lap and hide behind it.

'This isn't right,' Albert said.

Isaac was standing behind him, looking worried.

Having trimmed his beard back, Don opened the shaving set: a hard case with the words *Hale and Wigmore Hairdressers* printed on it in a white seriffed font, which had been a hand-me-down from his own father.

'And they say our bourgeois clutter only drags us down,' he said, clicking the latches, letting the spring-loaded mechanism lift the lid.

The velvet-padded interior couched a cut-throat razor with deer-hoof handle, a battery-powered trimmer, a china pot of Gentlemen's Balm and a stubby, wood-handled brush, like the one used for egging pastry. Don's father's initials, A.D.R., Albert's namesake, were embroidered in the velvet.

'You can stop now, Dad.'

'Thanks, Alb. But this is something I have to do.'

Albert was having trouble swallowing.

'You're making a big mistake. Wait till Mum gets here.'

Don attached a plastic grader to the trimmer and proceeded to chirpily buzz his jaw. Albert watched the fizz and spit of grey-black hairs. The tone of the motor changed – struggling – as it met his dense sideburns.

'Where's Kate? Is she back from hospital? She won't stand for this.'

Albert yelled her name three times at the top of his lungs. This brought spectators. Arlo emerged from the workshop, sharpening a carving knife flamboyantly. Janet – in rubber dungarees, spattered with pond slime – had been working in the three-tiered permaculture zone.

Albert knelt down to pick up the lopped-off hair, big nest-like chunks of it. Isaac was sitting on the bench now, looking upset. Albert held the clumps tightly as his father took the lid off the Gentlemen's Balm. It wasn't just the effeminate way in which he dabbed at the cream that was upsetting, or the long, lingering strokes he made along the length of his jaw, but that now he was humming, a kind of wartime picker-upper – a morale-raising jaunt – nodding his head side to side.

Albert said, 'Where's Kate?' again and ran into the house to look for her. On the hallway wall, above the table with guest and detest books, there was a photo-collage showing images of grinning volunteers, ambitious fancy dress and busy classrooms from the community's golden age. One image showed Kate, aged four weeks, naked, hanging from her father's beard. In the photo, Don was standing smiling with his arms out. Her eyes were wide open, her rugby player's thighs kicking at the air.

Albert went into the kitchen to look for her. That's when he saw the note on the round table.

Sitting on a log, now surrounded by his audience, Don pulled the blade out of its hoof. Isaac didn't like that and he got off the bench and went to find his mother and Freya. Don's snow-beard of shaving cream made his expression difficult to read and showed the real colour of his teeth.

After his visit to the hospital to see Patrick, Don had driven home with all the windows open, breathing loudly through his mouth. His jumper and trousers were in a plastic bag in a rubbish bin in the hospital car park along with, as he would never recall, the sealed letter to Patrick from Janet. His beard had glistened the way pastry glistens after an egg-wash. A note from Kate had been pinned under the Volvo's windscreen wipers. When he got home, Don, in only his T-shirt and boxers, couldn't face telling anyone the news so he left the note out and went immediately upstairs for a shower that kept going long after the water turned cold.

The note: *Pops, hope things went well with Patrick. I can't work at home so I'm going away for a bit. Let me know when you and Mum have sorted things out. Am taking the mobile, if you really need me. Tell Albert – sorry. K*

Albert came running back out the house and was now down on his knees, gathering up what hair hadn't blown away and balling it together. Don, working his crowd, tested the blade – drew blood – laughed – sucked his thumb. He was getting younger by the minute. He told the two Latvians that they had to stand up with the mirror, and they did what he asked.

Don delicately took the first cut, down the left cheek, the cream piling up against the blade, speckled with dark hairs – branches in a snowdrift. There was a badge of fresh flesh blinking in the daylight. Arlo clapped, using the palm of his free hand to beat his chest. Through default, he now had the best beard in the community. The little nick on Don's thumb was surprisingly bloody and there were drops on the blade and in the shaving cream.

Albert, with his head down, not watching, said: 'God.'

Wiping the blade on the edge of the log, Don went again, cleaning up the left cheek. The wwoofers held the big oval mirror awkwardly, like a big cheque from the lottery. Don's pale cheek shone. Albert's pockets were full of his father's beard.

Isaac held both Freya and Marina's hands as he pulled them into the yard. They stood still for a moment, trying to grasp the situation, then Freya went straight to her son, knowing what this would mean to him. She knelt down, hugged him and kissed the top of his head. Don started in on the right cheek, his mouth still hidden, any compassion disguised by shaving cream.

'Freya, now you're here, why don't you help with this last bit,' he said, stretching his neck out.

'Let me,' Albert said, his voice suddenly loud. He looked up at his father and held out his hand.

'Okay. Anyone else?'

'*I said* I'll do it,' Albert said, and he stood up, tufts of beard showing at the pockets of his jogging bottoms.

'You've never shaved before, son.'

'So now I learn.'

'I don't think you should practise on me.'

'*Who else can I practise on?*'

Don's cheek twitched, triangles of shaving cream here and there, spots of red.

'Okay,' Don said, 'but let your mum supervise.'

Albert wiped his eyes on his sleeves. The rest of the community were still watching, unworried, like they'd come across an impromptu piece of experiential theatre.

'It's *very* sharp, Albert.' Don handed him the razor.

He turned the blade this way and that, letting it blink in the sun.

'Can you lift his chin for me, Mum?' Albert said.

She raised her husband's jaw to the angle he used for making important statements.

'I'm going to start here,' Albert said, and he pointed with his free hand at his father's Adam's apple. 'Nice and deep.'

Don didn't laugh. Freya stood beside her son and lightly cupped the hand that was holding the blade.

Arlo stopped sharpening his knife. The wwoofers shuffled a few steps back, looking awkward and compromised. Freya guided the blade towards Don's neck. There was a certain childish brinkmanship about who was going to call this a terrible idea first. Don swallowed and the foam rippled.

With Freya's hand on his, Albert put the blade into the foam. It was clear Don wanted to say something but didn't want to move. Their son's lips disappeared inside his mouth and his eyes welled up. Freya could feel him gripping the blade so hard his knuckles stuck out. There was a high-pitched noise coming from his throat.

She drew back Albert's hand and peeled away his fingers. Once she'd taken the knife off him, he immediately stepped back and sat down, looking dazed.

'It's okay, Albert,' Don said.

Freya stood up and moved round the other side of the log to stand behind her husband.

'I can just finish it myself,' Don said.

She ignored him, placed her thumb on the tip of his chin and, concentrating, made the first upward stroke, going against the grain of his hair. He did not speak or swallow. Wiping the blade on her sleeve, she continued tidying up. She didn't recognize him. She didn't want to.

When she was finished, he rubbed his face with his hands and turned his head from side to side. This got a round of applause.

4   Animal, Mineral, Vegetable

When Kate arrived on Geraint's doorstep – with a plastic bag and a change of clothes – she had something about her of the convict on day release. Or that's how she felt, at least, as they brought her in, sat her down at the dining table, made her sweet, milky tea and asked what she'd like for her first meal, now she was on the outside.

'We've got,' Mervyn, Geraint's father said, swinging back the fridge door, 'drum roll . . . *streaky bacon!*'

Kate explained that, while the community wasn't vegetarian, actually, she was, although she'd be happy eating anything, and she pointed to the family-size box of Frosties on the counter.

The next day Liz, Geraint's mother, organized a symbolic gas-powered barbecue to clear their fridge of breakfast meats, Iberian chorizo, pork medallions and handmade lamb burgers. On the patio, topless in April, Mervyn wafted the meat smoke away with a tea tray, carrying himself in the manner of a man who has, at some previous time, worked out.

Liz had a kind of cycle helmet of blonde hair, raised from her scalp, sprayed stiff and sturdy looking. She was fiercely accommodating. Each night she said, 'Sleep well, Katherine,' and each morning she paid close attention to which cereal or muesli Kate chose, and then bought lots more of that brand. She never asked what had happened to drive her away from her home, but the implication was that Kate should feel free, at any point, to talk about it. In fact, Kate began to sense she was being treated like someone who had recently been through unspeakable trauma, so she started to wonder if she had.

Kate helped Liz to slice and salt aubergines and build a caponata. In tribute to Patrick, Kate taught Liz how to make red lentil dahl – *à la carcinogen* – with the bottom of the pan encrusted black. Over those first few days, Mervyn grimly, grinningly, tucked into three-bean stews, stuffed field mushrooms, huge walnut and beetroot salads.

Kate had texted her father to say who she was with, but since no one knew where Geraint lived, or even his surname, she was mercifully untraceable. Her only contact with the community was through her father's text messages, since she never answered his calls and refused to check voicemail.

> Sweets, it's been a week now – you okay? When will you come
> back? We're worried about you! Dad xxooxx.

She noticed that the message was sent at 2.13 a.m. and imagined him sitting alone in bed, lit by the light from the phone.

At Mervyn's request, Kate and Geraint slept in separate rooms. She got the guest room with reading lamps set into the wall and a bed half-covered by a silky turquoise spread. Prior to her arrival on his doorstep, she and Geraint had done all the things they could easily do in the back seat of his tiny Punto, which was a lot, but not everything. Now they were living together, however – and with the twin catalysts of Mervyn's disapproval and their being put in separate rooms – they quickly moved things forward, beginning with high-risk canoodling in the outdoor pool and ending with full, sacrilegious consummation in Mervyn's Jeep while it was parked in the garage. Cold and uncomfortable, yes, but fizzing with family scandal. Kate secretly enjoyed spoiling the father's pride and joy – both vintage vehicle and only son.

Considering that Kate had never spent any time in a suburban home before, she had a highly developed understanding of what to expect; during her upbringing, her father had encouraged her to make the most of his film collection, which had a lot to say on the subject, including *The Graduate*, *Edward Scissorhands*, *American Beauty* and *The Ice Storm*. One of the community's well-told stories was of Kate, aged ten, setting an alarm for herself to wake at 3 a.m. so that she could come downstairs and watch *Poltergeist*, the definitive suburban horror film. When Janet got up to milk the goats, she found Kate awake at dawn, alone, in the corner, staring horrified at the loom, which had more than once been talked of as a machine for chopping up children.

It was difficult for Kate to imagine that behind the contented atmosphere in Geraint's link-detached home, with garage, *especially* with swimming pool – there was not some kind of deviant interpersonal rot, rampant and unforgiving. By all surface assessments the Rees family were happy, which – according to Kate's understanding of suburbia – meant that they weren't. So it was with some relief that she discovered Mervyn's insomnia. Although he worked full-time on the *Evening Post* news desk, he also stayed up half the night watching TV in the lounge; she felt sure this was the key to the family's metaphorical basement. She remembered something her father had said: 'Insomnia is not a condition, it's a symptom.'

Why couldn't Mervyn sleep? What monsters emerged in his dreams?

One thing Kate did know was that, most nights, garden slugs came out from under the skirting boards and travelled across the lounge carpet. For some reason, Mervyn let them do their thing and, each morning, it was left to Liz to scuff away the glistening tracks. Kate liked that. The unspoken darkness between them.

That first night in the roundhouse, it was just Freya and Albert. They zipped their sleeping bags together, Albert showing her how to make a super-bag, and slept in the centre of the room on a sheepskin rug. While they were there, Freya talked to him about his sister and said that he wasn't to take her leaving too personally. It was by no means the first time Kate had run away. She was known for it. Once, famously, aged twelve, weighed down with a backpack full of tins, she had made her escape but was forced to jettison supplies, least favourite first. Her father tracked her via kidney beans, then flageolet, chickpeas, whole plum tomatoes and so on until he found her, exhausted, drinking the juice from a tin of pineapple rings.

Albert disappeared deeper into the super-bag and that was where he slept from then on, a warm globe near Freya's feet. She had brought an armoury of herbal teas in anticipation of waking in the quiet hours with something tugging at her, an invisible rope between herself and Don. The reality had been different. She slept deeply and, that first morning, when she woke up, found she was alone in a two-man sleeping bag. Albert had already gone back to the workshop to visit Marina.

On the second night, Isaac joined them and she and the boys went top-to-tail on the rug, with her in the middle. When they thought she was asleep, their pillow talk was alarming.

'Isaac?'

'Yep.'

'How do you think the world's going to end?'

'Um. It's going to start with a big noise like a bus noise and then ten buses' noise, then twelve, then there will be birds and if they write your name in the sky you can get on the buses and if they don't you have to die on the floor.'

Even that could not keep her awake. She had almost forgotten what a proper, unbroken, dreamless night's sleep was like. The feeling of being upgraded. Fresh eyes.

By the time Isaac next stayed over, two nights later, she had come to realize that few things are more exciting to young boys than the idea of the world suddenly and explosively ending, leaving them as lone survivors, walking the toxic earth with massive knives. That was what made Marina's theories so appealing. It would take more than drab rationality to distract them, which is why she made a concerted effort to get up before them and, when they woke, said: 'Today, we're going to have a lesson in time travel.'

She made them sit cross-legged on the rush matting while she sat on a stool opposite. It was a good exercise for the morning, while they were still in touch with their subconsciouses.

'Who here wants to drive a time machine?'

They both put up their hands. Albert raised his right buttock off the matting to give his hand an inch more commitment.

'Time travel is easier than most people think. Now, close your eyes and listen carefully.'

They looked at each other seriously, held hands and shut their eyes.

'Imagine you're in a lift,' she said, 'and there's a whole wall of buttons, numbered one to a hundred. Press the button that's the same number as your age. So, if you're six years old, Isaac, then press the button with six on it.'

Isaac's forehead ruffled. Freya watched him. His face seemed hyper-mobile, changing the whole time, a kind of human lava lamp, giving the impression that he had a wider emotional range than most children.

'Okay, once you've pressed the button, let the lift doors close and feel yourself move upwards.'

'Wo ho ho,' Albert said, bouncing on his bum.

'Ping!' Freya said. 'You've reached your floor. The doors slide back.'

Isaac's nostrils flared.

'Now, step out into the corridor. Feel the red carpet beneath your feet. Gold lamp fittings run along the walls. On this corridor there are one hundred rooms, doors on both sides.'

Albert's foot jiggled.

'Start walking slowly up the corridor, counting the numbers as you go. Say them out loud as you go past, and stop at the door with your age on it.'

'Onetwothreefourfive . . .' Albert said.

In his mind, he was running.

Isaac didn't count out loud. He traced a circle with his finger on the floor.

'. . . eightnineten*eleven*!'

'You okay, Isaac? Are you standing outside door number six?'

He nodded.

'Okay. That's your room.'

This was something she'd learned years ago when she and Don had attended a three-day non-denominational meditation course. She remembered Don used to say that every time he achieved 'thoughtlessness', he would be dragged back to the surface by his own sense of achievement.

This exercise was called 'Visiting Your Future Self'. Freya remembered her future self told her that she did not need to come on a meditation course to speak to her future or past selves, and that these were the sorts of internal conversations most people saved for long bus journeys. Even if Albert's 'future self' told him something as banal as that, Freya would just be glad to see him indulge in self-reflection. She imagined him meeting a version of himself who was Kate's age and whose concerns had shifted, as his sister's had, from the fate of the universe to the fate of a UCAS application.

'Now, walk down the corridor, until you're another five rooms along. What's six plus five, Isaac? Is it eleven?'

'Yes, eleven.'

'Good. You go to room eleven.'

'I'm outside mine,' Albert said. 'Super-sweet sixteen!'

'These rooms contain the version of you at the same age as the room number. So inside the door you'll find yourself five years in the future. He knows you are coming because he can remember sitting where you are, five years ago. If there's anything that's bothering you right now, then he'll be able to talk you through it. You can ask him what it's like to be his age. He'll know if you are scared or upset. He can offer you perspective.'

She could see by her son's expression that he was completely going with it.

'Turn the door handle and go in. Sit cross-legged on the floor opposite yourself, just like you are now. Take a moment to notice the room. Then notice your future self. Now, take this opportunity to ask – in your head – any questions you want to, and take note of the reply.'

Isaac's head dropped. He let go of Albert's hand, put his fingers in his ears and pulled them out again. He tasted the ends of his fingers, then wiped his hands, front and back, on his jeans. He opened his eyes and seemed surprised to see Freya watching him. His face passed through a series of emotions in the guilt / shame arena.

She mouthed the words *it's okay* and held out her hand to him. He dragged himself over to Freya and wrapped his arms around one of her calves.

They watched Albert. His face was moving: eyebrows tweaking, nostrils occasionally whitening at the edges.

– Albert!

– Yo!

– I'm sixteen!

– I'm eleven! How's the next dimension?

– Insano!

– I knew it would be.

– Non-stop *carn*age!

– So what happened?

– Well, it all started with the swarms. Not just one insect, but *all* of them, over land and sea, to desiccate the earth.

– You know some words.

– I was standing on the flat roof when they blocked out the sun. You could hear them. They were making a documentary about me and they got it on camera when I said: *Fetch the goddamn gasoline.*

– Wow, yes!

– Then I poured the gasoline through the woods, in a circle around the big house. My henchmen all stood at different points along the circle, each with a box of matches. I went up on the flat roof and everyone waited for my signal. I knew that the forest would only burn for so long, and we had to time it right so the swarm would pass by before the forest burned out.

– Makes sense.

– I could see the MegaSwarm coming over the horizon – locusts, hornets, wasps, horseflies, mantises, midges – and I was like: *Hold!* . . . *Hold!* And I could hear the scrit-scrit-scrit of the super-intelligent ant armies approaching, carrying hundreds of times their own weight in weaponry, and still I was like: *Hold!* And behind the ants, the legions of ticks, mites, beetles, rolling their ball bearings, even spiders, although not strictly insects, swinging through the trees behind and still I yelled: *Hold! Hold!* Then I said . . . *Let's watch this city burn!*, which was the signal.

– All of which was on camera?

– Of course.

– Fuckums.

– Yes. And the flames went racing up the trees, shooting into the sky, and my team ran back to the safety of the house, and we waited and watched as the hordes of ants fried themselves to the floor, huge clouds of flaming insects in the air, like fireworks in slow motion. The smoke acted as a force-field, directing most of them around us, but still a few broke through, spiders, alight but alive, running through the undergrowth, gnashing their mandibles, so we went out in the yard with cans of Lynx and lighters and we fought hand to hand with those homos.

– Who won?

– Guess.

– Boom town!

– Exactly.

– All in the documentary?

– *Oui.*

– You've learned French?

– *Oui.*

– Then what?

– Then we were the only people left on the planet. Kate was at her boyfriend's house and then at university, so she was dead.

– No!

– Sorry, but yes. Everyone else is fine. Mum and Dad are in the big house together again and I can do anything I want, like wander around in old libraries and castles and explore hotels. Living in the roundhouse will be really useful training for surviving in dangerous places.

– That's pretty cool. But I'm sad about Kate.

– It was her choice. You'll try to explain to her about how wrong she is, and that the world is really going to end, but she won't listen. She's sometimes very insulting. She even tries to *kill* Mum and Dad by telling them lies about how the world *won't* end. You may not want to hear this, but pretty soon you'll have to think of a way to stop her disrupting your vital preparations.

– Doesn't she realize that she is wrong and come back to the community just in time?

– In a fairy tale, maybe. But this is real life, champ.

On the way to the bathroom, Liz passed the room at the top of the stairs where Kate and Geraint were revising together. She stopped outside the door and watched their stillness, the backs of their heads occasionally bobbing, the heavy textbook split on the desktop. She signalled for Mervyn to come see – *shh!* she mimed, with a finger held up to her lips, as he lumbered over, still in his office shirt. They stayed standing, arm in arm, trying to concentrate on their son concentrating, but feeling too excited and blessed. Liz rested her head on her husband's shoulder as Kate's fearless hand reached to turn the page.

Mervyn and Liz had scoured their drawers for the appropriate office supplies. They would not be the ones to stop her squaring the hypotenuse. If tricolour highlighter tabs might undo the damage of her drab, loose-knit upbringing then she would have tricolour highlighter tabs. High-speed fibre-optic broadband had been installed to keep pace with her untethered mind.

She was, they both agreed, an angel sent to raise their son's grades by osmosis, a concept which was now well within his grasp. It was enough for him just to share a study with her superhuman concentration span. If their son seemed more subdued than normal, then that was only right because he was going through great changes, the painful retraction into his chrysalis. In the glimpses they got of his bedroom floor, they noted the slow retreat of foil trays, empty baggies, fried chicken boxes, piles of clothes, shattered jewel cases and snapped guitar strings until, one unseasonably warm day, they sat up in bed and listened to the burr of the vacuum cleaner coming through the wall. Their son's bedroom's famous smell – like damp cork, like the raw side of a carpet – started to sift and soften. Mervyn even claimed he missed it.

Thursday Meeting. 03/05/2012.
   Members present: Don, Freya, Marina, Isaac, Arlo, <u>Albert!</u>
   Visitors: Erin, The Tallest Man, No-neck Sally, 2 x Unknown.
   Members absent: Janet (Bristol) Patrick (ankle) and ~~Kate~~ (death)

Albert loved taking minutes in the community jotter.

'People, our battery is dying,' Don said, standing at the head of the table. The table was round, but still he managed to be at its head. He had a shaving rash, Indonesia-shaped, on his neck.

Although they were 'on holiday', Freya and Albert were still expected at the fortnightly meeting. This was the first time Freya had been back to the big house, though the same could not be said of Albert, who had been returning most days to see Marina.

Albert gripped his pencil and wrote: *Battery = dying.*

Freya divided her attention between peeling a wafer of mud off the back of her hand, reading Albert's minutes and watching her spouse's newly visible lips move. Don made a pestle and mortar motion. He was speaking slower than normal and the skin beneath his eyes was murky.

Albert wrote: *Last legs. Tighten belts. Membership drive.*

Freya looked across the table at the empty seat, Patrick's, a high Windsor chair with a patch of buffed wood where the rear of his head used to gurn against the backboard. Next to that, on the bench where Kate used to sit, there were the American newly-weds, Varghese and Erin, who had arrived last night to wwoof their honeymoon. They were smiling and tugging each other's jumpers.

Albert wrote down: *Patrick's departure = reduced cash flow.*

Freya watched Don chop the palm of his left hand with the blade of his right. His eyes went wide. He pointed at something in another room. Then he pointed at Freya and he gave her two thumbs up.

Albert wrote: *Be like Freya and <u>Albert</u>. Minimal living – Roundhouse.*

Everyone turned and nodded at her.

Albert wrote: *Half-life. 300,000 years. The dinosaurs.*

Don, still talking, pointed at each person around the table in turn.

Albert wrote down: *Responsibility. Equality. The children of our children. (My children!)*

Seeing Don without a beard made her think of him in the very first days of the community. Back then, he seemed to have a perpetual rant running inside him, sometimes silent, sometimes voiced, but always there. Whenever he emphasized a phrase, he used to lean forward, as though his torso became italicized in sympathy. *New structures for living.* Freya blinked and saw him now – trying to be reasonable. A small mound of dry mud had formed on the table in front of her, where she had been picking at her hands.

Albert wrote: *Go digital. Tight ship. Full circle.*

She noticed that, in-between taking notes, Albert used his pencil to colour in his arms, giving himself the grey sheen of someone with serious nutritional deficiencies.

Don looked around the room, catching each pair of eyes. Isaac, tiny in the wicker chair, drummed his fingers on the armrests, trying to synchronize left and right hands. Arlo held his tea in his mouth.

Don didn't look at Freya for long. He carried on speaking, raising one finger for emphasis. Albert wrote: *Reel ourselves in. Forge onwards.*

She watched Don lean forward, a little awkwardly, his sleeves rolled up, planting his palms flat on the table.

Albert wrote down: *Off-grid. Must vote. Now is the time. So little of it left! :-(*

All around her, hands went up.

One night, very late, when waking and going downstairs to get a glass of water, Kate saw the TV on through the rows of rippled-pond-effect glass squares in the door to the lounge. Mervyn was watching News 24 on mute with Live Text subtitles. It surprised her that he could bear to spend his sleepless hours watching the news, given that he was a current affairs journalist. She looked through the door and smiled in the small intimate way people smile to each other as they pass in a narrow corridor, late at night, on a sleeper train.

The phone lead stretched across the hall and into the toilet beneath the stairs, the door of which was locked.

'Hello. This is Albert Riley of The Rave House. I spoke to you a month ago . . . Yes, I've changed my mind.'

. . .

'I know. My parents say I must live my life my own way. Make my own mistakes.'

. . .

'Yes, they are both happy to sign the release forms.'

. . .

'You'll have to take my word for it.'

. . .

'They won't be around to meet you. Is that a problem?'

. . .

'You're making a big mistake.'

. . .

'Fine. Forget it. My father says your industry is inherently evil.'

. . .

. . .

'Hello. This is Albert F. Riley of The Rave House. I spoke to you a couple of months ago.'

A few nights later, in the spare room, Kate was woken by her phone buzzing against the floor. The screen said she had three texts from her father:

NEWS FLASH: BLAEN-Y-LLYN GOING OFF-GRID! Momentous Day Will Be Tinged With Sadness If All-Important Member of Community Not Around To Enjoy Momentous Day, Sources Close To The Community Reveal.

FYI – Off-grid day is being timed to coincide with F and Alb's return from holiday, next week. Twice the celebration!

Also, also, Albert's not washed since you left. Half expect to see centipedes, woodlice etc when he takes off his boots!

She lay awake, being alternately annoyed with, then sorry for, her father, unable to reconcile the ecstatic tone of his texts with the time on her phone's clock: 3:12 a.m. Was it possible that he did not know the messages were instant? Did he think they would arrive in the morning, like the post?

After being awake for some time, she became conscious of a high-pitched whine in the house. It took a while to realize what it was.

She went downstairs in her pyjamas. Her T-shirt, a baggy yellow vintage one, a hand-me-down from Janet, said: 'Life Begins at Forty'. The silky pyjama bottoms were Liz's.

Mervyn was again watching News 24 with real-time subtitles.

She opened the door and waved. He waved back, then made space for her on the sofa. The leather exhaled as she sat down and brought her legs up underneath her. He put down the remote on the coffee table.

'You okay?' he said, turning towards her. 'Couldn't sleep?'

She nodded. He made his face for supportive-but-not-intrusive.

'We'd best keep quiet,' he whispered, then pointed to the ceiling, where his wife was asleep.

'Can't stop thinking about my exams,' she said, which was half true. Two images had stayed with her from her open day at Cambridge: a professor in full subfusc billowing through a Japanese garden and a boy with one overdeveloped bicep punting along the canal.

'I'm sure you'll do brilliantly,' Mervyn said.

They watched the mute news with the coloured subtitles that came up one word at a time. He leaned towards Kate, and spoke quietly: 'The subtitles are written live by stenographers – like the people who record what's said in court. Fantastically skilled. They work in fifteen-minute bursts because it's so intense. Between 4 and 5 a.m., at the end of their shift, they make more mistakes, I've noticed. My favourite: "Russia backs away from Gran's missile deal."'

He laughed with no sound and she smiled.

More interesting to Kate than stenography was the question of what dark dreams kept a grown man with work in the morning awake in a suburban home watching rolling news. He came out like the carpet slugs, silent and lost, trawling the lounge by night. She cultivated thoughts like this – clues about the hollow core of link-detached living – and had more than once watched Mervyn and Liz in the raised pool at the end of the garden and thought that their heads looked severed, bobbing back and forth.

Mervyn was wearing a navy fleece dressing gown on top of his grey cotton pyjamas and he was seated with his legs wide apart, which she always thought of as a macho way to sit. Pretty much all the men of her childhood sat cross- or closed-legged. Open male legs would probably have been enough to get a black mark from Don, if seen at interview.

Mervyn smiled suddenly when another mistake came up. '. . . have developed body armour that is even resistant to snark attack . . .'

The words *body armour* made her think of her brother. She chose not to explore the thought further. In truth, she tried not to dwell on anything to do with her own family, preferring to analyse the Reeses instead. The last time she had seen Albert, he had been catching her tears and eating them. She listened to the small shifts in Mervyn's bodyweight, the leather creaking. The small outward expression of a large inward thing: sleeplessness as a symptom of the discontent that slithers through plush bedrooms at night, leaving a trail behind it. For her part, she angled her legs towards him and enjoyed breathing in a heightened way. It made living in the house more interesting, which was why she did it, she decided.

Freya woke up late and the roundhouse was empty. Blue and green daylight came through the recycled bottles that were plugged into the wall. This was the day that she and Albert were due to return home to the big house. Moving him down here had done nothing to change his outlook. His visits to Marina had continued apace. If anything, living in the roundhouse had given him a taste of the 'challenges ahead' and made his commitment more fervent.

Last night, after she had cooked him a special final-night meal of stewed aubergines followed by rice pudding, he had said: 'I'm excited about us going home.' Then, when she woke this morning, he had already packed and gone, leaving her a pan of porridge on the wood-burning stove with a note next that said: *Morning Mum! Porridge for you, here. See you at home!* She sometimes wondered if he felt like he was looking after her, not the other way round.

She got up and tried to eat, but found she had no appetite. She got dressed slowly, then, instead of packing, just picked up her empty suitcase and started off up the hill. Although the bag was empty, it seemed to her to weigh a lot. It was mustard coloured, a stiff old 1970s number with brown leather trim. For the first year of the community, she'd lived out of it – when their only private space was their luggage. It was still in good condition, largely because, in the intervening years, she had not travelled anywhere. In those early days, when a relationship wasn't working, everybody knew about it. In a way, that made it easier because you couldn't hide anything. Over the years, she'd seen some couples arrive at the community with, it seemed, the express purpose of putting pressure on their relationship. Famously, Tony and Angela Whishaw, too cowardly to end their marriage simply because they were miserable, came to the community and were relieved to find that temptation, jealousy and, as it turned out, serial adultery could be grown in greenhouse conditions. Freya remembered the couple she'd worked with in London. Five times a day, the *kerrrr-chisss* sound of his attempts to open Holsten Pils quietly beneath his desk and his wife, as though wearing her own Personal Instrument, selecting not to hear it.

When Freya got to the big house she could see, through the window, Don speaking to Isaac and Albert in the schoolroom. She left her case in the hall and watched them from the doorway. The boys had their back to her, looking up at Don, who was explaining the new charge controller: a machine to help them manage their electricity usage, to help their transition to being off-grid. It was made from off-white plastic and was the size of a shoebox, attached to the wall above the upright piano.

'So, what if there's a massive storm and the wind is blowing insanely and the sun is shining like a beast?' Albert said. 'What then?'

'Well, then we come inside, look at the meter, and if we're producing more electricity than we can use, then yes, it's in our interest to use that energy up. Because if there's nowhere for that excess energy to go, then it can end up burning out the circuits or even causing an explosion.'

'Hell yes!' Albert said.

Don frowned. The meter made a clicking noise, like a camera, every time they used a unit of stored power. Their battery was in a wooden beehive out the back of the schoolroom.

Click.

'Sah-weet!' Albert said, and he looked up at the ceiling. 'So, *if* there's a storm then we can install lasers in every room.'

'Well, I think the point is that we learn not to desire those things, Bert.'

'Not desire lasers?' Albert said, trying hard to raise one eyebrow.

Isaac watched them earnestly.

Click.

Don sniffed and tugged the end of his nose.

The tip of Isaac's tongue appeared between his lips when he was concentrating, like now. 'I don't understand,' he said.

Don went down on one knee to speak to him.

'Think of electricity like a river that runs through the house. Sometimes the river's full and sometimes it's dry. A river made of fire that you must *never go near* that flows in a big loop behind the walls.'

Isaac reached out and held on to Don's nose.

'Okay, boys. I think we're done. Go and get everyone together so we can make that phone call.'

Don looked up and saw Freya.

'You're just in time,' he said.

Albert stretched out the cord so that he could take centre stage in the middle of the hall. Everyone had gathered to listen to him phoning Swalec, the electricity company. Marina and Isaac were sitting on the herringbone woodblock floor, their backs to the wall beneath the coat hooks. The wwoofers were standing on the lower steps, arranged like a choir. Arlo was watching from the kitchen door, one of his hands cradling macadamias. On the landing halfway up the stairs, her back to the wall and looking down, was Freya. Just in front of her was Don, who kept looking back and forth between Albert's showboating and his wife, to check she was appreciating this monumental moment in the history of their lives together.

'This is Albert Riley. I'm calling to end our relationship.'

Albert twirled so that the phone cord wrapped around him.

'. . . No, we're not *switching* providers.' He had a piece of paper with a few notes on it. 'We've been drifting apart for years. It's not me, it's you.'

A small ripple of applause from the stairs. Don smiled with his mouth open.

'We don't need you. We've moved on. You should have seen it coming.'

Albert held the receiver away from his face and made a yapping mouth with his left hand. Everyone liked that. Don looked back to share this moment with Freya, but she'd gone.

'Are we sure?' Albert said, and he held the handset out to the crowd.

'We're sure!' they chorused.

Albert put the phone back to his ear. He read out their account number and address from a bill. But it turned out that a call wasn't enough. They'd need to do it in writing.

Freya went into Don's room and put her suitcase down beside the bed. She had the feeling Don had made a special effort so that the community felt vibrant and reinvigorated for her return, which it did. In their room, however, everything was exactly as she'd left it, right down to the glass of half-drunk water on her bedside table, the unwritten letter in the typewriter. The room had a curatorial atmosphere. It was expecting her back. She stood at the window, feeling numb, and watched a shadow move in one of the polytunnels.

After a while, she heard the bedroom door open, but she didn't turn round. Her empty suitcase was there and she waited for him to see it and realize what was happening. Perhaps there would be no need for her to actually say it, Don would just understand. He would wordlessly acknowledge her leaving. She waited and heard the floorboards ache beneath him. He was behind her. She listened, expecting the sound of his crying. It would be easier, actually, if he cried. Instead, she felt someone's lips on her neck.

As far as she knew, this was not the mouth of her husband. She had not heard the pre-emptive kiss-kiss noise or sensed the repression of that sound that would have signalled his swooping in. No small sealed bag opening. These were foreign lips on her neck, soft and a little tacky, possibly moisturized. She knew well the feeling of being kissed by her husband: the wet lips, the loofah of his beard, the enthusiasm. Like being worked on, somehow, buffed up. This was not that. It could not be him. Don did not have his hands on her, was not holding her at the waist then shoulders. She shut her eyes and focused on how it felt to be with someone new.

It was easier this way – so she rolled her head back and let his mouth attend to the curve where her neck became her shoulder. Then the stranger's hand groped her chest in a way that was unlike her husband. Then the stranger's other hand bunched her knee-length skirt up, lifting it, and all this in front of a window which made them visible to people for whom the husband was a figure of authority, and this was definitively not like her husband. The person went to work on her neck, breathing heavily. She pushed back against him, being careful not to look over her shoulder. It was still light outside and there was a girl down by the compost, hacking away. Freya heard the fizz of his fly. The stranger didn't care who saw, and he reached under her skirt and awkwardly pulled down her underwear. The stranger knew her name, it became apparent, because he started saying it, over and over.

She leaned forwards with her arms wide and planted her palms flat against the window casement. His mouth sucked her shoulder. The sun was falling behind the downs and she could see the first hint of her own reflection in the glass, and the silhouette of the stranger's head. He didn't bother with extensive foreplay, which was unlike her husband. She felt him bend his knees slightly then push inside her and she made the sort of sound she had long ago stopped making.

The light outside kept fading, and in the glass she could make out the outline but not the face of the man who was gripping her hips, his head down, watching himself. The stranger said he missed her. Then he came inside her and told her he loved her and he was glad she was back and he was sorry. Then she heard him sit back on the bed.

She kept her arms out against the window casement. The light outside was dim enough to see the details of her own reflection, and the expression she had was not at all the look of someone redis-covering sex with a new partner.

Pulling up her underwear, she adjusted her skirt and when she turned round Don looked up at her. Without his beard, the skin on his neck, his jaw and around his mouth was a pale pink colour, a litmus pink, and slightly raised, almost water retentive. He did look younger, but also smaller.

'Thank you for coming back. I wasn't sure you would.' He buttoned up his trousers. Standing, he went round to the suitcase. It became clear that he thought it was full, the case. He had the tensed shoulders and slightly widened stance of a man about to make light work of something heavy. He gripped the handle with two hands and lifted, but when it gave little resistance it put him off balance and he rocked back on his heels before coming forward again, dropping the bag on the bed. It was a couple more moments before the information was processed. She watched it happening. But he needed to see it, so he put his hand on the zip and led it along the edge of the old-fashioned case, the four curved corners. He lifted the lid. The inner lining was gold.

Kate couldn't sleep. She was surprised and disappointed to find herself thinking about the community going off-grid and wondering if it had been a success. She had even stooped to the ignominy of texting her father to ask but had got no reply.

At 2 a.m., she heard the bat-squeak of the TV coming on and decided to go downstairs for a glass of water. She got a drink from the kitchen and went into the front room, where Mervyn was watching his muted news. She waved at him and he waved back. Downing the lot in one go, she breathed hard and put the mug on the glass coffee table with a clink.

'Thirsty,' she said, and wiped her mouth with the back of her hand.

'You just missed it,' he whispered. 'Humanitarian aid to Gazza.'

She sat down on the sofa and tugged down her T-shirt.

'You okay?' he said, not looking at her.

'I'm fine.'

'Want to talk about anything?'

Her bare legs were tanned from being in the garden. 'No.'

She knew it was a cliché but she went for it anyway. She uncrossed and crossed her legs.

He blinked three times but still didn't look.

She liked passing the time this way.

The TV said: 'First UK tropes come home.'

Once they were fully off-grid, Don developed a new structure for electricity usage. There were grade-one appliances – washing machine, disc sander, bandsaw, computer / modem / scanner – which he said could only be used one at a time, and only when the battery was fully charged. He went round the community marking these with a red sticker. On the side of the charge controller, Don attached a small red flag, like the one on their American-style mailbox, which was raised if one of these core appliances was in use. The grade-two appliances (which he dotted yellow), including TV, DVD player and the hi-fi, could be used freely, and simultaneously, whenever the battery was 95 per cent full, or above, but were restricted to 'emergency only' below that. He said that he would verify what constituted an emergency.

Under Don's new regime, new behaviours developed. The smoothie maker ran just once a morning. To burn toast was no longer charmingly dappy. Electric blankets were a distant dream. There was an art to a responsibly filled kettle. If Janet blow-dried her hair she concealed it beneath a low-key hat. Despite Arlo's protests, the fridge and chest freezer thermostats were raised by three degrees. They took turns spending time with the wind-up radio.

The newly-weds, Erin and Varghese, acutely aware of not wanting to be a burden, had moved into Patrick's old dome, where they made cups of tea on a gas stove. Lit by candlelight, frail and sniffly, they were more in love than ever. Varghese, the giant, was making a video of their honeymoon. Filming at night with a time-lapse, he'd set up his camera in the yard, looking at the house. He was very pleased with a shot he'd got that tracked the passage of individuals, turning on a light as they entered a space and off as they left. A flurry between 3.30 a.m. and 4 a.m. showed that some of the residents' bladders had synchronized. One bedroom light stayed on all night and Varghese was thinking of reporting this to Don until he realized whose bedroom it was.

Kate and Geraint sat out on the shady grass and Mervyn reclined on the decking on a beach chair in his Speedos with *The Times* on one side and the *Sun* on the other like main course and pudding. On weekends, he dozed on and off through the afternoons. Liz, with the patio doors open, could be heard whizzing and blending, having graduated to vegetarian recipes that were not imitations of meat. Kate and Geraint both wore their swimming costumes and, in breaks from revision, cooled off in the raised pool. Her white two-piece with bows at the shoulders and hips had been bought for her, on a day trip to MacArthur Glen Retail Park, along with some tights that Liz said her legs 'deserved'.

Uneven stacks of books made a skyline along the walls of the round-house. Most of the rest of Freya's stuff was still in cardboard boxes, patterned with crossed-out labels in unfamiliar handwritings: Frag-iles, Sport Gear, VHS. In acknowledgement that this was now her permanent situation, she had dragged a mattress down from the big house. Being ancient and much communally used, it was in bloom with yellow daffodil-shaped stains.

It was hard to argue with Don that her experiment had failed; Albert was more fanatical now than ever. It was agreed, then, that their son spend weekdays at the community, where he could at least do his schoolwork, and weekends with his mother. The other news was that Isaac was no longer allowed to spend any time at the round-house. Marina denied him access, flat out. According to Albert, the reason she gave was that she wanted Freya and Albert to have more time together. But Freya had plenty of time to speculate on what this actually meant.

So when Albert came to stay, it was just the two of them, which Freya liked, though they no longer joined their sleeping bags together. One Sunday they went for a low-tide walk on Whitford Burrows, out to the cast-iron lighthouse, rusted and peeling, which would make, as Albert observed, a good bunker. She tried to make the time he did spend in the roundhouse pleasant: they baked bread together, har-vested horseradish and made onion marmalade. She got him the wind-up radio, some books and worksheets, an electric lantern, a proper pillow, and a Japanese dressing screen which allowed him a quarter-circle of personal space.

Of the weekdays Albert was at the community, every other night he slept on a camp bed in the workshop with Marina and Isaac. That made a three-way split in his sleeping arrangements.

Freya knew he needed a wholesale change of circumstances. But one of the reasons her options were so limited was that she had few contacts outside the community. There was really only one person she could think of who might help.

Don was standing on a stool in the entrance hall, reaching up, his right forearm hidden in the wooden, criss-cross slatted lampshade. He was replacing the energy-saving bulbs with other, more severely energy-saving bulbs.

'I appreciated your support on this,' Don said.

Arlo was watching from the door to the kitchen and chewing imported biltong. Over the years, Don had come to rely on Arlo to get behind most projects (the yurt village and the Ad-Guard, for example) so long as they did not affect the kitchen.

'About that,' Arlo said, flicking the switch to test the new bulb. A barely perceptible glow showed at the edges of the lampshade. 'It's great to see you so full of energy, Don, but I slightly wonder if this is necessary?'

'I'm just finishing what Freya and I set out to do,' Don said as he unboxed another ping-pong bulb and went into the toilet under the stairs, where his voice grew muffled. 'If anyone's not up to the challenge then they shouldn't be here.'

'You sound like Albert.'

Don went into the kitchen, followed by Arlo, and they looked up at the lights above the counter.

'Don't even think about it,' Arlo said.

'We all have to make sacrifices.'

'Yes but I actually need to *see* what I'm chopping. Unless you want me to sacrifice my fingers.'

'This reminds me,' Don said, 'I wanted to talk to you about catering for the party.'

'Right.'

Don was still staring up at the lights. 'I've been having thoughts about some unusual specialities.'

'Oh-kay,' Arlo said, frowning. 'Whatever you like. As long as my workspace is well lit.'

'Deal,' Don said, and he went through to the scullery. He pulled out a milk crate, stood on it, reached up and twisted the bulb free. Arlo followed and shut the door behind them.

'I can see why you are doing this,' Arlo said, his voice lowered, 'but I just wonder whether you and Freya should talk first?'

'This is about what's right for the community,' he said, and he screwed in the new bulb.

Arlo clicked the switch to test it. It was sunny outside and the light in the room didn't change.

Kate was sitting in the lounge on the black leather sofa, a dress over her swimming costume, wearing Liz's *Dallas* shades on top of her head, which she'd tried on as a joke but had grown to quite like, and was revising the Heaven's Gate cult when she noticed the dark silhouette at the bay window. Her mother was in the front garden, waving, not knocking.

It had been nearly six weeks since she'd seen either of her parents. She often thought of what they would think of her new lifestyle, lounging around with luxurious hair. Kate did not acknowledge her mother at the glass but enjoyed the feeling of being silently judged.

Then, after a while, getting up off the sofa, Kate went into the hall, opened the plastic front door, ignored the shape standing there, shut the door quietly, walked up the drive, along the street and out of sight. She stopped at a grass border between the pavement and the wide road. Watching her mother coming towards her, Kate was struck by how, in this postcode, her clothes looked sad – frowning, drooping, washed at low temperatures. She appeared to be carrying the woodland shade with her.

'How did you find me?'

'I rang your college.' Kate allowed herself to be hugged. 'So glad to see you.'

Freya had her back to the sun; the light picked out the wilder edges of her dark hair, which ran down to her armpits, parting over her shoulders. She had a quality of being impervious to light; Kate struggled to see her expression.

'You look well,' Freya said.

'I'm fine.'

'What are Geraint's parents like?'

'They're normal.'

'You wear shades now,' her mother said, and seemed really pleased. 'How *are* you? I've *missed* you.'

'I'm good. Fine. Revising.'

'In very glamorous surrounds.'

'Not "surrounds". This is what a normal street looks like. Why are you here?'

'Oh, *this* is a normal street. Of course. It's been too long.'

Her mother was trying to be jokey and warm in the way of best friends, but Kate was not willing. Freya grinned with all her teeth, which, Kate could see, were clean but not white. Her mother, looking around, seemed excited to be on the municipally maintained grass. Next to them, on a lamppost, there was a photocopied poster with a child's scrawled handwriting: *Your dog does the crime, you pay the fine.* Freya had the curiosity of someone visiting the set of a long-running soap opera. Kate could tell she wanted to be invited inside.

'How did you get here?' Kate said.

'I hitched.'

'You're too old to hitch.'

Her mother squinted at her. 'Are you eating meat?'

'*What?*'

'You just seem carnivorous, somehow.'

Freya rubbed her daughter's bare upper arms, then opened her mouth but didn't speak.

'Mum, has something happened?'

'Sweetheart. I'm sorry. I wanted to talk to you.'

Kate took off her shades and squinted. 'I don't have time for this. I've got revision to do.'

'I wanted to speak. You're my best friend.'

'I don't think it's healthy for us to be best friends.'

She watched her mother move from foot to foot.

'Is the grass *hot*?'

'No. It's fine. I'm just pleased to see you.'

'Mum, what's wrong? Do you need a wee?'

Kate looked around, her hand shading her eyes, checking to see if they were being watched.

'So,' Freya said. 'Can I meet them?'

'No.'

'I'll play it cool.'

'Do *not* play it cool.'

Kate looked her mother up and down. 'Why are you wearing so many clothes? Are you sweaty?' She leaned in and smelt her mother's neck, then sniffed her armpit.

Freya said: 'If I didn't love you so much this would be humiliating.'

The frosted-glass front door was unlocked. They went into the quiet, carpeted hallway and into the lounge.

'Okay, Mum. No specifics.'

Out the back of the garden they could see both Mervyn and Liz's bodiless heads moving in the raised pool. It was more expensive to get a sunken pool, Kate now knew. Two severed, free-roaming heads. Liz was doing breaststroke and had her hair held up with a crab-coloured clamp. Kate tried to read her mother's expression.

Stepping out of the sliding doors and on to the decking, Freya was hit by direct sunlight and she did not melt.

Geraint was on the shady grass, bouncing the football on his knees. Each time the ball went up above his head it moved into sunlight and reflected brightly, then fell into shade again. He made small unconscious grunting noises. The ball hit his shin and rolled into the flower bed. He looked up at the woodland troll on the decking next to his girlfriend.

He said: 'Mum. Dad.'

Kate waited until the severed heads had noticed that she had brought a homeless person on to their property. The two heads smiled.

'Guys, I'd like you to meet Freya, my mum.'

The woodland troll waved.

On fold-out garden chairs in a rough semicircle on the sunny decking, the mothers drank Pimms and lemonade, no trimmings, Geraint and Kate drank tiny Bière D'Alsace and Mervyn, who was topless, smooth skinned, drank cherry Coca-Cola from the can. Liz had put on a turquoise towelling robe with a big collar. Kate kept her shades on, tried not to look at her mother, and heard everything with live subtitles.

'You've a beautiful home, Liz.'

You're a bourgeois sham, Liz.

'Thank you, Freya.'

'I hope my daughter's been behaving herself,' Freya said.

'She's been an absolute dream!' Liz said. 'Wish we could keep her!'

Geraint leaned in. 'She's even got Dad eating polenta.'

'It's true!' Mervyn said, lifting his glass. 'I thought it was veal.'

Freya and Liz both laughed. Kate wondered how long she could endure this.

'Well, we're really glad to finally meet you,' Liz said. 'And how's – *Don*, is it? He didn't come with you?'

'He's okay, thanks. I was trying to tell Kate, we've been going through . . .'

'Oh . . .' Liz said, leaning forwards.

'Well, I'm just glad that Katie is staying with you at the moment.'

'Oh, sweetheart,' Liz said, and she put her hand on Freya's knee and kept it there. 'Is everything okay?'

Kate, behind her shades, was trying to feel nothing.

'Well, no, Kate's father and I are not living together any more.'

'Oh God!' Liz said, and she crossed the circle and threw her arms around Freya, spilling Freya's drink in the process, the Pimms and lemonade draining away between slats of decking.

'My God, you need something stronger,' Liz said and looked to Mervyn, who disappeared off into the house.

'If there's *anything* we can do to help.'

Then Geraint was kneeling next to Kate and taking her shades off. He hugged her and she couldn't see much because of the sunlight.

Her mother said: 'Kate's probably furious with me for making a scene.'

'This is not a scene!' Liz said. 'Merv, is this a scene?'

'God no,' came the voice from inside. 'I know a scene when I see one and this isn't it.'

Standing on the verge at the side of the North Gower road, Kate kept her thumb right out.

'I can't fucking be*lieve* you. *Why* did you have to tell them?'

'I didn't mean to. They seemed nice.'

'They're not your sort of people. You shouldn't make friends with them.'

On the moorland, they could see cows bathing in a murky pool, Serengeti-style. A family estate with bikes on a rack went past, kicking up dust. Freya and Kate both squinted.

'I grew up in a house a bit like theirs, you know,' Freya said.

'Did you have a swimming pool?'

'Well.'

Her mother was a little drunk and it was infuriating. In her hand she was holding a piece of paper with the home phone number of Bishopston School's headmaster, Howard Ley. Freya had told Liz and Mervyn that she had been thinking of sending Albert there in September, and Mervyn had immediately gone to fetch his little black book. He had all kinds of useful contacts, he said, and he would put in a good word.

A red minivan for M. Hare Period Restoration didn't slow down.

'Mum, you don't know them. They look like normal people but they're not. Mervyn's an insomniac and, I think, ex-alcoholic. And Liz is pathologically nice. She keeps buying me clothes she thinks make me look attractive.'

Two small cars went by, followed by a delivery motorbike. Kate extended her hand out straight, for more impact.

'Kate, you know that you, of all people, should be tolerant. You grew up with every kind of person,' Freya said, rubbing the small of her daughter's back with her spare hand. 'How many people have we seen touch each corner of the door frame and then touch the corresponding corners of their mouth with their tongue before they can walk through?'

'One person. Alan Medlicott.'

'Liz is being nice. Not everything is the tip of the iceberg,' Freya said. 'Sometimes it is just . . . a bit of ice floating along.'

Kate shook her head. Her mother was drunk, it was dreadful.

'Why are you being like this?'

'Like what? Non-judgemental?'

'Yes. It's awful.'

A car driven by boys with surfboards on the roof slowed and pulled up, flashing its hazards.

'Okay, Mum. Go now.'

07/06/12.
    Members present: Don (chair), Arlo, Marina, Janet, Albert, Isaac.
    Visitors: Varghese, Erin.
    Members absent: Kate, Patrick, Freya.

Albert was now banned from taking minutes. Don looked around the table. Janet had her Biro poised just above the lined pad in, he felt, mock anticipation. For any decision to be agreed, half the full-time members needed to be at the round table. Children counted for half, which meant that Isaac, although technically under the table, made a crucial difference. Freya was no longer expected at community meetings, though she had not been able to stop Albert attending. The newly-weds were settling in to communal life, ping-ponging a head cold back and forth between them. He coughed, she sniffed.

'A bit of naming and shaming,' Don said, turning to address his son. 'It's come to my attention that the young master has been speaking to a TV production company. He even sent them forged release forms. Anything to say in your defence?'

Albert was playing with his bottom lip, stretching it, turning it inside out to show off the forked blue veins. He let it *flup* back into position.

'Just trying to get the word out. People need to be warned.'

Don turned to Marina. She made a teepee out of her fingers. Janet frowned and wrote something down.

'Right then,' Don said. 'Moving on.'

He passed around copies of a document. It was a compilation of comments about the community dredged from the LiveWild.co.uk forum. One of the more notable contributions was from 'Coastnut', who used an extended metaphor, saying that Patrick had been 'like one of these "replete ants" – a colony's living larder, essentially – who they'd been fattening/milking for decades.' Firepoi88 said she had heard 'the children are illiterate and some of the other accusations really ought to be taken to social services' – and then a shocked emoticon face. Callum09 said: 'I've just come back from a week wwoofing there: NOT RECOMMEND.'

Don looked around, watching them go over the document. Some of the comments were a decade old but he didn't feel the need to mention this. He threaded his fingers together.

'Applications for membership are a quarter of what they were three years ago and we only have three visitors booked in for the next open day,' he said. 'But, on the upside, I hope you agree that since going off-grid we've really turned a corner. We need to let people know how much we've changed.'

Around the table, they were frowning and underlining.

At this point, Don turned to Varghese, the almost literal giant, the massive half of the honeymooners who Don had recently discovered had worked for many years in a Chicago-based ad agency. Varghese, who told Don he would be honoured to 'oversee a rebrand', was shuffling a sheaf of papers, graphs and inspiration material, shaping up to speak.

Mervyn began to wonder if Kate was timing her showers so that she always tottered back across the hallway with wet hair, chest flushed, wearing just a tucked towel, at times when he was picking out a shirt from the second wardrobe that stood on the landing. It happened every weekday. He tried to strike a naturalistic balance between completely blanking her, which was, in its own way, an admission of interest, and gawping. He said 'Morning', made eye contact but didn't linger or enjoy the smell that stayed in the air behind her as she made a point of squeezing past him to Geraint's room, where she now slept. Liz had said that it was time to let her 'come out of quarantine'.

He had to provide normalcy, he knew, during her time of upheaval. The last thing she needed was to be sexually harrassed by the adults she was trying to trust.

Early on in his marriage, Mervyn had cheated on Liz with an older woman he'd interviewed about the suicide of her grown-up son. He'd asked questions in the darkened back room of her house. She was a beekeeper and had been drinking Martinique white rum. She answered his questions by taking her tights off. She had red bumps on her ankles. They had sex twice, and Mervyn didn't speak to her again.

The day after the woman's son's funeral, he'd come home from work to find her in his back garden, getting on famously with Liz, who was on the verge of sending off for a mail-order hive. After that the beekeeper blackmailed him into having regular, admittedly thrilling, sex with her. For Mervyn, this marked the beginning of his problems with sleeping. All the while, his wife read up on hive intelligence. *Collectively, they make honey yet no single bee understands how it's done.*

Then the beekeeper's house got repossessed. Liz wanted to let her stay in their spare room while she got settled. Mervyn didn't think it was a good idea. He lied and told a story about her trying and failing to seduce him, using the detail about the tights and the bumps on her ankles. Liz instantly believed him, cut all contact with the beekeeper and ever since has enjoyed telling the story, among good friends, about the madwoman who tried to 'sting her husband' – and each time she told it, Mervyn had to shrug and chuckle.

All the while, the woman continued to threaten him. She was living in a council block in Clase. She warned him that she could describe his penis in a way that his wife would instantly know was authentic. The colour of it, she said. To this day, there had never been any genuine resolution – just her demands, first for sex and later for money, growing more and more infrequent. He hadn't heard from her in years, but that didn't mean it was over. Mervyn believed that since he had created the problem, he deserved to take the burden of worry that, any day, if she was feeling drunk, sad, jealous, spiteful, she might call.

Over the years, as the *Evening Post*'s go-to death-knocker, meeting people at times of heightened emotion, Mervyn had been in more than one tempting situation. His method – post-beekeeper – was to take the time to imagine the true details of what it would be like with that person: turn something romantic into something journalistic. Acknowledge the inappropriate feeling, then flesh it out with details until reality leaches the charm out of it.

So it was, that afternoon in the office loos, he imagined Kate's body. In his fantasy, she was double-jointed. After he'd filled a hand-towel which he imagined to be her flushed chest, he made himself keep the fantasy going in his mind, her weeping in the back of the Jeep, digging her nails into her palms and, through strings of saliva in her mouth, saying she loved him. He kept the story going: he and Kate having a nocturnal relationship, silent orgasms in front of muted News 24. After a few weeks, Kate convincing him to elope with her in the Jeep – an implication that she might kill herself, if he didn't go along with it, is how Mervyn imagined it happening. A queen-size foam mattress squeezed in the back, driving through the Irish lowlands, and at first it being exciting but by the fourth day it already becoming clear that, although they got on okay and the hyper-mobile sex was fun, they were too different for it to work in the long term – and the cold-weather mosquito bites made her calves and ankles swell up in a strange, watery way. Then, one morning, Kate disappearing, lost among the hills and suicide-friendly cliffs south of Galway, and Mervyn searching for three days before returning home to tell Kate's family what had happened – only to discover she was back there with them.

Now they were sharing a room, Kate and Geraint felt a pressure to act like a proper couple. This meant bed-sex, which felt somehow much further along the relationship timeline, much closer to marriage and therefore death than Jeep-, woods- or pool-sex. Quickly, they formed a routine, a side of the bed, a sleeping formation ('the turnstile') and pet names that will not be recorded here.

Geraint had started to change. He'd put his name on the waiting list for an allotment. He'd been reading about Blaen-y-Llyn online and kept signposting his knowledge, in conversation: 'I can see the value of a sustainable housing village.' He kept asking her when they were going to go for dinner at her mother's. He'd Googled Freya Riley and unearthed some of the dreadful articles, hatchet-jobs, written about the 'Lost Tribe of Gower'. It was when Kate spotted Geraint in the utility room, turning electrical devices off standby, that she felt a portcullis come down between them.

More and more she looked forward to the thrill of her secret visits to the lounge, to sit next to insomniac Mervyn. She liked the extra risk of being careful not to wake Geraint as she got out of bed.

She brought her goose-pimpled legs up on the sofa, didn't tug down her 'Life Begins at Forty' T-shirt, which, having now experienced Liz's washing temperatures, had shrunk.

She watched the screen. It said: '. . . school spells fifty truants . . .'

Mervyn didn't notice. He kept watching the TV.

She breathed. He turned to look at her and they made eye contact with each other and she smiled. He had a sympathetic expression and she imagined it was the one he used for interviewing the recently bereaved.

Although they were already off-grid, Varghese had said it was important to have something up online so that people could understand, visually, the dramatic change. As such, they shot a short film of the community chopping down the electricity pole at the bottom of the garden, although now no power was running through it. Varghese got various talking heads on video to describe it as sticking out of the ground like 'a crucifix', 'a middle finger' and 'the hilt of a knife'. Isaac said electricity was 'like a waterfall of fire inside the walls of the house'. He looked unfeasibly cute and muddled. A tracking shot followed Arlo with an axe over his shoulder and Don carrying pruning shears, both men side by side down the stepped path. It was clear by the way they walked that they imagined their own theme music. Having climbed the pole and severed the cables, Don sat on top like an awkward, judicial bird, squinting down at the camera, only sky behind him.

Everyone had a go at chopping, and when they heard the wood creak they ran back and watched. It fell slowly, hitting the ground like a last-round knockout, like a victory for the featherweight outsider. Varghese asked them to hold each other's hands aloft, then made them do it again, in better light. He made Isaac hold up a piece of slate with a message chalked on it:

A-Level Results Day Party, 2012
All Welcome.
At Blaen-y-Llyn (aka The Rave House), North Gower

The apple tree in the yard had been first planted to mark Don and Freya's wedding day. In turn, it produced the fruit which made the gum-tingling cider that they got drunk on before conceiving Kate, loudly, on their platform bed. Their daughter's birth, in turn, had an impact on the community at large: raising morale and, in time, bringing in young families. This allowed for sharing childcare with other parents, which gave Freya and Don more time for each other. And so on. It was symbiotic, Don knew, the relationship between his marriage and the community. They fed off one another.

He was standing in the entrance hall, by the phone, turning through the Yellow Pages. He noticed there were several punctures right through it – they looked like bullet holes – which he had not seen before. He turned to *P* and dialled in the number carefully.

'Hi there. I was wondering about hiring a sound system.'

Just as Kate's fifteenth birthday party had created its own legacy – The Rave House – Don hoped that this summer event could build a new reputation for the community. By making it an A-level results-day party, he hoped to guarantee his daughter's attendance.

'An outdoor event.'

It would change public perception and bring in new, younger members and remind Freya of the reasons they started all this.

'About 300.'

He'd suggested to Arlo some special dishes that would utilize Freya's unique talents as slaughterer-in-chief, some way of involving his wife in the party preparations, investing her in it. Arlo wanted to help.

'Naturally. How much?'

He lifted the receiver away from full contact with his ear, as though it were hot. There was a long silence, then Don got out his rarely seen personal debit card and, bravely, two digits at a time, read the long number.

Kate had two minutes remaining on her last exam, and was now checking for spelling errors. The light came in from the sport's hall's high windows.

She was almost sad they were over. There was something enjoyable about the tarot of turning over an exam paper: a whole gymnasium full of people reading their fortunes. Kate had hit her specialist subjects on both sections, first the French Revolution, then German Resistance, allowing her to helicopter in an aside about reweighing contemporary German guilt.

She found no spelling mistakes.

Outside the hall, she stood at the top of the stairs that led down to the car park, letting other students stream past her. Geraint was standing at the bottom holding six balloons, red, yellow, green, two of each. Since having his final Geography exam three days previously, he'd had time to get his first decent burn of the summer and looked good.

She skipped down the steps and the six coloured balloons jostled and squeaked above him as they kissed.

'How'd it go?'

'I destroyed it,' she said.

He smiled and admired her and she imagined the balloons, carried by the wind, slowly lifting him out of the car park.

There was someone calling her name. She looked around and saw Patrick standing in one of the empty diagonal bays beside a bright new Mini Cooper. It had an advert for *John Burn's Gym* on the driver's door and, on the bonnet, *Walkabout Bar*. He waved a big, two-armed wave.

They were sitting on the flood barrier eating North Poles with chocolate sauce that Patrick had bought for them. Kate was in the middle. Patrick wore a white shirt with red pinstripes that was only on its first or second outing, judging by its stiffness.

'So where do you live, Pat?' she said.

'Right on the seafront. I can pretty much swim to my door.' He seemed pleased, and sucked on the little red spoon.

'Is that your way of saying that you're homeless?' she said.

'You can see my house from here,' he said, and pointed along the cycle path.

'You live in the little shed where they keep the pitch and putt clubs? You've done well.'

Patrick laughed. 'And this,' he said, pointing up and down the coastal path, 'is my commute. You're speaking to Mumbles pier's most senior croupier! You two should come and redeem a free game of Bowlingo.'

'Thanks, we'll definitely do that,' Geraint said, then, leaning forward to make purposeful eye contact with Patrick, 'Do you mind if I ask you something?'

As they drove to Kit Lintel's house in Llanmadoc, Geraint could not stop talking about the community. Despite the fact that Patrick's account of life there had included choice phrases such as 'the longest winter of my life' and 'the deceit of kinship', this had only succeeded in piquing Geraint's interest. She tried to explain to him that the reason Patrick had seemed so contented now was because he had finally escaped the community. Geraint did not buy it.

Kit's parents' cottage overlooked the salt marsh. He had a big garden with a swing. Geraint had suggested that to celebrate the end of their exams they should do something different. As Kit represented the entirety of their college's alternative scene, he had been chosen.

Kit brought a cassoulet pot out on to the dining table. His black hair had an ambition to become dreadlocks but currently resembled a bird-eating spider clambering out of a nest. The smell was rank, like old flannels, and it stuck in the back of their throats. The mushrooms looked absurdly phallic, twenty severed dicks sliding around in the bottom of the pan. Geraint smiled nervously as he poured the dishwaterish liquid into three mugs. She smelt hers and wrinkled her nose. Kit held his mug out for clinking.

Geraint downed his and wiped his mouth with the back of his hand. Kit did the same and picked a slimy whole mushroom out of the bottom of the pan, simulated oral, then chewed it. Kate mimed sipping hers but didn't open her mouth. She had no need for mind-expanding drugs. Her mind was at its perfect width and depth.

'Mine's too hot,' she said, and she got up to go to the sink. She ran the tap and held her finger under it. With the other hand she discreetly poured hers away, then half filled it with water.

She turned back to the boys and made a show of tasting for temperature.

'Better,' she said, then necked it.

When it got dark, the moon was out and bright enough to see by as they walked down to the estuary's salt marsh, which Kit said was a guarantee of sensual overload, containing every kind of spongy texture, from foam to blow-up mattress to stress-relief toy. They walked across it, wrapped up warm but barefoot, leaving their footprints in the goo. Kate hammed it up, twirling her arms around, looking up at the sky – 'I can see, like, all these dudes playing guitar solos' – and pretty quickly they were calling the moon a paracetamol, a glass of milk, a shower head raining stars, a Nazi prison searchlight ('Don't dark me out, Kate, please . . .'), and Geraint announced that paddling through a shallow sandy stream was 'just about the fucking greatest thing of all time', and Kate watched Kit do graceless roly-polies and she quite enjoyed herself – the feeling of a secret separateness – and she and Geraint held hands and laughed and he asked, 'Are you laughing at what I'm laughing at?' and Kit had to sit down for a while, and they asked him if he was okay, and he said, 'Give me a minute' and then later decided he had to go inside and listen to Greek myths on cassette, read by Stephen Fry, which left the two survivors sitting on the circular bench that went round the ash tree in Kit's garden, and he said, 'I love you, Kate' and she didn't feel the need to respond.

Back in the house, they found Kit Lintel pouring orange juice into Kit Lintel's father's laptop.

'I feel fantastic,' he said.

A day later, they were lying under the duvet in the lower bunk bed. Kate was wearing his tartan pyjamas. Geraint was naked and only now coming down.

'Do you think we'll stay together when you're at university?'

She was on her back; he was on his side.

'Of course,' she said. 'When *we* go to university!'

Everyone spends their lives with everyone else, philosophically speaking, if we're to think of human consciousness as a permeable membrane and time as a concertina'd illusion.

'I'll probably go through Clearing. I don't want to lose you.'

'You won't lose me.'

'I feel sick, I've never felt like this,' he said, and he sucked his lips in.

'Aw, sweetie.'

Geraint, I liked you better when you were a meathead.

His skin was clearing up now that he ate what she ate. She missed the inflamed pores that ran round his neck.

'I've never felt like this either,' she said.

'You know, I really want to see the community. I feel like I'm ready.'

He'd stopped calling it The Rave House or The Commune.

'I just want to see where you come from,' he said. 'Who you are.'

'It's not exciting.'

I want to be able to leave you without feeling bad about it.

'I don't care whether it's exciting. It's a part of you. That's why. I want to see your origins. Meet your favourite goat. Bellamy?'

'That's sweet,' she said.

Then he leaned over and gently – lethally – kissed her on the fore-head.

I only came here because I wanted to do well in my exams. I am only with you because you seemed different from what I was used to. I will leave Wales as soon as I can. I will have written the letter breaking up with you before my first day on campus. I will walk straight to the postbox in the autumnal sunshine in Cambridge/Edinburgh or, at a very outside chance, Leeds, and I will never think of you again.

5   Outage

The schoolroom windows rattled as the sleet came in slantways. Everyone was standing around the charge controller, watching the hydro and wind needles creep up. The newest wwoofers, four Dutchmen on an alternative stag do, had their arms round each other's shoulders in the manner of Eurovision contestants awaiting their scores. Early that morning, Arlo had walked through the community beneath paunchy clouds, cranking the wind-up radio, announcing a storm warning: 'Severe weather for Wales and west!'

'Dad, is it dumping yet?' Albert asked.

Don peered at the dials. The wind played a minor chord across the chimney.

'Alright,' Don said. 'It's dumping.'

That was the signal. The community set to work. There was a moral responsibility to use electrical goods. To avoid the excess energy burning out the circuitry, they needed to plug in. It was wasteful for Albert *not* to turn on a hairdryer, play a CD of Harry Belafonte's 'Jump in the Line' and film Isaac with his swishy blonde hair dancing in a wind tunnel. Clothes that had gone unwashed were washed, then dried in the microwave.

Don prowled. It disappointed him to know that so many of the people he trusted had secret pluggable devices in their rooms. In the kitchen, Arlo, with an electric whisk, made raspberry meringues and pushed carrots and ginger into the blender. On the table, an electric carver. In the pottery shed, Marina was filling the electric kiln with new work. On the bench next to her, a laptop he'd never seen before.

By dusk, everyone was gathered in the schoolroom, ballroom dancing. The music was loud enough to distort and it skipped each time Isaac ran past, arms out, pretending to be an aeroplane with one engine down due to bad weather. Marina was dancing with

Arlo, with Albert on his shoulders, the stag do paired off in two couples and the newly-weds span in circles. Janet was away again with her boyfriend. Flashing fairy lights were wrapped around the two horizontal roof beams and Schubert's 'Kupelwieser Waltz' was on the record player. They danced and listened to the gap close between the lightning and its sound effect. Every now and then the windows blinked white and the room bleached. Don, watching from the doorway, felt that everyone was too pleased, too relieved – that this betrayed their true longings. He leaned against the door frame, watching them slowly turn, standing on each other's toes, laughing it off, whispering little jokes, clinging to a world they claimed not to miss.

Don thought about the forthcoming party. Varghese was building online buzz by harnessing the already existing reputation of 'The Rave House'. In the dogsonacid.com forum, he had posted 'the tech spec' of the Funktion One sound system alongside a row of gurning animated emoticons. Don had told Varghese he was worried that the party was going to be too wasteful, and that it might not reflect the values of the community. Varghese had explained that with some of today's young people there was a conflict between a party being overtly low impact and being authentically cool. It was either/or. Responsibility vs Freedom. But, Varghese said, by encouraging the young people to have the best night of their lives, Don could create a bond with the community that would, in time, develop into an interest in sustainable living. That was why it was vital to get them on results day. They would be at an apex of open-mindedness and ready to make lifelong emotional attachments. They would do most of the work themselves. All the community had to do was not get all heavy on the first date.

Varghese suggested Don think of sustainability as an embarrassing uncle who, although invited to the party, should be kept out of sight. Young people were attuned to being manipulated into thoughtful behaviour, he said. *Slam-dunk your green glass bottles here, dude!* That wouldn't do. A generator running on used vegetable oil and biodegradable cups and plates was about the limit of it.

Don sniffed. He watched the ballroom dancing and missed his

daughter and wife. It was usually only at night, in his room, that he let himself feel what he was feeling now. He went into the hall. While putting on his coat, he could hear boots in the washing machine thumping like a heartbeat. In the scullery he grabbed a torch, then went out the back way into the weather. He heard the three-blade wind turbine going *whup-whup-whup*, its metal struts creaking.

Looking back from the bottom of the garden, he saw the house lit up, shapes passing the schoolroom windows, and the distant crescendos of swing jazz behind the big band of rain and wind. Ambient light poured out through all the piecemeal windows: bay, skylights, portholes, the stained glass at the top of the stairs – a testament to twenty years of cooperation, not a single vision but many visions patched together. It looked like the big house might explode, like it was molten in the centre and getting hotter.

Varghese had told Don about a nightclub in Rotterdam that had a piezoelectric dancefloor which harvested the energy given off by the stomping feet to power the lasers, which, in turn, promoted more ambitious dancing, and so on, until the whole club, Don presumed, got vaporized.

The first thing that came through the draught curtains of the roundhouse was a raised hand, followed by its owner, waltzing, partner-less, spinning through the room, dark spots specking the matting as drips fell off the hem of his coat. Don did a couple of turns and then stopped.

'Everyone's pleased about the weather,' he said. 'They're dancing in the schoolroom. I thought you might like to join us?'

Freya was smiling, watching him from a stool next to the ex-milk-churn wood-burning stove, which was glowing orange at its edges. She was drying off – steam rising from her arms, her thighs, as though she were evaporating.

'You bring glamour wherever you go,' she said. 'How are things?'

'*Things* are terrific,' he said, opening his eyes wide, starting to dance again. 'And full of electrical appliances on standby.'

'Well, you might need to use them in a hurry,' she said.

'Exactly!'

She watched him slow down, stop, lower his hands. The wet had come through his boots and there were dashes of mud up his trousers.

'Why don't you come up to the big house?' he said.

He waited for an answer, and when one didn't come he turned and started looking around, first at Freya's bed, the Celtic knot of dark hairs on her pillow, then at Albert's quarter-circle of the room. His made-up bed was demarcated by the Japanese dressing screen patterned with clouds and non-Welsh dragons.

'I overheard Albert describe himself as being *of no fixed abode*,' Don said.

Freya watched him. Some thunder revved and white light flashed at the porthole window.

'I've been speaking to someone,' she said. 'The headmaster at Bishopston Comp. He says there's room for Albert to start school in September.'

Don turned to look at her. 'You never mentioned that.'

'I'm mentioning it.'

'We need to discuss this.' He tugged up the thighs of his trousers and sat down on a stool opposite her. 'I thought we agreed that learning should be child-led. Look at what Kate's achieved. She's way ahead of her peers.'

'It was different for her. Albert's got no one to learn with. Besides, I worry that without contact with people his own age he'll get too . . . strange.'

'Right now he's ballroom dancing on the shoulders of an ex-professional chef. How will that go down in Bishopston Comprehensive?'

'All I'm saying is he might *benefit* from a teeny bit of peer pressure. He'll make friends. He always does.'

'I'm sure he and the school psychiatrist will get on well.'

Don was a little pleased with that, she noticed. Her socks were drying on the wood-burner. She turned them and they sizzled like rashers of bacon.

'You know,' he said, 'since Varghese has been handling our online presence, we've had loads of emails from teenagers as well as their parents, because the system they're part of is failing them. By September, the community'll be overrun by young people looking for a decent education. We'll be wishing the little sods would leave us alone.' Don stopped speaking as the sky grumbled but no lightning came. He went on: 'And what about the things school can't teach Albert?'

'Like what?'

'Like a million things. Like how to build his own home, live with other people, grow his own food, *kill* his own food – now you're gone, there's nobody to pass on that knowledge. Another skill-set slips between the generations.'

'Get someone trained up then. Train *yourself* up.'

She watched him. Don stared at the stove.

'You know I'm not cut out for that kind of thing.'

She opened her mouth with an impulse to say something cruel, but decided to let it go.

'Just for example, Arlo's been looking forward to making this traditional Sardinian meal for the party,' he said. 'He's been going on about it – *sanguinaccio!* Blood soup, basically. But without you, we can't do it.'

'*Take* the *goat* to an *abattoir*, Don. I don't live at the community any more. I'm not killing your animals for you.'

'No, of course,' he said, then stood up off the stool and started looking around again. 'But it's an example of how skills and traditions get lost over time.'

She breathed through her mouth. He examined the fanned, self-supporting pattern of the roof beams. Raising his arms to test one, he grunted as his feet came off the floor.

'But Freya, the thing is, the abattoir's in Cardiff and the blood needs to be fresh that day. Arlo says it has to be *straight outta de throat and onna de stove.*'

'Tell him to cook a different recipe.'

'Have you ever met Arlo?' Don said, in a funny voice.

'Then *do it yourself.* Christ.'

'You know what I'm like,' he said.

You know what I'm like. That was it for Freya.

'I won't let you put this on me. *You* do it. *You* should do it.' Her voice suddenly loud. 'Then the *skills and traditions* won't be lost, if you fucking do it.'

She breathed hard. Don had a dazed look on his face. She turned the socks again. This time they didn't hiss. She felt the same impulse as before, but now gave in to it.

'I went to see Kate,' she said.

'*What?*'

'I went to see Kate, at her house.'

'Why didn't you tell me? What's the address?'

'I don't remember.'

'What's the street name?'

'I've forgotten.'

'She won't answer my calls. I'd just like to know, for my own well-being, her postcode.'

She shook her head.

'I'm her father, Frey.'

As she opened the stove door, flames flared in the rush of oxygen. He walked a full loop round the edge of the rug.

'You're just doing this to be cruel,' he said.

'You're right,' she said.

'Okay, well, good then. *Good.* Now we're getting somewhere.' He slapped his hand against the beam above his head. 'And tell me – how else would you like me to suffer?'

Patrick watched the storm through the floor-to-ceiling windows that ran the length of Mumbles Pier Arcade. He was in his booth. The weather had kept away the regulars, leaving only Karl Orland, his ex-dealer and now occasional dinner companion, who some-times dropped in at the end of Patrick's shifts. Karl was playing Cash Invader, crouching down to peek up the reels.

Patrick's official title was croupier. The title he gave himself, however, was Human Change Machine. He didn't just slide stacks of ten-pence coins across the counter, but also sometimes laminated pamphlets from Proclaimer's Mental Health Support. This wasn't his dream job, but despite early success as a businessman and landlord, twenty years at the community had left him with a pretty wonky CV. Mortgage lenders no longer considered him 'a worthwhile gamble', which was appropriate.

He was renting a little sea-view two-bed with a back patio that opened on to the cycle path. It was paid for by the rent from his student house in Norwich, which was still, according to his agency, 'attracting moderate interest'. He had no desire to ever go back there or to discover how badly the agency was ripping him off. All he knew was that each month the cash which arrived in his account, along with the piddling wage he earned as a Human Change Machine, allowed him to live in what felt like extravagance – relative to the geodesic dome.

Karl jabbed the spin button with his knuckles, then kept standing there frowning for a while, waiting for the music to return to idle and the lights to start swirling. Patrick had discovered the real reason Karl had never turned up that week, back at the community. Jury duty. It really tickled Patrick – to think the hand of democratic bureaucracy was still able to influence the community, and drag him back to the mainstream.

It was Friday. On a normal weekend night, the arcade would be full of gamblers exploring the impact of lager on probability, but tonight, with the weather, Patrick decided to shut early. He locked the front and side doors, then put the cashbox in the safe.

He and Karl went outside to the little smokers' area and sat on the covered bench that overlooked the sea. Behind them, the noise and patterned lights from the machines – cartwheels, snakes, tractor beams, sunrays, building blocks – and, in front of them, the bay and the seafront lights curling round.

Patrick coughed steadily until something came up, which he spat into the water. Karl patted Patrick on the back. He was the sort of drug dealer who genuinely supported a client's attempts to quit.

A sheet of lightning hit out at sea; grey cloud appearing in a chamber of sky then sucked away into the night's black lungs. Thunder followed.

'The sky has chest infection too,' Karl said, and was pleased.

They heard the oddly homogenized and comforting noise of drunks walking along the seafront. Girls screaming, either in hysterics or terror. Boys in tight white T-shirts and Italian jeans walked like Ken dolls towards the pier. When he had come to Swansea from London, Patrick had at first assumed that this was a sign of a really vibrant and open gay scene: tanned men in muscle tees, walking with their outsize arms around one another's shoulders, openly checking each other out.

Lightening hit again, flashing the city's off-colour teeth.

'A beaut,' Karl said, and he brought a spliff from behind his ear. 'Do you mind?'

Patrick shook his head. He no longer felt the remotest temptation. Then there was the opposite of a sound as the city suddenly flickered out and the lights went off in the arcade behind them. Every machine, swirling, running rivers of colours with fairground noises, suddenly went blank and quiet. Swansea had disappeared. Either a blackout or the world was ending. There was just the tip of Karl's spliff, flaring in darkness, and, at the far side of the bay, the tops of the steelworks' smokestacks burning.

It was midnight as Don drove through the storm with Radio 3 on. In return for his daughter's address, which was in Three Crosses, Don had agreed that he would slaughter the goat at the party, under Freya's supervision. Supervision, as far as he could tell, was her way of saying she wanted to be there to watch him suffer. He tried to explain to her once again that killing was just not part of his nature, and that perhaps she should view that as a good thing, but it didn't go down well. She had always thought he faked his fear of animal slaughter, and in all honesty he had hammed it up a little, but, he asked her, if a person feels the need to ham something up, then isn't that evidence of a genuine problem? There had been no response.

On the upside, this did all mean that she was now tied to spending a few hours at the community, on the morning of the party. If he could just get her to start enjoying herself, see some old friends, have a drink, then there was hope.

The windscreen wipers briefly conducted Dvorak before falling out of time again. In preparation for the party, Don had started trying to enjoy music. An example of how he was willing to develop himself, to change.

He turned in to Three Crosses. It was only then he noticed that none of the street lights were on.

It had been Geraint's idea for them to come together and 'enjoy the power cut'. Gathered in the double-glazed conservatory, they were watching the weather with their backs to each other in the style of superheroes surrounded by foes. Kate was wearing a gingham shirt-dress that Liz had bought her. Against her will, she rather liked it. The rain made a satisfying *takataka* noise on the plastic glass. There was lightning and Mervyn laughed and Liz screamed in a theatrical way and Geraint told his mother to grow up. It felt like they were in it, the storm, as a family. They unfussily held each other's hands behind their backs, and she was holding one of Mervyn's, she knew, because of its size and the seams of rough skin at his joints. The ground shook, and in the lightning flash Kate thought she saw a figure standing on the hyper-fertilized lawn. She didn't say anything. It could have been her imagination. The killer who comes to torture suburban families when a power cut disables the burglar alarm. Just then, her pocket buzzed. She pulled out her phone and read the message.

Hi sweets, mum told me you live in Three Crosses. Very posh! I was just driving back from town and noticed the power cut. Are you guys okay? xxxx

She put the phone away immediately and prayed to all gods that the man on the lawn was a serial killer and not her father. Her back stiffened and she gripped Mervyn's hand behind her.

There was another flash and this time, Geraint saw.

'Oh my fucking God, there's a man in our back garden.'

Mervyn put his hands against the glass and looked outside.

'Maybe he wants to borrow a torch,' Mervyn said.

'Then why doesn't he knock on the door?' Liz said. 'He's probably a looter.'

'It's my dad.'

She let that piece of information sink in, then she read the text message aloud to her family. Ever since she'd arrived, she'd been enjoying painting a picture of her father as a kind of lunatic, and now he was living up to it. Liz said Kate was well within her rights to call the police. Mervyn and Geraint said they'd be happy to have words, on her behalf. Her new family made her feel brave. She rang his number. In the darkness of the back garden, they saw a dim light ping on. As the number started calling, she turned on speakerphone and put her mobile down on the wicker and glass coffee table.

'Kate!' came her father's distorted voice. 'I'm so glad you called.'

They could hear his voice outside, as well as in.

'Dad, what the hell are you doing? I can *see* you.'

'So I found the right house then! I just wanted to check you're okay, because of the power cut.'

'You're in our back garden.'

'Couldn't read the house numbers in the dark, but knew I was looking for a place with a swimming pool. Did I ever tell you that your mother and I did our courting in a swimming pool?'

'You're on loudspeaker. Say hello to the people on whose property you are trespassing.'

Out in the rain, they could make out the blue-lit outline of the side of his face. Kate thought there was something different about him.

'Hello there?' he said.

Not a peep from her new family, and Kate liked them for that.

'What I wanted to say was that you'd all be very welcome to stay the night at ours – until you get power back. We've got plenty of room. There's music, lights and salsa dancing' – he tried to laugh but it sounded robotic through the phone's crappy speaker – 'we're really enjoying ourselves and you'd all be very welcome to join us.'

They saw the phone light grow larger as Don came towards the conservatory. She realized what was different. No one had told her about his beard. Through the tinny speaker, there was the crackling sound of him breathing.

'Dad, you need to go home.'

They watched the floating phone light get closer.

'Right-o, well maybe I could –'

She ended the call. The pale blue light came closer to the glass, seemed to be waving. They couldn't make out what he was saying. Then the light blinked off.

On the drive home, Don tried hard to enjoy Radio 3 because he knew how effective most people find music as a form of emotional release.

Liz and Kate were upstairs in the big carpeted bathroom, lit by two fragrant candles on the windowsill. Kate held the glasses while Liz unscrewed the wine.

'You deserve a drink after that.'

They sat next to each other on the step up to the circular, two-person bath.

'Things are going to get better,' Liz said.

'I hope so.'

They clinked.

'And I just wanted to say . . .'

Kate scrolled through the things that Liz might say next: *My husband said your name in bed; if you break my son's heart I will kill you.*

'. . . you've been living with us for a while now and God knows how hard it must be but I want you to know we think of you as part of the family. This might sound weird, but we've never been happier. Mervyn, especially . . .'

Kate covered her mouth with her wine glass.

'. . . you've made us appreciate what we've got. I hope you're happy living here too.'

Kate nodded, drank, swallowed.

'That'a girl,' Liz said, and took a big swig herself.

Kate imagined telling Liz that she had taken her only son's virginity in-between the vintage benches of their four by four. Liz reached behind her and pulled, from the empty bath, a paper Topshop bag. She presented it to Kate.

'Surprise! Mervyn's naive but I'm not. Now you and Geraint share a room. I'm too old to wear this, but you'll do it justice.'

When Kate didn't immediately look inside, Liz pulled the two items out herself – high-waisted black lace knickers with beaded detail and a matching bra, longline, studded – which Liz held up against herself, laughing. Kate hoped her face for stunned horror was the same as her face for happy surprise.

Liz put the clothes in Kate's lap.

'Put 'em on now if you like. And the rest of the bottle's yours too. A power cut's good for one thing: candlelight.' Liz winked. 'And, by the way, Ger' told me what you two got up to in the back of the Jeep.' Liz clapped her hands together. 'Priceless! Just don't tell Merv!'

Geraint was in bed, reading by torchlight. He shined the beam on Kate as she came in.

'Who goes there?'

'Me.'

'Hi, me.'

She walked over and sat on the edge of the bed. 'What you reading?'

'Don't ask. I'm a loser.'

She lifted up the big hardback book. *The New Complete Book of Self-Sufficiency.*

'Ask me *anything* about chutney,' he said, and closed it. She actually felt like Geraint's mother, sat on the edge of his bed.

'Are you okay?' he said.

'Fine, I guess.'

'Want to talk?'

'Nope.'

'You coming to bed?'

She shook her head.

'I'll be back in a bit,' she said, and then, feeling a bit bad for him, and bad for herself, she rubbed his back before leaving.

Downstairs, she was sitting in the dark lounge with two wines.

Mervyn wasn't awake and this annoyed her. Over the last few days, he hadn't been regular in his sleeplessness. She thought of the words *we've never been happier*.

Kate drank from both glasses, spilling spots on her gingham shirt-dress. She held up a candle to look around the room for slugs on the carpet, but couldn't see any. Something, perhaps a non-lethal house fire, some trauma, would be appropriate at this point. She stayed seated trying, through the force of thought, to summon Mervyn, and when he didn't come she tried summoning Patrick, and when he didn't come, she even tried bringing back her actual father until, finally, she fell asleep.

She only woke up because the shell-motif wall lights had come on, and so had the hallway light and the TV standby LED. The power was back. Outside, the storm had given way to steady rain. The candle was a puddle. She blew it out. There was a gentle throb behind her eyes and two empty glasses of wine on the coffee table. Next to the glasses, the bottle had a little left in it. She turned the TV on and, for old times' sake, watched rolling news on mute with real-time subtitles. 'Bad weather causes rolling power cuts across South-West' with stock footage of lightning.

She batted away her headache by pouring herself the last of the wine and taking a big drink. Flicking through the channels, she eventually stopped at a cartoon. When she was young, she and Albert hadn't been allowed to watch them very much. Her father's line was that they eroded the link between cause and effect. But this was one of the few she had been encouraged to watch – *Steamboat Willie*, the first Mickey Mouse cartoon – because it represented 'a pivotal moment in the history of the moving image'. As an eight-year-old, the scene that had really stuck with her – and came back in her night-mares – was of Mickey, sent below deck as punishment, peeling potatoes. He had a pile to the left and an empty bucket to the right. He'd pick one off the pile, take a couple of swift swipes with his knife, then throw it over his shoulder into the bucket. Grab, *switch-swatch*, throw. But the thing was, the pile of unpeeled potatoes never got smaller and the bucket never filled. This being one of the few kitchen jobs that an eight-year-old could tackle unsupervised, it scared the hell out of her.

She didn't hear Mervyn coming downstairs, just saw the light in the hallway go off and a shape behind the squares of ripple-effect glass. He went into the kitchen, turned off the light in there and came back to the lounge, pushing open the door. He had the puffy face of the just woken. He seemed surprised to see her.

'Have you not been to sleep?'

'I think I must have.'

He closed the door behind him and, barefoot, wearing jogging shorts and a white T-shirt, padded over to the sofa and sat next to her. Roles were reversed.

'Anything you want to talk about?'

'Not really,' she said.

He examined her face. 'I'm worried about you.'

'Don't be.'

She didn't feel sleepy.

'Liz gave me a present,' Kate said.

She got out the underwear and laid it out on the sofa between them.

'Very becoming.'

'I haven't tried them on yet.'

She held his gaze then, and lifted the bra up to her chest. Her new family sometimes treated her as though she was damaged, and sometimes it was easier to play along.

'Do you think it suits me?' she said, which was cheap, she knew, but she was impatient. He looked.

'Oh, definitely,' he said, and then chuckled in a way that felt forced.

She shifted her legs so that the leather sofa made a creaking noise as though a door was opening.

'How about these?' she said, and held up the knickers.

The eye contact kept going and she wasn't going to back down. He broke the tension by laughing a little, and when he laughed his eyes fell, and when his eyes fell he saw her legs, and when he saw her legs he stopped laughing. Then the lights went off again and the TV died. They were sitting in silence and Stone Age dark. The storm hadn't quite finished yet.

'You still there?' she said.

'Still here.'

'Will you stay?'

'Of course. I'm with you. Do you want to talk?'

'I don't want to talk.'

They listened to the wind whip round the corners of the house. The double-glazing made a deep *wub* sound when the wind pressed against it. She could feel him sitting just a few feet from her and she felt he was looking at her, or at the blank space where she was, or at the version of her that was wearing elaborate underwear in his mind. Neither of them said anything. They waited to see who was going to break the silence, but she knew it wouldn't be her. The one sure way to spoil this would be to name it. She heard him breathing. The sofa creaked and she wondered if he was moving towards her. Leather was useful like that, amplifying every shift of weight.

She road-tested some heavier, sexualized breathing.

She heard him respond with the same.

The wind, also, joined in.

They kept this going until their breathing synchronized. She felt far away from herself. Inching along the sofa towards him, she slid her hand ahead of her. His breathing sounded like a recording of breathing.

He had *decided* to come downstairs. To sit down next to her. His decision was bigger than hers. Three times her age, married, kids: this was the full deal. She listened to the compulsion to act. The bare ends of her knees touched his left leg. He didn't flinch but he held his breath. It felt as though a circuit had been completed; the only switched-on machine in a world without power.

She knew how he liked to sit, legs wide, thirty-five degrees, with his statuette displayed. All she had to do was put her hand over and bring it down in the right place. This would be something she could navigate from – a reference point, moral north. She visualized his position from what she could feel of his leg, and by the lean of the sofa cushions and the sound of his breath, which had grown a little feminine. He couldn't do it himself, was the implication; it was her responsibility to lead, to reach across and put the thing in gear.

She put her hand out, through the blackness. It helped to think of her body as remote controlled. *Reach, descend, hold.*

The hand met some fabric. He made a sharp inhalation noise. His crotch would reveal the truth about this family. It did not know how to lie. Time passed and her hand stayed there. She wondered whether this moment was perhaps not a good thing after all, not even a good-bad thing, not *even* a bad-but-useful-for-moral-geography-in-future thing – just bad. There was a humming noise first, a subterranean noise, a low buzz barely perceptible behind the wind and rain. It was automatic. Street lights came back on. Ambient light highlighted the drizzle outside the bay window and some very faint light reached them in the lounge, where she could just make out Mervyn's profile, his head back, lips slightly parted.

The shell-motif wall lamps came on. Kate kept her hand where it was. Mervyn's eyes were closed, his throat exposed, the swell of his Adam's apple. It was a face of precarious ecstasy, maybe.

Either that, or it was the face of a man who, having forgiven himself for some bad decisions in his past, was finding sleep came to him often and inappropriately: with total darkness and reasonable quiet. As Kate imagined it, she had provided an opportunity for him to display his reliability as father and husband and he now dreamt of slugs moving over his body but they weren't scary or nightmarish, quite the opposite – he was finding their progress relaxing.

She felt a buzzing against her thigh. Taking her hand away from Mervyn, she got out her phone; messages from her father pulsed in her palm. She felt sick. More thunder outside and then the distinctive churn of Mervyn beginning to snore.

Freya was woken by her bladder. The tip of her nose was wet. The storm had passed and there was the sound of drips coming off the leaves. Leaning out of bed, she opened the grate and jabbed the coals with half a table leg. She peered behind the Japanese screen but couldn't see Albert. Standing up, she looked closer, still couldn't see him. She pulled back the duvet. Her boulder was asleep, curled up, arms crossed, hands tucked under his armpits. He had come down here to sleep because he said it was too noisy up at the big house. She had asked why he didn't just stay in the workshop with Marina and she had seen the awkward expression of his being caught red-handed, missing his mum.

She put on her dressing gown over her green nightie and went outside. The air needled her ankles, wrists, neck. The storm had passed and taken the warmth with it. She ought to have made it to the long drop but couldn't be bothered. Her bladder ached. Holding a tree for support, she swung open her dressing gown, hiked up her nightie, crouched and let rip. The steam rising up between her legs, the crinkling sound like embers, the smell of her vitamin C supplements and the feeling that she was being watched. She looked over her shoulder – the evidence she was being watched.

Patrick lay in bed, trying hard to believe that the noise of an armed intruder entering his seafront home was an auditory hallucination. Although it would be upsetting to discover that, after three drug-free months, he was having a paranoid delusional episode, this was still preferable to an actual, real live burglar downstairs.

When driven by fear, the imagination creates reality, he thought, listening to the astonishingly lifelike and left-to-right panning footsteps. It was, he hoped, an internal burglar. A groaning sound very much like the kitchen door opening, or a groaning sound very much like a burglar who – having been recognized as fictional – was slowly dying on Patrick's mind's patio.

Scientifically, it was entirely reasonable to suppose, Patrick supposed, that as a mind reopens its neural pathways and locked memory boxes after an extended cannabinoid addiction, trespassers must be allowed to clatter around in the internal kitchen before they will leave for good, empty handed.

Since his accident, it hadn't been easy reclaiming a secure mental footing. His key anxiety was that his mind was doughy and easily shaped. Paranoia about his susceptibility to paranoia. He had a feeling that all those years ago, when he first met Don, Janet and Freya, he was the dupe, the tasteless money-man, the rich patron who was allowed to believe that he 'got' the art when in fact the art was an attack on all that the patron represented.

If this was an imaginary burglar then, reasonably, Patrick ought to be able to apprehend him or her simply by thinking of something else. So he thought back to his time in the hospital with the mental health assessment officer, Kim, a young Christian with round teeth. She was the one who had suggested he might want to visit her church while he got back on his feet or, more accurately, crutches. 'I think of religion as the opposite of mental health,' he had told her, and she had laughed generously.

When he left hospital, he had assured the doctors that he was going back to the community, where he would be looked after. In reality, he left Morriston, swinging his blue cast out of the car park, past the workers' cottages and up to the double doors of the unpretentious, red-bricked Proclaimer's Church. A poster pinned to the wall said: *God is a DJ. Got any requests?* If he was soft-brained, Patrick had thought, then he would soon know as much, when tested by Kim's righteous enthusiasm.

The church had a guest bedroom, which they also used as storage space. It contained a giant octopus costume, nativity sets, old arcade machines and, in one corner, a mattress, sleeping bag and bedside lamp. They gave him a bowl of the most astounding split pea and ham soup. He hadn't smoked in weeks; his taste buds were as new.

That first night the church had a party for the local young people. They invited Patrick to join them. On the dancefloor, loosened by three times his recommended dose of codeine and with certain frequencies vibrating the pins in his ankle, Patrick bobbed on his crutches and swung the bad leg. He thought again of his desire to pass on something of his life experience to the new generation. He had a semicircle of dressed-up teenagers giving him the thumbs up every time he tried a fresh move. Behind the DJ, a video screen showed stills from the Chandra observatory. When he went to bed, they gave him a pair of fluorescent foam earplugs. Patrick was nearly sixty. At midnight, on the dot, the music stopped.

The week he spent in the basement of the new-build church, his bowels were still so clogged up from the morphine that he felt like he was sleeping on pebbles. While attractive men and women brought him glasses of prune juice, he spent time mentally cauterizing his feelings for Janet. The metaphor he had developed, while in hospital, and which showed a trace of the morphine's imaginative flamboyance, was that Janet conducted relationships like a stunt pilot, flying as close to her spectators as possible, without actually touching them. Patrick thought of himself as a spectator – one of many – grinning and laughing idiotically with his hands in the air, every time imagining that he'd be able to grab hold of her long scarf as she sped by.

He counted himself lucky, in a way, that the damage to his ankle had provided a telling illustration of Janet's feelings: on first seeing his injury, she was stricken, desperate, willing to do anything and, judging by the way she passed her body heat to him, most people would have assumed, in love. But when offered the chance to spend two days at his hospital bedside listening to his unappetizing breathing sounds – a commitment which would have shown a deep connection between them – she declined.

In many ways, that time in the dome, long ago, when they had come close to sex but without the sex, was her ultimate loop the loop: getting as close to him as she could possibly be, absorbing maximum attention and love, without giving any of herself away.

Then, one profound morning which for Patrick was the key religious revelation of his life thus far, the prune juice finally had its intended effect. Kim offered to change his sheets. Such saintly hospitality, Patrick thought, would have been enough to lure in a weak-minded individual. But he was relieved to find he still had his rational disgust, and although he liked the engaging young people, the basement had given him new ambitions: to live out his years in secular hopelessness and never see Janet again.

Patrick heard the unmistakable hush of drawers being opened downstairs. He could think of no psychological analogy for this; it sounded like a bona fide robbery in progress, someone searching for jewellery. Pulling back his duvet, he sat on the edge of the bed in his boxer shorts. He leaned forwards to the fireplace and grabbed the coal shovel.

Slowly making his way downstairs, Patrick held the shovel like a baseball bat. Adrenalin allowed him to take each step without wincing. His thin blue boxer shorts were the kind that mushroom up around the elasticated waistband.

He got to the bottom of the stairs and looked at the plastic front door for signs of forced entry. It was locked and untampered with. The door to the lounge was closed and he pushed it open with his good foot, his bad ankle tweaking under his weight. The room was quiet. Walking slowly back through the house, he tested the lock on the door to the basement as he passed. Stepping into the kitchen, white-knuckled with the shovel high, he quickly checked behind the door, but there was no one.

He was now starting to realize: a psychological burglar was, in truth, *worse* than a real one. A real burglar was for one night only; an internal one was for life.

But then, looking around, he noticed the back door was open a couple of inches. He clicked on the garden's security light and looked out through the big window above the sink. The only living thing was the pygmy palm at the back of the patio.

Swinging open the door, he stepped outside, raising the shovel. His ankle ached and tightened. A big moth butted the security light. There were dark footprints, unevenly spaced, marked out across the light condensation on the patio stones. They led to the double doors at the back of the garage, which were wide open but with no light showing through. He took a couple of small steps, barely lifting his feet off the ground. From inside, he could hear a snuffling noise, a nose-breathing, a crunching, like a hog troughing through human remains. He waited, gripping the coal shovel. He wanted this to be real. He stepped through the doorway.

A square pale light was floating in the blackness. A portal.

There was the smell of garlic and chicken. He flicked on the two strip lights, which batted awake in sequence.

Kate was standing behind the meat safe, hunched over a bowl of Indonesian jellied chicken, a tray of grilled garlicky aubergine and a lentil salad. She was using her mobile phone as a torch and in the other hand was holding a drumstick. There were black marks on her face and arms and streaks of spiced jelly down her dress. She was eating meat. *She was eating meat.* She was wearing a gingham shirt-dress. *She was wearing a gingham shirt-dress.* This was not the Kate he knew. Her mouth was half full, and chewing. In the snow-globe moment of the strip lights, she stopped.

He was either Mr Universe or he was wearing the mother of all Puffa jackets. It was knee-length, collared, black, with a furred hood.

Freya squinted at him while still pissing, making mist.

'Sorry. It's me, Geraint. Something's happened to Kate.'

She looked over her shoulder at him for a long time. His eyes were puffy and half shut. He had a quarter moon of toothpaste at the edge of his mouth.

'I'll wait back here,' he said, and retreated behind the curve of the roundhouse to wait for her Morse code to stop. It was just getting light. She stood and tightened her dressing gown.

'It's okay,' she said. 'You can come in. Albert's asleep.'

She waited while he knelt to take off his complex walking boots, then they slid through the draught curtains. She slotted some bits of broken-up pallet on to the coals, and they sat on stools beside the wood-burner. Geraint kept his voluminous coat on, his delicate nose poking out of his hood.

'She's gone. I rang the community. Nobody's seen her. I tried her mobile. My dad's driving round looking. He dropped me here. We thought she might be with you.'

His breathing was shallow. The fire popped and Geraint glanced at Albert, hidden beneath his duvet. As far as he knew, Albert still wanted to kill him.

'Could she be with a friend?' Freya asked.

'Can't think of any,' Geraint said, and held his stomach.

Then a duvet-muffled voice spoke. 'I wouldn't worry,' it said. 'She's almost certainly dead.'

*

Kate woke up in a strange bedroom and either her brain had swollen or her skull had shrunk – whichever, the fit was not good. She massaged her forehead. Her most recent memory was of entering a house via a coal chute. From that image, she worked backwards. She had been sitting on a doorstep, drinking whisky from an Evian bottle. The doorstep was Patrick's. She had got there by walking the streets along the seafront with her bag of clothes, looking for a convertible car paid for by advertising. Before that she had been at Blackpill, already drunk, cooling her feet in the lido. Her feet had needed cooling because of a long walk along the old train tracks through Clyne, overcoming the fear of rapists and slashers by taking shots from the sports-lid Evian. The bottle, as she now remembered, had been filled, just before she left their house, from Mervyn's expensively packaged Oban whisky (which she never once saw him drink). Then she remembered the reason she had left their house. It went beyond shame, what she was feeling. Darkness and the texture of his jogging bottoms. Two kinds of heavy breathing.

The room she was in was filling with the smell of death. This was what she deserved.

When Kate finally stepped into the kitchen, Patrick was in flip-flops, boardies, T-shirt, and a Slanket, holding a metal spatula: an alpha male at a one-man barbecue. She was wearing a silk-hemmed dressing gown, another Liz donation, and her skin was blotchy.

'Oh ho ho, look who it is!'

'Pat,' she said, swallowing.

'Hello, Burglar Bill.'

He put down the spatula and came towards her with his arms raised.

'Sorry,' she said, shivering on the tiles. He wrapped himself round her.

'Don't be sorry. I'll take whatever visitors I can get.'

She kept her arms by her sides as he hugged her. She had forgotten how much torso he had. He smelled of moisturizer.

'You're still not *great* in the *mor*-nings,' he said, and let her go. 'Or should I say . . . afternoons.'

'Please.'

'Just so you know, I rang the community to let them know that you're safe.'

'Oh God.'

He went back to the cooker, pulled a plate from the oven and put it on the table. There were beans, toast, two portobello mushrooms, grilled tomatoes, a hash brown and a poached egg. She sat down and stared at the plate for a while. He watched her staring and made the sound of cogs turning.

'Something missing?' he said.

'Okay, Pat.'

'What?' he said, and he did a little Charlie Chaplin dance with the spatula, his flip-flops clacking on the tiled floor. He had a mid-price haircut.

'You win,' she said.

'What on *earth* could you mean?'

He did a twirl on the spot, his Slanket pirouetting out. He was really enjoying himself. He swung open the oven door, pulled out the middle rack.

'I've waited years for this,' he said, shaking the baking tray a little.

Scraping back her chair, she sighed and took her plate to the oven. She forked in three chipolatas, two pieces of bacon, a load of quartered potatoes which were fried with the meat fat and then, hesitating for a second, lifted a slice of black pudding aboard.

6   Preparations

Click.

Don was standing in front of the charge controller, staring.

Click. A counter read 459.

He had already checked every room in the big house, the workshop, pottery shed, the barn and the dome. He had interrogated a number of day visitors and cross-questioned Marina about rumours of an undeclared printer.

Click. 458. This number showed how charged the battery was, 500 being full and 000, empty. Don had set the controller so that if the reading ever dipped below 450, the whole community's power would cut out. This had not made him popular. Publically, he said it was a necessary restriction, to maintain the battery's lifespan. Privately, he felt the community had become too easy-going. Since the storm, a month ago now, when they had tasted limitless electricity, everyone was struggling to embrace a more careful lifestyle. Don wanted the community to be streamlined, in time for the party. He didn't like the way Varghese, who was working hard at promoting the event, kept calling it a 'blow-out'.

Click. 457.

He was becoming emotionally linked to the charge controller. To him, each *click* sounded reproachful: the noise people make in slow-moving post-office queues.

Click.

Between the charge controller and the party preparations, whole days could go past without him having to think deeply about his family. That left only the nights, stretching out limitlessly, with Don finding books that used to guarantee him sleep in under a chapter now seeming, if not exactly riveting, then at least back-lit and light-weight.

Click.

The only community members whose electricity usage Don had not yet accounted for were Isaac and Albert. The community had no official term dates, especially now there were only two students, so it was generally agreed that whenever the microclimate served up a stretch of genuine warm weather, the student body could make the most of it. Since the start of the 'holidays', he had only seen glimpses of his son, walking across the yard holding something unnerving like a screwdriver or the Yellow Pages.

Click.

Don shook his head and went outside. He decided to do a lap of the house, which is when he saw a black extension cable snaking from the kitchen's back window, down through the garden. Running now, he tracked it past the fire pit and into the musty dark beneath the Douglas firs as it connected with a chain of linked five-plug adaptors. Don slowed as he approached a clearing where there was an old, overstuffed armchair, one that had been in the bottom of the garden for years, rotted down to its bones. It looked like a seat that someone had died in, which was clearly the look that Albert, who was in it, was going for. Don had assumed his son's uncleanliness had plateaued, but now, perhaps slightly for the camera, he saw this was not true. With dirt-mascara and his hands gloved with mud, he looked like he was presenting an episode of *Tales from the Crypt*. He didn't see Don.

'Hit it, Eyes,' Albert said.

The chain of plug adaptors led towards a camera – Varghese's camera – on a tripod, facing Albert, and to the Korg Trinity keyboard belonging to Isaac's mother lying on the ground, off to one side. Isaac was sitting cross-legged in front of it, lowering his finger on to a single key. A supernatural wind, the creak of a ghost ship.

Albert stared at the camera, eyes wide. 'Ladies and gentlemen, fellow humans, I bring grave news. The world could end any time now. We are reaching final days,' Albert said. He gripped the armrests like a pilot in an ejector seat. 'Prepare! Choose weapons! The monsters are almost upon us!'

Which is when Don stepped in front of the camera.

*

Albert unplugged the adapters, one by one, his father standing over him. Isaac, with his head down, dragging one end of the expensive keyboard on the ground behind him, sulked off through the woods. Albert passed each unplugged adapter to his dad to hold. The mud on his hands was flaking off as he worked.

'Albert, you know I like to see you follow your interests.'

'It's not an interest.'

'And you know I'd be thrilled to see you take up film-making.'

'I'm not taking anything up,' Albert said. 'Varghese said I could use his camera. So I did.'

'And that's one thing about being educated at home, you can learn about film-making. We can get Varghese to teach you about lighting and editing. And you and I could study contemporary cinema, if you wanted. I think you're mature enough to see most films. It wouldn't be like that at school.'

'Okay, thanks but no.'

'Whatever you're interested in, you can learn about. That's the real heart of home education. Have you decided what you'd like to do about next year?'

Albert was concentrating on a particularly sticky plug. Don had seen, in his son's room, that his bedside reading was a copy of Bishopston Comprehensive's glossy brochure.

'Well, make up your own mind. Don't let me and your mum push you around. You'll probably want to rebel against us, and that's fair enough. Most teenagers do. I did.'

'I'm not a teenager. I'm eleven, nearly twelve.'

Albert was done with the five-plug adaptors. He started winding up one of the cable-reel extension leads, walking forwards as he turned the crank.

'Did I ever tell you about when I ran away from home?' Don said, watching his son. 'For two months, I stayed in a squat in *London*. An amazing old house. We had a tennis court. We used to play tennis.'

Albert shook his head.

'When I first got to the squat, I fell in love with one of the girls,' Don said. 'She had a great name. Sheila La Fanu.'

'Why are you telling me this?'

'She was the most beautiful girl – a climber, climber's hands, fingers squished, nails cracked, do you know that move?' Don flattened his right palm and jabbed it in the air. 'Wedging? Where there's a crack in the rock and if they can't get a grip on it, they just squeeze their fingers in there. Her fingers looked like parsnips, tapered. A Greenpeace climber. Used to be the one who'd scale the power station at night and drop the banner: "London Cancer Factory".' Then he leaned down to Albert's ear and whispered conspiratorially in a tone that he hoped would show his son that, one day, the two of them could be friends. 'She had a climber's body but alpine tits.'

Albert turned the crank as fast as he could. They passed the fire pit.

'Don't ever say that word, please,' Albert said.

'I fell in love with her. I was your age.'

'You were eleven?'

'You're almost twelve. I was not much older than you. Seventeen maybe.'

'Kate's age,' he said. He handed his father one of the cable reels and moved to the next one.

'She took me out to the Mile End climbing wall – she was seven years older than me. I lived for those sessions, me belaying her, watching her mechanical thighs as she sprang up the wall. Every session, she'd say how much I was improving and I'd tell her that it was her teaching that was the reason.'

'I don't know what you're trying to do. This is not enjoyable for me.'

They were going up the woodchipped steps through the kitchen garden, and Albert changed cranking arms as his right got tired. Don wasn't going to help him.

'After a month, she took me to the Munros in Scotland – just me and her – and said we were going to camp up there. Sleeping on a ledge up a mountain with this girl. We climbed all day and I sunburned my back so badly I couldn't lie on it. We stopped at this ledge. It was more of a plateau. She put aloe vera on me.'

'Oh my God, Dad.'

They were approaching the kitchen window. Once Albert got there, he'd be able to get away. Don started talking a little faster.

'She had to sleep on her back on account of her breasts. Me, I had to sleep on my side or my front 'cause of the sunburn. It was meant to be. I thought, *If I can't tell this girl now that I like her, then when?* So I said: "Sheila La Fanu, I'm in love with you." I used her full name. Sheila La Fanu.'

'I'm asking you to stop,' Albert said, his nostrils flaring. 'Whatever you're trying to do, please don't.'

Albert was on the final cable reel, whizzing his hand as quickly as he could. Don was now weighed down with extension leads.

'She said, "You're too young, but I like you, and we can have a kiss and you can touch my breasts," so we kissed. The wind and her tongue and she put my hand under there. It was momentous.'

Don gave his biggest smile. His arms were full of adaptors and cable reels. They were at the kitchen window.

'Is that it? Can I go?'

'I'm telling you – one of the greatest experiences. This is all to come, for you, in the future, if you'd just choose to believe in it. If the world doesn't end, you've got lots to look forward to. Then she paid for my train home. You can't know the value of it until you experience it. You're becoming an adult.'

'I'm not.'

'You may not know it, but you are.'

'If I was an adult then you'd let me have responsibility for things, and you don't.'

'I am giving you responsibility. Remember what we talked about?'

'You said I'm allowed to watch. That's not the same. You need to let me be in charge.'

'You're still eleven.'

'You just said I was basically seventeen. Am I an adult or am I not?'

'Look, okay. A compromise.' Don knelt down in front of his son. 'How about I let you take charge of the selection process?'

Albert brightened up. 'Really?'

'Yes, I'll rely on you to do the research.'

'Okay, good, I will.'

He hugged his father, the power cables between them.

'Now tell me. How's your mother?'

'I don't know. She's okay, I think.'

'I miss her. Does she know that?'

His father was getting upset.

'She knows.'

Don's Adam's apple bobbed in a way that signalled what was coming.

Albert looked around to see if they were being watched.

7 Results Day

'They don't smell like failure,' Patrick said, sniffing each envelope in turn.

He and Kate were sat on a bench next to the cycle path, looking out over the bay. It was raining at sea but Mumbles was bright.

'Open them,' she said.

Two rollerbladers went past, sweeping their feet behind them.

'What does it mean if you get into Cambridge?'

'I won't have got in,' she said.

She'd spent the last two months working through her reading lists, and when not studying, imagining Mervyn and Geraint bonding over her disappearance with fishing trips, remote control helicopters and a compensatory meat-marathon. She visualized their house suddenly brimming with chorizo, Coke-boiled hams, shanks and T-bones. Or even worse, she thought, the continued path towards vegetarian enlightenment: walnut oil, a veggie box, sunflower seeds in clamp jars. The disappointing news from her time in Three Crosses was that, where she had hoped to find suburbia's dark and seething underbelly, she had found the potbelly of contentment.

'Put me out of my misery,' she said. The electric tourist train went past incredibly slowly. Patrick's wide fingers struggled to tear the paper.

'Oh ho ho,' he said.

Kate stared off at the pier, imagining herself high up in the sky and falling with rag-doll limbs into the green-blue sea.

It had been agreed that Varghese could make a filmed record of the party because new content would need to be online, in the days afterwards, if they wanted to see long-term impact. 'Stickiness,' Varghese called it.

Don said he could film whatever he wanted, on the condition

that he steer clear of the goat pen between 10.30 a.m. and noon, though he didn't tell Varghese why.

Just after breakfast, Varghese captured the party's first genuine *moment*. Don and a team of wwoofers were building the live music yurt in the long field when three young lads turned up, carrying buckets. Although the party had been advertised as 'an all-dayer', Don had assumed that guests wouldn't arrive until lunch. These lads had been up since dawn, low-tide fishing. They showed the camera the buckets of whitebait, razor clams and wild oysters. They didn't like oysters so Don took as many as would fit in the pockets of his tweedy suit jacket. 'If all the young people who come today are anything like you,' Don said, 'then our future is in good hands.' Varghese had to explain to him not to make direct eye contact with the lens.

At the last count, Varghese's YouTube video of the community felling their electricity pole had almost 10,000 views and the requisite mixture of abusive and incomprehensible comments that, he reassured Don, were a mark of growth, 'like zits during puberty', and not to be taken personally. On the BassMusicWales.co.uk forum, genuine ravers now outnumbered Varghese's various avatars on a thread entitled 'Rebirth of the Free Party!' Likewise, the environmentally conscious GowerPower.org had included them on its list of local days out.

Patrick drove Kate in his sponsored Mini Cooper with the top down and she sang, 'If you'll be my bodyguard' and he sang, 'I will be your long lost pal.' Her hair made a comet's trail behind her as she yelled, 'Aaaa!', which was a representation of the four key letters she'd seen when she'd looked at her exam results. Patrick slalomed slightly once they were out on South Gower Road and honked at everyone. They were going for overpriced lunch.

Kate was too busy miming the bass solo to notice when he didn't take the turning for Llanmadoc. In fact, it took Patrick coming to a full stop before she looked up and saw a poster attached to a tree that read: *This Must Be the Place*.

'Strange,' she said.

He tapped his fingers against the steering wheel.

'I know what you're trying to do,' she said. 'It's a nice idea, but I don't want to come home. It's not like I secretly want to but I can't come to terms with it. Let's go order food we can't pronounce.'

He turned off the stereo.

'You should at least go and see your parents. Tell them the news.'

'Don't do this. Stop being grown up. Let's hit the road.' She thumb-pointed over her shoulder. 'I'll text them.'

She turned the stereo back on. 'If you'll be my bodyguard . . .'

Patrick killed the engine and pulled up the handbrake.

Kate let her head loll forward. '*Really?*'

He centrally unlocked her door.

'Okay, listen. I will tell Dad the news and have some kind of epiphany, since that's probably what you're imagining, but there is no way in the world I'm staying, so I'm going to come back and you'll still be here – *won't you* – and we'll go and eat hand-dived scallops, am I right?'

He nodded.

'You're lying,' she said, then, holding out her hand, 'give me the keys.'

It was both pleasing and disappointing that, walking into the community for the first time in months, nobody recognized her. After looking around, unnoticed, she finally spotted Don inside a chill-out teepee that was set up beside the fire pit. Through the arched entrance to the tent, she could see him, kneeling, arranging cushions in a diamond formation.

'Hello, Father.'

He stopped for a moment, spooked-seeming, and shook his head.

'It couldn't be,' he said, not turning to look. 'It must be her ghost.' He plumped a beanbag in a way that tried to be wistful, then turned and crawled out of the teepee, pretending not to see her.

'Dad.'

'*So* sad,' he said, standing up, his eyes wide, 'to be haunted by my own daughter. Such a sweet girl.'

'Da-ad. I've got news.'

He started walking up the shallow steps to the big house, shaking his head.

'Oh we'll miss her, I suppose. She wouldn't even come home for the party in her honour.'

She bounded towards him and took a running jump on to his back, swinging her arms round his neck and her legs round his waist, yelling 'Aaaa!' as he huffed and gripped hold of her and turned back down the steps at a canter, already heaving under the strain but *absolutely not* willing to put down his seventeen-year-old daughter until she explicitly said so. He started doing loops of the fire pit, neighing, and Kate's laughter went up and down as the air got knocked out of her. She raised one arm in the air – rodeo-style – and didn't say stop until she could hear some unsettling congestion in her father's lungs. When she did say 'Okay! Okay!' he halted instantly, gracelessly, falling to his knees on the soft ground, his face now a purplish, almost glans-like colour and sweat beading between his eyebrows. His tongue was slightly out. He was old, she noticed.

Kneeling down in front of him with her full-beam grin on, the wonks in her front teeth, she said: 'I got into Cambridge.'

Just saying those words made her capable of compassion. She watched his chest go up and down. He coughed a little and it became clear he had something in his mouth. Even this could not dim her torch of empathy. She handed him a tissue. He made the transfer, subtly, turning his head to the side. It was a big one. She glimpsed it, just for a second. The phlegm in the tissue like a sunrise through mist. Everything was beautiful.

'I'm so glad you came back,' he said.

There were two wet patches forming in the pockets of her father's jacket.

'I'm not actually *back*. I just came to let you know.'

From the patio at the back of the big house, Kate noticed a tall South Asian man pointing a hand-held camera down at them.

'You're back,' Don said, glancing at the camera. 'Here you are. Back.'

'I'm not staying. We're off for extortionate lunch.'

'This is your celebration. Everything you see was made for you.'

'I don't want that.'

'Anyway, who's *we*?'

Patrick was sitting with his hands in his lap, the roof and windows down. He didn't hear them approach. A solemn, narrator's voice began: 'Nearly a quarter century ago, in an office block in Lambeth, you introduced me to something that changed my life for ever.'

Patrick turned to see the narrator standing at the passenger side door with his head bowed slightly and oysters, one in each hand, shucked and on the half shell. Of the first few months he and Don had spent together in London – their honeymoon period – the moment of greatest romance was spent shucking a dozen natives with a penknife, arguing about landownership, on a bench on Primrose Hill. Kate, behind her father, held up her hands and mouthed: *Sorry*.

'Come on, old pal, a peace offering,' Don said, presenting them, reaching into the car. 'An invitation to the celebration.'

Patrick pressed a button and slowly, excruciatingly so, slow enough to allow the childishness of the gesture to really ring out, the soft top's exoskeleton unfolded itself and pushed forward over Patrick's head, forcing Don to take a step back as it clicked into place. He walked round the front of the car and came to the driver's side window.

'Fresh off the beach today. Gower's own.'

'Which one is poisoned?' Patrick said, and sniffed them.

One was huge and one was tiny. They were both bloodshot with Tabasco, which was how Patrick liked them. He took the small one. Without even getting out of the car, he necked it, took a couple of bites and felt it slide down inside him. Don held up the huge one in his hand and seemed unsure. Patrick allowed himself to make a small *ch* noise that he knew would be just enough.

'Fine,' Don said, and lifted the frilled edge to his lips. It had real depth, the shell, fist-sized, definitely a wild oyster – an alpha male. Patrick thought about something sarcastic along these lines but decided it wasn't necessary. Don had the creature in his mouth and, it became clear, could not swallow.

Patrick looked around for Kate so that they could enjoy this moment together, and saw her, but also, next to her, an outsize brown-skinned man pointing a hand-held camera at Don. His giant finger was on the zoom, and it was apparent that Don realized he was being filmed. A little creamy liquid eked out at the edges of his mouth as he finally swallowed, a full chest gulp, leaving him bent over, his hands on his knees.

Patrick felt unthreatened and reckless.

'Right, I'm off,' he said.

'Don't leave me,' Kate said.

'It won't be the same without you,' Don said, still bent over, mouth open.

Patrick imagined Don telling everyone at the party: 'I held out an olive branch, but the old man's still not ready to grip on.'

'You're really just going to dump me here?' Kate said.

'I really am.'

'You'll be missed,' Don said, unconvincingly.

'Give me the car keys, Kate.'

'Come get them,' she said, and held up the key on the palm of her hand.

He raised his eyebrows. 'Are you really going to make me?'

'I really am,' she said.

Patrick shook his head and breathed out. He got out of the car and walked around the bonnet. She took a few backward steps as he approached, now dangling the key from her index finger.

'This is not dignified,' he said.

'How's your ankle for running?' she said.

He stopped. Behind Kate, the cameraman stepped back for a wide.

Albert swung and felt the compost give. 'She's back.'

Isaac stabbed the thick gunge, climbed on to the garden fork's hips with both feet and waited there, elevator-style, as it sank in.

'She's come to fuck things up,' Albert said.

He had heard someone yelling 'Aaaa!' and, going to investigate, had seen Don giving Kate a piggyback.

The mattock's blade went *shung* as it entered the mulch. Albert yanked it back and a green-yellow pus seeped out of an eggshell. The smell was vicious. Isaac dropped his fork and ran back towards the polytunnels, both hands over his nose. Albert was immune.

'But don't worry because I have everything under control,' he said.

In-between each swing, he looked up towards the goat pen. Isaac walked back over, sniffed the air and picked up his fork.

'Total fuck,' Isaac said, and frowned.

'You got it, Eyes.'

Isaac seemed surprised to hear himself swear. He looked down at his muddy hands.

Don was shortly due to meet his wife and he had still not changed into his slaughterwear. Kate had asked him to give her and Patrick 'the tour' of the festival. It would have been strange, given the enthusiasm with which he'd just welcomed them, to decline. He wanted to explain that the tour would need to be very quick because he was going to meet Freya for the first time in weeks, and he really wanted their meeting to go well – which his daughter would understand. But he could not risk telling her that he also needed enough time both to change into clothes that he was happy to see spattered with goat's blood and to access a meditative state of pre-slaughter calm. This she might find upsetting. So he said nothing.

They started at the bottom of the long field, beside the yurt, which had its sides uncovered and a low stage at the back.

'The live music arena,' Don said.

'So who's headlining then?' Patrick said.

'No one. Or rather, everyone. *Everyone* is headlining.'

Don ushered them towards the top of the field where the first visitors had arrived from other communities, Teepee Valley, Brithdir Mawr, Holtsfield. They had to walk at Pat's pace, which, with his ankle, was approximately that of a pallbearer. They passed a converted Royal Mail van, a Honda Civic, an American school bus and a bathtub, all parked at angles. A pony drank from the tub. Don kept getting a few paces ahead, then waiting for them to catch up.

Don stuck to firm ground to allow for Patrick's ankle, hoping it would help him pick up the pace, but it didn't.

'Would you like a hand?' Don said finally, and he honestly hadn't meant it to sound patronizing, but sometimes old patterns of communication have a way of asserting themselves.

Patrick said nothing but walked quicker all the same, just the tiniest of hobbles creeping into his gait, clearly unwilling to express any discomfort. Kate put one arm through Patrick's, like husband and wife, to support him.

They stopped at the goat pen while Kate jumped the fence to say hello. They heard her apologizing for having gone away. Don looked around. It was a matter of minutes until he was due to meet Freya at this exact spot.

They walked over to the front of the big house, where the sound system was being set up beneath a big blue seven-cornered tarpaulin, amoeba-shaped. It shaded half the yard, having been stretched and tied between the guttering of the schoolroom, the apple tree and the roof of the workshop.

'The Rave Zone,' Don said, with audible capitals, then looked at his watch.

Kate watched two young guys – not much older than her – carrying speakers from a white van, setting them up on a row of pallets and lashing them together with buckle straps. There were eight cabinets, two high by four across. The upper ones had militaristic casings. By the looks of it, the sound system had been her father's key investment in the future of the community, that and the semi-circle of Portaloos set back behind the workshop. On a plastic school desk next to the speakers there were CDRs, a mixer and an amp. One of the boys opened the driver's side of the van, came back with a disc, held it up in the air – flashing sunlight off its underside – and said: 'Soundcheck.'

'You know, Don, this system's gonna project like billy-o?' Patrick said. 'Good morning, pensioners of Gower!'

They looked around but her father had gone. Apparently the

tour was over. Kate hadn't been able to work out if his nervousness had been just a symptom of the party, or if that was what he was like all the time, nowadays.

As the boys switched on the equipment there was a sense of air moving, of latent energy. The first sound was of a helicopter landing. Patrick actually looked up. Then the beat came in. It was physically loud, akin to being groped. Kate put her fingers in her ears and watched the boys bounce together behind the school desk, lip-synching. The noise brought people out of the house and gardens and into the yard. A woman with an intricate facial birthmark emerged with her hands over her ears. Marina appeared from her bedroom at the far end of the workshop, making the universal hand signal for *turn it down*. More people came out of the big house: a pale man in his early thirties making gang signs; Arlo doing the robot, holding tongs; Janet, squinting, wearing a straw hat; two new wwoofers and then Isaac, sitting in the dirt at the side of the workshop, making mud pies, drumming his pan on the off-beat.

Everyone saw Kate and Patrick. They saw everyone.

'We're back,' Kate yelled, barely audible, raising both arms.

Patrick held up a hand in acknowledgement.

Arlo slotted his tongs into his back pocket, wiped his hands on his apron and led the charge. Janet followed, removing her hat to reveal blow-dried hair. Everyone held out their arms – too many hugs to choose from – all smiling and calling their names; people Kate had never seen before, moving towards them with arms extended like the undead. The first hug was from Janet, who put her arms round Patrick's waist and her ear to his chest; he kept his arms up awkwardly, as though wading through pond water. Then the rest fell on them, one after another, Kate's vision darkening a notch as she was enveloped and squeezed and told that she had never left their thoughts.

Someone turned off the soundcheck. Through the clot of heads she saw Albert, watching from the side of the workshop, holding a three-quarter-size wheelbarrow of compost. It was not the circumstances in which she had hoped to have their reunion – her suddenly famous and swamped by groupies. Marina squeezed Kate's shoulders and whispered 'Your brother missed you' into her ear. Albert dropped the wheelbarrow, made serious eye contact with his sister, pointed towards the house then ran inside.

As the giga-hug disbanded, only Janet and Patrick remained, Patrick trying to peel off her arms. Kate excused herself, saying she needed to catch up with her brother.

In the schoolroom, there was a man with an alcoholic's ripe nose making paper lanterns, two non-identical twins cutting colourful people holding hands out of tissue paper, drawing a unique expression on each, and a boy with a square fringe folding origami cranes. They looked up at her with the non-judgemental but slightly questioning expression that she herself used to adopt when finding unknown persons wandering the house.

In the kitchen, a skinny woman fed a breezeblock of cheese into the industrial grater, producing a blonde wig in the bowl below.

She finally found Albert in the scullery, wearing an apron, washing potatoes at the butler's sink. It was odd to see him washing them because he still had not washed himself. He had a kind of Hollywood tan. He wore special black scrubbing gloves that said POTA across the right knuckle and TOES across the left. The way he rubbed his gloved hands around the potatoes reminded Kate of an evil genius formulating a plan.

'Hey, bro. I'm back.'

He ignored her. His hair looked salt-stiff, almost glued. Her instinct was to smell him, to take a hit off his neck.

'Don't mind if I help, do you?'

She picked up a peeler and started skinning, slimy strips piling up on the counter, their wet sides glistening. He kept on formulating. She looked across at him with a half-smile to convey impending fun – the kind of smile you do before tickling someone.

'Albert, I want to say I'm sorry that I went away. It can't have been easy for you.'

He stared straight ahead, gazing at the paintbrushes in a jar of dark water on the sill, then glancing up at the community's only wall clock. It was 10.27. She tried to think of some common ground between them.

'Guess what I saw the other day? *Steamboat Willie*, remember that cartoon, where he peels potatoes?' she said. 'How scared we were?'

She mimed throwing the potato over her shoulder and whistled the tune.

'Why would that scare me?' he said.

'You used to have nightmares,' she said, nudging him. 'We both did.'

He responded to her nudge with an elbow, then reached down and got another potato. There were only ten or so left. Outside she noticed Patrick, now Janet-less, making his escape, gingerly moving down through the kitchen garden.

Albert reached down and grabbed another.

'I've missed you,' she said.

'Gotta problem, you fuck?' His voice suddenly loud in the brick-tiled room.

She examined his profile, imagining licking her finger and writing something witty on his cheek. 'I just want us to be friends, shithead.'

'I'm not letting you near me. You're not getting anywhere near.' He looked up at the clock. 'And stay the *hell* away from Mum.'

He still hadn't turned his head towards her, not once. She saw that Patrick, despite his weak ankle, was already way down at the bottom of the garden, disappearing into the trees beyond.

'Two left,' she said.

'You're either part of the solution or part of the problem,' he said, 'and Arlo says he wants the skins left on.'

Mud swirled down the plughole. He looked at the clock and tossed the last one in the colander. Turning round, he picked up a fresh sack of potatoes, unwashed, and poured them in to the sink with a flourish. He took off the gloves and handed them to his sister.

'This is the least you can do,' he said, and was gone.

It was 10.31 and Freya and Don were standing by the goat pen. He was wearing grey joggers, a Phoenix Suns T-shirt with the basketball bursting through the front and a blue baseball cap. His slaughterwear. They heard a blast of hip-hop from the sound system and Don turned his cap to the side. No response from Freya, who was not about to let him start enjoying himself. There was the sound of hooves clacking on wood and they looked across. All six goats were standing on the roof of their pen, huddled together in sunlight, as though longing for a crag to inhabit.

'Are you ready?' she said.

'I'm waiting for my helper.'

'You don't need a helper.'

'He's on his way.'

'Which goat are you choosing?'

'Belona.'

'But she's four years old. She'll taste like boots.'

'I delegated the responsibility for choosing. I just want to say, before my helper gets here, he's been fantastic. Really thrown himself into the research.'

Freya squinted. A voice came from behind her. 'Belona will have a delicious gamey quality, ideal for stews and curries.'

'Oh no, Don, please,' she said, as small arms reached around her waist.

As Kate washed the potatoes, she came to terms with her own brother distrusting her. Although he could not have known about her behaviour with Mervyn, she worried that Albert understood instinctively the type of person she had become. She was glad, then, of this punishment, the endless-seeming potatoes. The job took quite a while, and once she'd finished she took the clean ones through to the kitchen.

After that, she went and sat up on the flat roof, watching silhouetted paragliders turning this way and that above the downs, more today than she'd ever seen. They looked like a child's drawing of a flock of birds. She had a good view of the party taking shape: the kitchen garden and polytunnels were busy with people she didn't recognize, kneeling, crouching, bent at the waist; one figure she found familiar but couldn't name was moving along the runner beans; a rash of tents had spread across the top of the long field; a hay-bale pyramid was halfway to completion, making arena-style seating for the music yurt. At the blind bend, good-natured car congestion formed, people waving each other on, and above the downs she watched a paraglider either in a death-spiral or really showing off, disappearing behind the hill before she could find out which.

The familiar-looking slouched person was now in the polytunnel, obscured by plants. Whoever it was moved instinctively among the tomatoes, plucking the ready ones with a firm tug, filling a salad bowl with reds and yellows. She only realized it was Geraint when he stepped out of the tunnel, framed by the doorway. He had grade-three'd his whole head and was wearing a white vest. He had a farmer's tan with arms the colour of teak. She felt dizzy and unsafe to be on the edge of a roof. He noticed her watching. He stopped and squinted.

He made binoculars with his hands to stare back at her.

All the years that Freya had known Don he had talked a good slaughter. She remembered that before eating roast dinners, he often took a moment to visualize the relevant animal's living conditions and the circumstances of their death – to check that he was morally comfortable (he always was) – before digging in. If Freya walked away from this now – and she had a good instinct to – then Don would be let off the hook again. She wanted him on the hook. And although Freya didn't like her son's involvement, the truth was that Albert would probably be calmer than most of the wwoofers, and certainly calmer than his father.

She and Albert led Belona to a secluded spot, a clearing between trees behind the barn. There was a young tree, she knew, that had a low branch they could use as a gambrel. Belona had two leashes round the top of her neck. Freya held one and Albert the other. They stood on either side of her, keeping the ropes a little slack so that she could scoff from her feed pan.

'Will this be painless?'

'It'll be as humane as is possible.'

Belona tried to jump but the leashes kept her grounded. Albert dropped to his knees, let go of his rope and hugged the goat round her middle, resting his head against her warm flank.

'Hope you enjoy your last meal.'

'Try not to make her nervous, Al.'

Don came round the corner of the barn carrying a moulded plastic storage case with the word *Blitz* in red on it. In size and shape, it resembled his shaving kit. His cap was facing forward now. Belona made a noise from her stomach as he approached.

'Albert, would you like to say a word of thanks?' Don said.

'Don – please.'

'Thanks for everything,' Albert said, still with his arm round Belona's neck, speaking into her ear. 'This will teach me how to kill goats. It will allow us to survive in the end days.'

Freya made a small *tsh* noise. Don knelt down, laid the briefcase on the grass and clicked it open. The bolt gun resembled a relay baton, but nickel plated. He lifted it out and hefted it in his hand. Albert stood and, copying his mother, picked up his leash and wrapped it twice round his wrist.

Don was testing his grip – one-handed then two – on the trigger lever.

'You've got to load it first,' Albert said.

'I know.'

Don spun the gun's lid until it came off. Opening the small tin of 9mm cartridges in the carry-case, he carefully pinched one out and immediately dropped it in the grass. Freya breathed deeply while he scrabbled around looking for it. She chose not to think about him doing the job badly and something terrible happening to Belona. He'd be relying on this weakness in her, she knew, hoping his incompetence would oblige her to step in.

'Take your time,' she said.

Eventually he found the cartridge, loaded it and screwed the cap back on. By now, Belona had already half emptied her feed pan. Once she finished eating she would be that much more difficult to control.

'She looks nervous,' Albert said.

'Don't anthropomorphize,' Don said, and with his free hand he reached forward and stroked the goat's jaw tassels. Then he rubbed the spot on her forehead where he would be aiming for. A look came across his face. He stood up, turned his back, walked towards a patch of nettles and let out some excess saliva.

Freya took deep breaths. This was part of her husband's show. She remained calm. Eventually, he came back towards Belona, whose head was still down, the bottom of the feed pan just visible now. Don held the baton in both hands, out in front of him, the way Italian waiters hold pepper grinders. She felt he was trying to seem ill-matched for the task.

'Dad, the firing pin's still down,' Albert said.

Don nodded. He took one hand off the baton and, with difficulty, lifted the safety.

'Mum, I don't think Dad's very good at this.'

'Let your father be.'

'I'm fine,' Don said, and he dropped to his knees to get a better angle.

'I've been practising on the Yellow Pages,' Albert said. 'I'd be way better than him.'

As Don shuffled a little closer, Belona made a quick wail. Her tongue darted around the bottom of the pan, dabbing up the last of her food. Don's lips disappeared. Freya could tell he was making the internal 3 . . . 2 . . . 1 . . . of children on high diving boards. At least she could see he was genuinely trying.

'It will be part of my education,' Albert said.

'Let him concentrate.'

'I just need to do it,' Don said, speaking to himself. He made a kind of two-handed stirring motion with the bolt gun as he tried to get himself in the mode.

'Don't think,' she said.

'Easier said than done,' he said.

His eyes were half shut and this was the first time it really struck her that this was cruel.

'It would help me learn about responsibility and consequence,' Albert said.

Belona finished her food, made a throaty noise and brought her head up to look at Don. He made the mistake of looking into the goat's eyes, the letter-box shaped pupils.

Albert said: 'Why don't I take over?'

'Leave your father alone.'

Don was still making eye contact with the goat, whose jaw was masticating.

'Young people are fearless,' Albert said.

'Don, you're doing fine,' she said, surprised to find herself becoming straightforwardly encouraging now, wanting him to do well. Don noticed it too and glanced up.

'Okay, okay, *fine*,' he said, and his jaw tensed. 'I *will* do this.'

As his voice grew loud, Belona kicked and pulled against her leashes, and Freya and Albert both had to step back and tighten their grip. Now the goat was without the distraction of eating, which had kept her head lowered, Don had to stand up to get a better angle. He took a step back, as though a short run-up might help.

'I would be ruthless,' Albert said, leaning back. Belona's head was stilled by their leashes.

Don began nodding now, redoubling his commitment. His knuckles showed white and he seemed to be saying something under his breath. Belona made a vibrato noise and a look passed across Don's face.

'She's nervous because you're nervous, Dad. Probably best for me to take over.'

'Don, now's your chance.'

His back hunched and he raised the bolt gun above one shoulder. He held that position, the shiny baton aloft, the fact that his hands were now shaking making him look a little, Freya could not help but notice, as though he were preparing a cocktail. In truth, he did not resemble a killer.

Don's expression was of a man who had surprised himself. He'd secretly thought that, for all his avoidance over the years, when it came to it, he would probably be able to go through with this. For Freya, here was his moment of self-awareness that she had been hoping to provoke, only now it was in front of her, she realized they would both have been better off in ignorance.

Albert said: 'Let's face it. I'm the man for the job.'

Then Don, still with that same startled expression, held out the baton to his son.

Geraint was in the coop, lifting up the swing-down door on the hutch.

'How long have you been here, Ger?'

Kate watched him through the chicken wire as he reached in and stroked one of the hens.

'Basically since the day you left. I came here looking for you, but then decided to help out.'

Kate wondered why no one had told her this.

'What do your mum and dad think?' she said.

'They've been really supportive.'

'Have you found out your results?'

'I haven't had time,' he said. 'Liz and Mervyn might bring them over later.'

He used their first names. He held a podgy hen and nuzzled its wing feathers with his nose.

'I'm really sorry about leaving,' she said.

'No need.' It looked like he was talking to the hen. 'You handled it badly, but you did what was right for you. Things worked out. My fault for not seeing there was a problem.'

He put the hen back down, felt around in the straw and pulled out a small pale egg. He held it up and admired it. There didn't seem to be much of his old self left, and for this she felt responsible.

Just then they heard an impact somewhere and saw birds complaining in the sky above them.

When Don heard the shot, it took him by surprise and he put his hand to his chest. He was standing in the corner of the barn, not more than ten metres away from his wife and son but no longer visible to them. He had been listening to their muffled voices, unable to make out exactly what they were saying so filling in the gaps himself. He was still wearing his slaughterwear but had taken off his cap while he leaned his forehead against the brick.

Behind him there were two long tables and, on each, stacks of wooden plates and a cutlery tray. On stands on a workbench there were four barrels: mild, dark, perry and 'Lucky Dip Cloudy Cider'. He went to the table, took a reusable pint cup, held it beneath the tap and watched the glaucous yellow liquid dribble in. A memory of Patrick and a golden balloon. Once the glass was full, he took a long drink. In the corner of the barn, a red light came on.

'You okay, boss?'

Varghese stepped out, his camera held up.

'Yes.'

'Everyone's arriving. You ready to give me that tour now?'

There was the *eek-eek-eek* of the rope working against the branch as the goat's body jolted, the muscles still contracting.

'How do you feel?' she said.

'Sad.'

Albert watched the blood stream from the tip of Belona's tuft of beard. As the metal bucket filled, the sound changed from *tacktack-tack* to a pitter-patter.

'Mum?'

'Yes.'

'I'm worried about Dad's survival in the next stage. What will happen to him?'

'He might adapt.'

Albert watched the bucket. Once it was half full, a raspberry red, Freya swapped it for an empty one.

'You can take that to the kitchen.'

'Okay.'

'You did very well,' she said, and kissed him on the head. 'Do you want to help me with the rest or have you had enough?'

'I think I've had enough.'

'Okay.'

He held the full bucket carefully, both hands on the handle and carried it through the grass, across the yard. It caught the light: a full moon.

In the kitchen, Arlo was dicing onions with ex-professional flare.

His cheeks were wet but he did not wipe his eyes. Albert clanked the bucket on to the tiles.

'I bring-ah blood,' Albert said, but didn't feel up to giving his Mediterranean accent the usual oomph.

'My boy! My butcher!' Arlo said, and he knelt down and hugged him. Albert felt Arlo's tears wet against his cheek.

'Okay. Now, say after me: co-ag-u-*la*-re.'

'Coagu*la*re,' Albert said, without enthusiasm.

'Perfect, Albert. Benissimo.'

'I would like to be crying too.'

'I can make that happen,' and from the hugging position, Arlo picked him up with a fireman's lift and held his face above the onions.

Sitting on a garden chair with a chopping board on his lap, Arlo cut the seams of fat out of the liver. In an iron pan on a trivet over the fire, there were onions, chilli, mushrooms, garlic and fresh kidney sizzling. Albert was standing by the fire with a long-handled wooden spoon, prodding at the pan. They heard footsteps and looked up to see Kate coming down the stepped path towards them.

'I smell death,' she said.

As his sister got close, Albert wiped his eyes with his forearms. He took a paper plate and served himself an unnecessarily large portion.

'There was no suffering,' Arlo said, red-handed from the liver.

'The hens can tell when something bad has happened,' she said, quoting Geraint now. 'They won't lay any more today.'

Flopping down on to the bare grass near the fire, she lay on her back and stared up at the sky.

'Nice one, bro. Your first kill. One notch on the bedpost.'

Albert kept tucking into his food, undisturbed.

'First a goat, next your parents,' she said. 'How do you feel?'

'Your brother is upset, actually, Kate. I think he surprised himself.'

'I was *not*. I didn't surprise myself,' Albert said, and he put a big forkful in his mouth. 'Killing her was easy.'

The pan applauded as Arlo threw in more liver.

'*Her*? Don't you always kill a billy?' Kate said.

'That is the usual,' Arlo said.

Kate breathed out heavily. Albert was chewing and now bobbing his head side to side, as though listening to a song he liked. The fire popped and the alignment of the wood changed.

'So who did you go for? Better not be Belona. You know she's my favourite.'

Arlo stopped chopping and looked into the fire. Albert made appreciative food noises. Kate got up on her elbow. The smoke was drawn towards her.

'Arl?'

He didn't move; he had a stained chopping board on his knees. Kate held her hand in front of her eyes.

She blinked. Her eyes were reddening – the smoke from the fire.

Albert had got a chunk of liver on the end of his fork. He was chewing. He stopped. He looked at his sister and – with blood on his teeth – he smiled.

She actually ran away. She ran, into the woods, rubbing her eyes as she went, trying not to think about Belona rotating, the queue of people with paper plates, the disappointing, chewy meat, dry and overpowering, the pile of scraggy bones on the compost heap. She tried not to think about that. Just because she now ate meat did not mean that it stopped being murder; it just meant that she had become a murderer.

When she stopped running she found she had arrived, without consciously deciding to, at the place she always used to come when she was upset: where a chain-link fence dangled in the river, catching inexplicable bottles of Japanese bleach and blue rope. This was where the old version of herself would have come to wipe her eyes when someone had failed to live up to her high standards. Instead, she carried on into the woods, away from her special place, away from the sound of the cattle grid rattling in the distance as more people arrived for the party.

As she walked, she tried focusing on the letter *A*, and what it meant to her. She tapped into that part of her that was already in Cambridge, reading difficult fiction in a quadrangle.

She walked until she didn't recognize the path any more. After a while she saw, up ahead, smoke coming out from some tall grasses. Getting closer, she realized that it was, in fact, the roof of the round-house, its stovepipe breathing.

The last time she had seen the roundhouse was years ago and she was surprised how cosy it looked: a rack of pots and pans by the front door, pairs of boots lined up either side of a welcome mat and, looking through the porthole washing-machine window, Patrick, brewing industrial-strength chai, and Freya, unzipping a suitcase.

Don had reached a point, somewhere between two and three large cloudy ciders, where he wanted to be in front of a camera. Varghese filmed him, still in his basketball tee and joggers, but mercifully hav-ing given his cap away. He stood in the middle of the long field, called for the Frisbee, made a difficult catch then threw it again, as hard as he could. It went off-camera, so it didn't matter where it landed.

Varghese filmed Gower's only magician, Herod the Significant, who was having trouble convincing anyone to lend him their valu-ables until Don took off his watch. Don preferred being in front of the lens; there was something transformative about it, in the same way that a miserable holiday, for the brief moment when a photograph is taken, becomes infused with joy. He now had a glass of perry, which he sucked through a straw as Varghese followed him past a band who were practising, sitting on stools outside the back door of their van, one playing a melodeon, one a mandolin, and a harpist who took away a hand to wave at Don; he blew a kiss back and tried ostenta-tiously counting them in ('Ah one, ah two, ah one two three four . . .') and it actually worked, they played a silky two-step as he rumba'd up towards the kitchen garden, where he called hellos by name to the wwoofers whose names he knew and just hellos to those he didn't. Don went through a polytunnel, joking that a hanging cucumber was a boom microphone, tapping it – 'Is this thing on?'

Kate had reached a point, somewhere between two and three large mugs of chai, where she felt numb. This was a useful emotion because, since stepping inside the roundhouse, she had learned two things. First, she discovered the real reason her father had been in a hurry that morning. Secondly, and this was the big one, Freya had now decided, unilaterally, that Albert would start school in September. Not only that, but she had arranged with Patrick for her and Albert to stay at his house in Mumbles during term-time, because it was close to the school.

So Kate now found herself helping to pack up their stuff. While Freya folded the Japanese screen, Kate put clothes in a suitcase. It didn't feel great to be taking an active role in dismantling her own family, but she couldn't disagree that her brother needed help. Patrick, meanwhile, had gone to bring the car round so they could start loading up. Kate had noticed he seemed pleased. He had even offered to 'nip up to the party' and 'run it all past Don', since Freya was unwilling.

'Okay, I can finish up,' Freya said. 'You should get back to celebrating your genius.'

Kate carried on folding a collarless shirt.

'Hello?' Freya said. 'Are you there, overachiever?'

'I'm not going back to the party.'

Her mother frowned and they listened for a moment to the distant noise of the sound system. 'You'd rather pack suitcases with me. How sweet.'

'I'm just trying to steer clear of my brother.'

Freya frowned for a long time. 'What did Albert tell you?'

'He told me that being a murderer is easy.'

'Ah,' Freya said. She leaned the Japanese screen against the wall and came to kneel beside her daughter. 'Sorry to tell you this, Kate, but your brother couldn't go through with it. He's not the psychotic he'd like you to think he is, I'm relieved to say. He got very upset.'

'So who did it?'

'You can probably guess who the real murderer was.'

Kate realized, then, she'd been folding the murderer's cardigans.

Albert and Isaac were in the upstairs bathroom, pissing into the same bowl. Isaac had wanted to get his face painted but Albert said that they needed to stay focused.

'We're lucky, Isaac.'

'Why's that?'

'Most people in the world don't even know it's going to end.'

The sound of drunk people ignoring their inevitable fate drifted through the open window.

They double-teamed a dried-on streak on the bowl.

'Get it,' Alb said.

'I'm trying.'

'You and me together.'

The stain started to disintegrate and fall into the pan.

'Spraying hot acid, you and me.'

Albert got a single sheet of loo roll and dropped it into the toilet water. They watched the paper dissolve into tiny bits, churning in the water, a yellowy cloud, an open portal.

'I'm done,' Isaac said.

Albert zipped up, then Isaac did the same.

'Good,' Albert said, and he reached to the windowsill, pulled the toothbrushes out of their mug and held it up for Isaac to smell the rank bacterial backwash. Isaac shook his head. Albert looked stern and brought the mug closer. Isaac sniffed, then gagged.

They climbed in the bath, shoes on, to further their plans. Sitting cross-legged, they faced each other, Albert with his back to the taps.

'Remind me, how will the world end?' Albert asked.

'Um.' Isaac looked around. 'It's gonna come up through the plug'oles?'

Albert reached into the plug and pulled out a slug of human hair.

'Like this?'

'Like that.'

'Smell it.'

'I don't want to.'

'We both smell it.'

Albert held up the rag of greasy of hair and they both sniffed, both gagged.

Just then, through the open window, Albert heard a voice he recognized. Immediately he climbed up on to the sink and stuck his head out, looking down at the patio.

'I thought I'd driven her away but now she's back and putting on a disguise,' he said. 'My sister is evil.'

'Is she?'

'Yeah, she is. She wants us all to die. We have to get rid of her or she will undermine our message.'

'Okay.'

'But we probably shouldn't kill her though, before you say it.'

Varghese was showing Don some of the footage they'd shot. With each new scene Don's on-screen face got a shade redder, so it looked like a continuity error. As he watched, however, Don did not notice this. In fact, through his cider-fug he imagined that off the back of this short film a series would get commissioned – and the money would be enough to put them in the clear – and they would attract new members: bright, forward-thinking, child-laden people – enough children to make Freya see that sending Albert to school wasn't necessary and from that point on his son would return to being the bright, hopeful boy of old and Freya would try to kiss Don, having seen him represented in this way, natural on screen and heading up a worldwide growth in secular but authentic communal living.

When Kate had cautiously approached the patio at the back of the house, which was now the designated fancy dress area, she had been intending to apply only a couple of tasteful tribal stripes, to give the impression she was getting into the party spirit without actually getting into the party spirit. Her mother had convinced her to find her brother and try, *again*, to connect. But as she approached, someone had called her name – it was Geraint or, as he was now, The Hulk, sitting on a school desk, his green legs hanging in the air, surrounded by pots, tins and tubes of face paint, jam jars full of brushes, cubes of sponge, pallets, rags, torn clothes and the oval mirror. Being The Hulk just meant being algae-green from head to toe and topless, with his newly acquired farmhand's body and small cut-off jean shorts. He had called Kate over and demanded complete creative control, which he was exercising now, as she stood in front of him, letting him take aesthetic revenge. It seemed like the least she could do.

With everyone painting each other's faces, there was a kind of domino effect, each person avenging the botched job that they'd received at someone else's hands.

Next to them was the wicker dressing-up box from the attic, its leather straps untied, vomiting woollens, leggings, Babygros, a ball gown, a straw hat and an old stripy shower curtain on to the grass. Around them, people were becoming blocks of colour, breakfast foods, worms, skulls, X-men, robots, suns, munchkins, devils, Oompa-Loompas, peacocks, lions, elephants, minstrels. All human life was there.

It was almost dark. Patrick squeezed the last of the cardboard boxes on to the passenger seat and locked the car. He had parked at the top end of the new-build cul-de-sac development – scene of his injury – because it was the nearest spot for vehicle access to the roundhouse. The homes were lived in now, with cars in some of the drives and a basketball net screwed into the wall above a garage. He felt a twinge at the memory of his lying there in the turning circle incapacitated. Of all the sensory revelations of that evening – the pain, cold, mind-bending paranoia – he was disappointed to note that the most persistent memory was of how Janet's body felt against his back. In particular, her nipples. He also found he could clearly recall Don showing off his knowledge of hypothermia, displaying his talent for hijacking someone else's life-changing trauma. This thought might have made Patrick angry had he not just finished carrying Don's wife and son's belongings to his car.

Freya had gone back to the roundhouse, where she claimed she was going to try and sleep, in preparation for the big move tomorrow morning. Patrick said that he would go back to the party to have an 'air-clearing' chat with Don. He strapped on his head torch.

In the long field, the upper area was now so busy with tents that he had to walk a zigzagged route to avoid getting tripped by guy ropes. He passed four full-size teepees, their spikes prickling the dim sky. In the distance he could hear the bass. It sounded gastric. He could see, at the bottom of the field, the hay pyramid and the main stage where alt-folk four-piece Endless End were creating the evening's first proper dance: a ceilidh-cum-circle-pit. There were probably close to 200 people standing and sitting on the grass, smoking, eating and drinking.

As he strolled among them, he imagined what he would say when he came across Don. *Hand in your badge, old man.* Or, more realistically, but just as cruel in its mannered way: *I know this must seem like I'm moving in on your patch but I want you to know that I'm motivated purely by what's best for Frey and Albert.*

Patrick peeked in the barn, where the big vat of blood soup, labelled *Very Non-Veg*, was on a long table. Nearby, a small dog had climbed into the tray containing a whole salmon, and was currently holding the head in its mouth.

Skirting the rave arena, Patrick watched the young and relatively reckless dance under tarpaulin, lit by the house's outside lamps and lanterns stuck in the ground. Patrick noted, with some affection, the three boys he used to buy weed off smoking ice bongs in a flower bed. The party, as far as Patrick could see, had funnelled into two camps: the young, up here, with the sound system and the unyoung at the live music stage, with cross-pollination at the fire, food, booze and toilets. The only exception was Don, who was standing just beyond where the dancers' limbs could reach him, dressed now as the Sun, with a rubber Statue of Liberty souvenir crown painted yellow; his face, his drink and the basketball bursting out of his T-shirt were all coloured yellow too. He was having his ear chewed off by a girl who was entirely blue. To Patrick, she seemed to be the Sky, though she was supposed to be Mystique from *X-Men*. Don spotted Patrick and immediately started waving him over.

Kate was an endangered megafauna, with big white eyes and black earmuff ears, smoking Benson & Hedges on the pyramid of hay. Everyone on the flammable pyramid was smoking. It felt huge in her hand, almost like a wand, and she sucked on it and sprayed the smoke, turning her head back and forth while looking for her brother in the crowd. She couldn't see him. People were watching the band in threes and fours, all drinking perry then slipping away to piss in the nettles. So far, the bands had been sharing their gear with good humour, except for some inevitable queenyness over snare drums.

'Hello? Delivery for Kate.'

She looked round and saw Isaac beside her, holding a tray, a tea towel over his arm.

'From your brother,' he said. 'He's sorry. He sent this tomato soup and salad that he made himself with a little help from Arlo which I walked all the way down from the big house without spilling any.'

He handed the tray to Kate.

'Okay. Where is my brother?'

'He drew a letter *K* in coriander, which is the first letter of your name.'

'Great. Tell him he's forgiven, and to come and see me. Where is he?'

Isaac bowed then turned and climbed down the pyramid and went away. She held the bowl up and took a big sniff and felt better. Geraint, who had been clambering up and down the pyramid like a temple monkey, asking for filters, leaving scuffs of green paint on the hay, returned. He smiled at the sky, which was dark now, then tried to pick something out of the small, impractical pockets at the front of his jean shorts.

'I saved you two greenies,' Geraint said. 'They're a*maz*ing.'

His bin-lid eyes stared at the pills in his hand the way children stare at emergency stop buttons they're not supposed to press. He put one on the end of his tongue and stuck it out towards her. She'd never taken one before, though everyone assumed she was an old hand. She thought of Kit Lintel, and mushrooms, and the evening she had spent pretending to have a life-changing experience. Growing up in a community she had always found drugs a bit embarrassing, something that old people did, the way most teenagers think about opera.

His eyes narrowed as his tongue started to burn from the chemicals. She looked at her soup and was glad to think her brother might have mellowed. It was beginning to seem like she might be able to enjoy herself this evening. Geraint put his hands on her knees and wagged his tongue like a dog. She sucked it off in a quick hard slurp that tasted of smoke and ketchup, and washed it down with soup.

Patrick and Don kept walking through the market garden, away from the noise, until the geodesic dome emerged into view, Patrick's old home, looking like a testicle veined with fairy lights. It had been made available to the revellers – a banner read THE THUNDER DOME! – but it was empty, which, for Patrick, said everything about its eternal position in the community. They went inside, shutting the door and the windows, which just left the sound of the kick drum pushing through, a feeling in their chests of perpetual resuscitation.

'Phew,' Don said, and he sat down on the low futon-sofa.

'I think that girl liked you,' Patrick said.

'She liked *everything*.'

It shouldn't have surprised Patrick that they hadn't kept the dome as he had left it but, nevertheless, he was standing, looking around at the bare, triangulate walls. The only decoration was a photo of whoever was sleeping here of late, a giant brown man and his miniature girlfriend, holding hands in a park. In anticipation of the difficult conversation ahead, Patrick instinctively checked the cupboard where he used to keep his stash. Inside were rows of labelled tapes and a pile of cue cards, each of which had handwriting on. He read one:

Day Sixteen. Tape 3/5. 00.00–00.41 audio only – Marina interview** (thoughts on D, F, A and 'The Future'.) 00.42–00.58 audio only – covert recording of communal meeting. 00.59–01.20 long of D in garden, lecturing wwoofers on power usage (audio not usable but good video)

'She thought we were a cult, Pat. She asked me how many wives I have.'

Patrick shut the cupboard and turned round. Don had scuffs of blue on both cheeks where the girl had said goodbye in the French manner. He was filling two wooden cups with Merlot from a box by his feet. He passed one up to Patrick.

'And how many wives did you tell her?'

Don didn't find that funny.

'Have you seen Freya?' he asked.

'Actually, she did ask me to pass on a message. Said she's too tired. Gone to bed.'

Don inhaled for a long time.

'I know it's not what you wanted to hear,' Patrick said. 'But you should try and have a good time anyway. You've worked really hard to make all this happen, and you deserve to enjoy it.'

Their relationship was not built on kindness and Don squinted in non-recognition. Patrick took note and tried to even things out with a bit of trademark banter.

'I am reminded of something you said to me once. "Get stuck in, Pat. Sixty's not too old."' His impression of Don was camp. ' "All these tremendous women, intelligent, free-thinking, body-confident."'

'Are you trying to tell me to get laid?'

'I never said that. I'm just saying there's a little secret that I know. You take this table leg off,' Patrick nudged the one he was referring to with his foot, 'and feed it through the coat hooks on the back of this door. *Et voila* – privacy.'

'Oh Christ,' Don said, and he put his head in his hands. 'Is that what Freya hopes will happen? I'll get laid and forget about her?'

Patrick didn't reply; he wasn't used to seeing Don vulnerable and it unsettled him.

'You know she's talking about sending Albert to school?' Don said.

'I actually wanted to talk to you about that,' Patrick said.

Finishing off his wine in one, Don leaned forward and squirted himself a top up from the box.

'I just don't think it'll do him any good. School won't suit him. Maybe when he's older, Kate's age, it will. Plus it's miles away. He'll lose half his life going back and forth.'

'That's what I wanted to talk about – the commute,' Patrick said.

He knew there was a spot in the middle of the room that, because of its shape, produced a kind of reverb. He had always disliked how it made him sound, but for now he decided it would be better to speak with a certain omnipotence. He knew the spot by instinct; he took a couple of steps and one to the side, then raised his chin: 'Freya said it wouldn't take so long for him to get to school if she and Albert lived nearer the school.'

'You can't teach that kind of rational thinking, Pat. That's why I married her.'

Patrick stayed where he was. To get the special effect he had to keep his head in that position.

'And she asked me if she and Albert could live in my house, for a bit.'

The reverb smoothed the harsh edges off his voice, he felt.

'And what did you say, old pal?'

'Well, Don. I mean. To be totally frank, I said ye–'

It was the purest kind of uppercut. Don, seated on the very low futon-sofa, had made a fist and pushed himself up, reaching full height as he caught Patrick under the chin. His fist must have travelled four and a half feet along a vertical axis. At exactly the point in the word *yes* where the tongue darts out before the sibilant, it hit.

Patrick took a couple of steps back and held his throat. It hadn't been that hard, both men knew, but it counted.

'Okay,' Patrick said, his voice no longer omnipotent.

His tongue was bleeding. Something in the less than whole-hearted way Don had hit him – at about 65 per cent strength – suggested a kind of resignation. It was almost an *okay, you win*. Don sat back down on the sofa and said: 'Damn.'

At this point, Patrick had expected to feel more victorious.

She'd never heard music like this before. This was not normal dance music. Closing her eyes, Kate clearly imagined robotic dogs coming towards her over the horizon. Giant robotic dogs. Their feet were the drums and they were growling the bassline – no, they were chasing the bassline – the bassline was chasing them! Always running towards her but never getting any closer, like in the *Steamboat Willie* cartoon, but not scary at all. A guy without face paint danced against her. His features looked squashed but she didn't mind so she pushed her bum into his crotch and laughed over her shoulder. He was one of the free-party heads who had arrived at midnight, easily recognized by the girls' fluorescent leggings and the boys' sleeveless tops. Whenever the music dropped away, she heard the hydraulic rush of an entrepreneur, somewhere, doling out nitrous. There was someone who looked like her father, if her father had jaundice, standing near the edge of the dancefloor, speaking intensely to a girl who was one of those blue-skinned aliens in hot pants.

She found The Hulk next to the speakers, watching his own hands with interest, dancing by a girl dressed as a peacock. He reached into the condom pocket of his jean shorts and teased something out, another pill, which he pressed into Kate's palm. Gazing up at the amoeba-shaped tarpaulin, she felt an affinity with everything, right down to the single-cell organisms within her. She took a moment to contemplate the inside of herself, her internal neatness, before becoming aware of her bladder. She could not wait to go to the toilet, Kate suddenly realized. She was excited about it.

Avoiding the Portaloos, she went to the toilet under the stairs. She felt her breath go in and out and she looked at the ceiling and the walls and the toilet scrubber and the curlicued *H* and *C* on the taps. She sat down, giggling, then read and reread the note that said: 'Hello. If you're reading this, you must be sitting on me. I like organic waste (that means piss, shit and toilet paper – yum!) Everything else, feed to my friend, Senor Bin. Love, Joe Bog.' It was brilliant and clever. Then she wiped herself and saw red on the tissue paper. She stared at it. A watery red. She looked into the bowl and saw all her piss was red. Internal bleeding. The pills.

Fucking cheapskate pills, just typical, for me to die on the day of my unconditional acceptance. So this is how Geraint gets his revenge.

She pressed her hands on her stomach. Suddenly there were no unthreatening robotic armies, just a slow, painful death in a brightly lit hospital, and she thought of Patrick, the forked capillaries at the side of his nose. Kate realized she would never stride purposefully through the university library's impossibly complicated annals.

Annals. Never annals for her. She would never have one-on-ones with outlandish lecturers. So many stains on their jumpers, shoelaces untied, that she would never see. She would never punch well above her weight, academically and romantically, would never fall in love with a boy of an opposite social background – even more opposite than Geraint's, the son of a wealthy foreign diplomat, perhaps – and they would never toss off the shackles of each other's ideas of what a relationship could be, and discover that, when it came down to it, they were similar – both fleeing their childhoods, both social explorers – and they would never hold each other in a postgraduate carrel amid the smell of rare and expensive books and wake full of knowledge, not the kind of knowledge found in books but something deeper, about themselves, about each other.

She stared into the bowl. What was she worried about again?

Oh yeah, the watery blood that suggested a slow, agonizing death – with hours to decide her final words, hours to edit and redraft. She couldn't think what her final words would be. *I love you.* Was that an awful cliché? It felt true, though. I love *you*. I *love* you. *I* love you.

'He-llo? I'm dying out here,' a female voice said.

Kate pulled up her knickers and flushed. She straightened her black skirt and unlocked the door. As she came out, a Pierrot clown shoved past and slammed the door behind her. Kate went back to the kitchen, where there had been a fight with raw onion. It was everywhere. She felt her eyes start to sting. She sniffed and remembered that she was going to die. She'd forgotten. She started crying. There was a big red bloody patch on the chopping board on the table. She stared at it. Next to the board were a pile of beetroot scalps.

She stared back and forth between the board, the bloodstain, the beetroot.

The board. The bloodstain.

The beetroot.

She was like some completely useless detective.

It took maybe eleven seconds.

'Beetroot salad,' she said. 'I ate beetroot salad.'

There was a boy she didn't recognize at the fridge – not in fancy dress – digging at a carrot cake with his hand.

'I thought I was dying, but I'm not!'

She pulled the other pill Geraint had given her out of her pocket and took it with a glass of Five Alive.

The last image that Patrick had of Don was of him, with a frightening intensity, twisting out the last dregs from the foil bag of box wine, as though breaking the neck of a rabbit. Don had asked to be left alone, and so now Patrick was standing at the edge of the live music yurt. He kept deliberately clipping the cut on his tongue against his front teeth, wincing, then doing it again. The band were called 'Palindromeda'. As they finished one particularly awful song, Patrick heard a voice at his shoulder.

'You've been avoiding me.'

He knew who it was. Only now, somehow, with his car full of another man's wife's belongings, and with his tongue swollen in his mouth, did he feel able to see her. He turned to look – her face was flushed at the forehead from dancing and wearing a neckerchief – then he went back to watching the band. The frontman said: 'This song's called "Called songs, this".'

She said: 'I've missed you.'

Patrick felt the back of her hand against his cheek.

'What happened to your face?' she said.

Albert wandered the party, trying to decide on the best position from which to make his announcement. He needed to take into account where the biggest crowd could gather, the audience's sight lines and which position would give him the best silhouette. They would not be getting any more trouble from his sister, who, Albert could only assume, had tasted the soup, realized that she was drinking one of her oldest friends and was right now releasing tears into the wild, somewhere very far away. He walked past the fire pit and saw Zinia, a woman whom he had once loved like a grandmother until she left the community to live in Christiania years ago. She had curly hair and an Alpine chest.

'Bertie!' She used to call him that. 'My boy, you're *huge*!'

'I know.'

'*Slask fitte!*'

He repeated it. 'What does it mean?'

'I saved it for you. It's Swedish. It means something unspeakable.'

'Okay, thank you.'

Up at the yard, he tried to ignore his father seated on the bench by the schoolroom with a Smurf on his lap. Albert examined the flat roof as a possible podium. He walked back towards the dance-floor, into the noise, avoiding the flailing elbows, to check that he would still be visible from there. When he heard his name yelled, he turned round in time to see someone who resembled his sister wrap her clammy arms right round him, wetness and heat coming off her neck.

'Bro!' she said. The hug went on and on. Her face paint was smudged to an ashy grey. When she let go, there were black smudges on Albert's forehead. She looked him up and down.

'What are you?' she said, dancing as she talked. 'Are you a sea captain?'

He was wearing wellies and a blue naval utility coat. The coat, which he'd got from the dressing-up box, was to give him authority as a public speaker and to point towards the possible floods ahead.

'Why are you still *here*?' he said.

'I came to see you!'

She bobbed her head from side to side. She was holding a bamboo pole, the panda's glow stick, twizzling it. He could feel the music in his lungs, the air moving. The smoke machine exhaled, the green laser came on and his sister reached up to break the beams. He needed to hurt her more.

'The soup,' Albert said. 'It was made with the blood of your goat. Belona's blood.'

'Cool,' she said, and she tried to get him to dance, taking hold of his hands and puppeting them up and down.

'It *was* cool,' he said, in an overly sinister way, then waited for her to scream.

'What did you say about Belona?'

He cupped his hands round her ear and yelled.

'The soup was made with her blood!'

Her dancing slowed a little. Just her feet going.

'I thought it was tomato.'

He didn't mind repeating himself.

'You drank her blood. We mixed it with tomato to fool you.'

'Oh my God, that's weird.'

He watched her smudged face crack. Her teeth floating there amid the black paint. It was a smile, he realized. An unfathomable response. Her feet were still going from side to side, shoulders shifting.

'Brother of mine,' she said, kissing him in the middle of the forehead, then leaning right into his ear. 'If there's one thing I've learned tonight, it's that I love you so much. And you'll never stop loving me either. I know why you do everything. I love everything you are.'

She pulled his head into her chest and kissed him again, really hard on the crown. He could smell her. Maybe she was in shock – that was the problem. He had to make her understand.

'I stuck her, Kate. She was pissing blood like a fountain pissing blood.'

He felt her move in time to the music.

'I know what happened. That you weren't capable of pulling the trigger. I spoke to Mum. It's great that you're sensitive. Don't fight it – you're a good person by nature!'

She wouldn't let him go, squeezing him and trapping his arms at his side and moving his body in time with the music as though dancing with a doll.

'That's not true,' he said.

'I'm so proud of you!'

Letting go of him, she put her hands in the air as the synths came in. The bass dropped monumentally – a dynamited tower block.

As the smoke cleared, Albert looked to where his dad had been sitting but he was gone.

'Yeeeeeaaah!' she said, her voice going scratchy.

Little bits of spittle got Albert in the face. Her head went back, looking up at the tarpaulin. He gazed inside her nostrils, tiny nodules of dried snot attached to hairs like a miniature and impractical abacus. He did not know who this person was.

'Don't feel bad. She had a good life. Better than most animals' lives. Mum said Belona was pretty chilled out, even at the end. Come on, come dance, this is amazing,' and she pulled him closer to the speakers, his heels dragging in the grit. He yanked his hands away and put them over his ears. The bass rattled his insides and he thought of the way the innards had flopped out of Belona on to the grass, and of how there had been a sound like hundreds of people licking their lips all at once. He thought of the way the heart had kept thumping after the brain was mush. He looked around at the brain-dead people, his sister among them. There was an apocalyptic clown, blood around his mouth, with a top hat and cane, the white paint cracking at his jaw where he was gurning.

'You should think about how she bled to death and seemed to be in pain,' Albert said, though he was starting to get upset.

She mimicked using a steak knife and fork, cutting off a chunk, chewing it, but all this in rhythm with the music.

'It's fine. I love you. And you may not know it but you love me.'

He was blinking a lot. 'I don't.'

She did the one where electricity runs up one arm, across her shoulders and down the other arm.

She tried to pass it to Albert, but he'd gone.

Don was in the dome, down on one knee, tipping the table up with his shoulder as he took one of its legs off. The Sky was above him on the mezzanine bed, swinging her blue legs in the air.

'What you gonna use that for?' she said. 'And will I get splinters?'

He wedged the table leg into the coat hooks and tested the door to make sure it didn't open.

'You know all the tricks,' she said.

Don was full of different drinks and his ears were ringing and he had even slightly pulled his hamstring when dancing. It made him sad that the thing he was doing might be the thing his wife hoped he would do. He climbed the few stairs, holding on to the rail made from an elm tree branch, while trying to disguise a limp.

He crawled on to the bed, took the girl's drink out of her hand, then leaned in and put his tongue in her mouth. Her skin was soft, even with paint on. He experienced dizziness, having recently downed a Martini, and he worried about a possible fall from the mezzanine.

She lay back on the mattress and he carried on kissing her, leaning over with an arm either side of her upper body. She felt the crotch of his trousers. He asked himself a question he had not asked in some time: did he have clean genitals? Yes, thoroughly so, because he'd hoped that something might happen with Freya.

She pulled off her top and revealed the parts of her body she had not painted. He tried not to think about anything and groped her and kissed her. She slipped her hand down the front of his trousers and tugged inexpertly.

'This is probably pretty normal for you,' she said. She had to stop kissing while she concentrated on his belt. 'It's cool that here sex can just be sex and nobody has to get het up about it.'

Her speaking reminded him of how young she was, so he kissed her to keep her quiet. She shoved off her jean shorts, along with her underwear. He didn't want to say that this was moving too quickly, but he wondered if it was a generational thing: this *was* moving too quickly. She was of his daughter's generation. Twenty-four, he had discovered, a graduate. More white clouds now, among the blue. She had shaved all her pubic hair off. He had never seen that in person before. It pretty much appalled him. He tried to buy time by going down between her legs. She was scentless. These weren't real genitals, as far as he knew. So much had changed since he was young.

'I'm married,' he said, from between her thighs. 'I have a wife.'

'I know; I get it. Do you want me to meet her later or something?'

'I mean I'm properly married. Legally.'

'I understand.'

'I don't think you do. I think I might have to stop what we're doing here.'

She looked down at him.

'Yes,' he said, 'I definitely think I'm going to stop.'

'Weird.'

'I just realized. I've also hurt my hamstring.'

'Fuck you.'

'I'm really sorry.'

'Whatever.'

Isaac was standing in the gloom behind the generator, yawning a lot and feeling sick from the fumes but knowing that the human race's survival depended largely on his standing there, staying awake, feeling sick. He looked up at the flat roof of the big house and could make out a shape moving around. He waited for the signal. Isaac was happy that there were lots of other children at the party, some of whom he knew from before, like the three blonde sisters from Tinker's Bubble who he used to be friends with when he lived there. They were all wearing bridesmaid dresses and had jumped on him when they first saw him. They called him 'Eye Sack', which he always found funny. Then, later on, he had been riding piggyback on the oldest sister Anya, whose plaited hair swung so high as they ran that it tickled his ears. That was when Albert saw them and made a deadly face so that Isaac had to climb down and take Albert's hand and come stand here in the dark behind the generator to finish the plan. Albert had explained that his sister had not been upset at all by the blood soup. She was now entirely without a mind, so there was nothing more they could do. Isaac thought about how his mother had said they would be moving on again soon, to a new community. She said that she was unsettled and that the energy interplay was shifting and she did not want to be here on the 15th October when Mars came a-knocking. She said the party was a good opportunity to meet people from other communities. She had told Isaac to let Albert know it was possible they might leave in the morning, if they met someone who was willing to give them a lift. His mother didn't like the party being filmed and photographed as she believed that films and photographs took something away from you that they could never return. There was the shape on the roof, silhouetted by the dusky clouds, dragging a rectangle out of the skylight. His mother had very small eyes, eyes that always looked closed in photos even when they were open. He had heard people taking photographs say 'Let's try again, you blinked' so many times that in the end she had to say 'That's just how my eyes look.' He had not got his mother's eyes. He had someone else's eyes. For some reason the fumes made Isaac never want to eat bacon again. Isaac had seen a number of photos of himself and was extremely pleased with all of them. No one was noticing the noise the generator was making because of all the other noises. Don sometimes called the generator 'Jenny'. His mother said that Don was 'messed up on some deep level' and that any community with someone that competitive at the heart of it would have problems. His mother said that they needed to find somewhere more genuine because it was important to be somewhere genuine, especially now. Isaac had not told Albert that they might be leaving so soon. He was scared about what Albert would say. His mother had been invited to a community in Northumbria and had printed off pictures and Isaac could not deny it looked nice with a big wooden structure for morning meditation and a choir that did not care if you could sing. He stared up at the flat roof above the kitchen. There were a few rectangles up there now and a shape tending to them. His favourite place had been Tinker's Bubble, where he'd had three girlfriends, all sisters, all blonde, and sometimes they'd carried him around like a corpse. There was a waterfall there that trickled down the side of the hill and the posh house at the bottom had a trampoline in the garden which he and the girls used to sneakily bounce on until lights came on in a window and someone yelled. His mother became friends with a nice man named Daniel who smelt of damp woodchip, which was a good smell. Daniel wrote a song about his mother that rhymed *Marina* with *hyena* and *ballerina* and was Isaac's favourite song for a good while, until his mother said it was not a good song any more. Then they went to High Copse Court, which his mother tried to become a member of but was not allowed because, as she explained to Isaac, their minds were locked shut like a beehive. Then they came here and Marina told Isaac to be extra nice, which he was. He was happy to meet Albert, and Albert was happy to meet him. The shape on the roof wasn't moving any more. He heard a woman's voice nearby, saying in an American accent: 'Varghese, I think you should come up the house quick and catch this. Albert's on the roof.' This made Isaac pleased that they were doing something important. Then there were the torch flashes. Dot dot dash. Dash. Dot dot. The signal. Isaac knelt down, gripped on to the thick textured plastic where the lead went into the generator. It would turn off the music and lights in the rave arena but would not affect Albert, who was plugged into the river behind the walls of the big house. Before he'd even pulled the plug, somewhere someone screamed really loudly and for a long time. Isaac held the cord with both hands and leaned back.

Patrick and Janet took their shoes off at the door to her room. At the end of the corridor, power leads were running through the window and out on to the flat roof. As they went inside and Janet shut her door behind them, the dance music stopped. She nodded as though the ability to mute the outside world was well within her powers. Through the walls, they heard a muffled, amplified voice and the sounds of cheering. They sat on school chairs opposite each other.

'I'm so glad to see you.'

'Sure.'

Their voices sounded intimate in the sudden quiet, which Patrick didn't approve of. She examined his face in the light from a double-helix lampshade that hung above them. She smoothed out his forehead with her thumbs, which made him realize he was frowning.

'I never got to say sorry in person for not coming with you in the ambulance. I desperately wanted to but I was worried that I'd make things worse – since you seemed to believe I was plotting to *kill* you.' She opened her eyes wide in mock horror.

Patrick tried not to take in what she was saying. She looked down at his ankle and asked if she could have a look, which was just the sort of thing that he had been training himself to avoid. He wanted to say: *No, that's not appropriate*. But he didn't say that. Instead, in the quiet room, he stayed silent. She put her hands on his knee to see if he reacted, then slid off her seat and knelt in front of him, running her hands downwards, feeling his left shin through his trousers.

He gripped the sides of the chair and stared at her work table: four ice-cream-cone devil horns were drying on newspaper. Underneath the desk was a mound of bubble wrap, Jiffy bags and antique presentation boxes printed with 'Accessories to Murder' in an italicized font.

She took hold of his left foot and lifted it up, straightening his leg out. He watched her. She pressed the sole of his foot to her hip, then reached up his trouser leg, found the top of his thick walking sock, and rolled it down and off.

Smells are good for bringing back memories.

It was the first week they lived in Blaen-y-Llyn together. They all shared the schoolroom, eight of them. No stench or bulge or habit was disgusting. Janet's hyper-sonic bat farts in the night. She and Patrick would sometimes lock together, him waking with her tucked in flush against him.

Outside there was more cheering.

She pushed up his trouser leg, then ran her fingers down the flat of his shin towards his ankle, its yellow skin, the hair worn away by the cast. She watched him breathe in, his chest expanding, those lungs. Then she found it, the scar.

'What was the real reason you left?' she said, while examining the marks, which looked like a quadratic equation. Locating two metal screws, just below the surface of the skin, she pressed her thumb against them and Patrick inhaled.

'Don says the only reason I stayed here so long was because I was in love with you, but being in love with you was the reason to leave,' he said.

She smiled and slid her hand up to his knee, just beneath his trousers. Her other hand held the underneath of his calf. It felt like she was ready to draw him in, hand over hand.

'Am I really that bad?'

'I'm afraid so.'

'Am I doing it now?'

'Oh yes. Absolutely.'

She looked down at her hands.

'Sorry,' she said, and let go.

He stood up from the seat and moved awkwardly to the door, hobbled by a hard-on as well as his ankle. She threw him his sock. He was unable to bend to put it on. They listened to the crowd outside. Some were chanting.

'You never replied to my letter,' she said.

'What letter? You never sent one.'

'The one I sent when you were in hospital. I gave it to Don to give to you.'

Patrick pretended he hadn't heard that and leaned back against the wall, managing to get the sock on.

'Well, if you didn't get it, I'll tell you what it said. It said I was so sorry about your accident and that I had wanted to come in the ambulance but didn't want to upset you. I wrote about why I was awake that night, and drunk; it was because things weren't going well with Stephan. I laid all my feelings on the line. How much I care about you.'

'Was it a love letter?'

He thought of the way she sealed her letters: pink wax stamped to look like a man's nipple.

She looked at him. 'Maybe not in those exact terms, no. More of a kind of get-well letter, but with added content.'

'Did it suggest that we start a full sexual relationship?' His voice was loud.

She showed her teeth. 'Not that I recall.'

'Sounds like your typical high-grade bullshit then.'

'So that's what you want? A full sexual relationship.'

'Yes. Or nothing.'

'Right.'

It had taken him years – actually, decades – to say that. Among some other emotions, there was definite relief. 'The answer is nothing, isn't it?' he said.

'I think so,' she said.

'Fine. Good. That's cleared up. Anyway, where's old Stephan? I looked for his Saab,' Patrick said, 'but couldn't see it. I wanted to key him a message in the paintwork.'

'He's not here,' she said, sitting back on her seat and looking up at the ceiling. 'He's back with his wife.'

Patrick felt giddy. He was close to laughing in fact, but then told himself that this could be one of her stunts, though her expression said that it was not. Something about knowing she had been hurt made certain conversations more possible. Patrick smoothed down his trousers. His hard-on was gone. He felt freed.

'You need inequality. That's what you get when you're with someone like me. What could be simpler, more pure, than one person unfalteringly adoring another person, and that person quite liking being adored?'

'Right.'

'You don't even need to find me attractive. In fact, it's better if you don't!'

'The type of relationship you are referring to is called friendship. Happy to renew that with you, Pat.' She looked at him. 'You're pretty much perfect, but I just don't want to fuck you.'

It was a kind of exhilaration to hear those words.

'I'm hoping for early onset menopause,' he said, his voice suddenly cheerful. 'Take sex out of it and I'm looking like a strong contender. Au revoir, libido; hello, Patrick.'

She nodded slowly twice. 'You're playing the long game?'

'Twenty years in, no turning back now. Let me know when you feel the hormones dwindle,' he said, and looked at his watch. 'How old are you?'

'Forty-two.'

'And counting,' he said. 'You're just entering the zone. Keep me on speed dial. You may find your priorities change. Oh ho, I wish you'd told me this a long time ago.'

She stood up and came towards where he was standing by the door.

'I did tell you. I told you by never having sex with you.'

*

When the outdoor lights and music shut off, everyone beneath the rave canopy made a big synchronized *boo*, which, Albert knew, was just a small slither of how bad they would feel when the world as they knew it really did go through the industrial cheese grater.

Albert had hooked himself up to the big house mains. He had the karaoke machine from the attic and a microphone on a stand. He was on a low stool that was so close to the edge of the flat roof that if it were to tip forward he would be hospitalized, he estimated. He was ghoulishly lit; in a circle beneath him were five upturned reading lamps, each installed with contraband 100-watt bulbs. He lifted the clay megaphone that Marina had made for him to his lips and yelled at the microphone.

'I have something important to tell you!'

In the yard, the only remaining light was from the mosquito repellent lanterns. He couldn't make out the faces of the people who were turning to notice him, spinning and pointing up in the way that people point at superheroes. There were some people still talking loudly, and some laughter.

'Listen to me! This is important!'

Having never been to school, he had never seen the silence-produces-silence technique.

'Listen!' he said.

Someone shouted: 'We love you, Albert. Don't jump!'

There was a round of applause and a hydraulic gushing sound, then everyone went quiet apart from one or two drunks somewhere singing 'Heeeey-ay-baby', but Albert decided that it was fine for those people to die in the paradigm shift so he ignored them.

'I have invited you all here today to tell you some very bad news.'

Huge, panto-style, sympathetic *aww* sounds from the gathered throng.

'We have a limited number of days remaining on this planet.'

The quiet held for a moment. The clay megaphone hurt his lips.

'We must learn to discard the material world.' There was a shout-out for Madonna that Albert didn't understand. 'Pass this message on. If everyone here told just two people a day, and those two people told two people, and so on, for all of the remaining days, then we would reach the whole world.'

He started to hit his rhythm and was getting some strong calls of support.

'When it happens we are going to have to be ready. Before we enter the next paradigm, we must learn to perceive it. Some people will try to tell you lies.'

A scattering of applause and, it was hard to be sure, some kind of bowing hero-worship happening in one section of the crowd, which was the sort of thing he had been hoping for. Possible Mexican wave. There was a red light too, pointed at him, like a robot eye.

'Who's with me?'

He'd hoped a few natural leaders might emerge in the crowd and start organizing people but, as yet, that hadn't happened. Down by the generator he could see someone had a torch, and just then there was the tinnitus of the sound system coming back online, his audience suddenly visible to him, expressions lit by fairy lights on the trees and security lamps in the grass. Perhaps they were turning on the sound system so that they could plug Albert's microphone in and he could project his news even further. The red light was Varghese's camera. That made sense, because it was important to record a moment like this.

'Thank you for listening!' Albert said. 'Go – now – it's time!'

He dropped the megaphone and it fell off the roof and landed in a plush flower bed below, although it didn't smash dramatically; it just cracked in two.

Someone in the crowd pointed and yelled 'It's behind you!' at Albert, and there was a huge cheer, bigger than anything he'd got for his speech. He turned round and saw something terrifying: sea mist. It was coming in quick, thickening tangibly, smudging everything out. The revellers were captivated. It was quite possible this was the beginning of the end, in which case his speech had come too late. This would be permanent darkness. The world was shrinking. As Albert walked off stage, someone had lined up Prince's '1999' as the first record and everyone went absolutely nuts.

*

Smoke machines were obsolete. Albert walked out of the big house and across the yard, which was now a grey room. He found Isaac and took his hand. The DJ couldn't resist putting the strobe on. People kept coming out of the mist and patting Albert on the back and saying things like 'Nice one, dude' and 'Thanks for the tip-off' and 'The prophet walks among us' and Albert tried to give them all the death-eyes but it wasn't having any impact. *They* gave him the death-eyes, though none of them seemed to realize.

Isaac was fidgety and had stopped speaking. He had a look on his face that Albert didn't like. The mist made them feel that, wherever they went, they were still inside.

They looked in Isaac and Marina's bedroom at the far end of the workshop. It was bare, apart from a load of cardboard boxes and suitcases stacked at the far end. Isaac was upset and Albert told him to grow up.

'Where's your mum?' Albert asked.

Isaac squirmed and Albert gripped him by the wrist as they walked back along the candle-lit path through the market garden to check for her in the pottery shed. As they got close they saw that the shed's strip lights were on. Albert wanted to ask Marina what the best plan was, now that the world was officially full of idiots who would soon be dead. He found her, kneeling, wrapping a fruit bowl in newspaper and putting it into a cardboard box full of other parcelled-up shapes. There was a can of Red Stripe by her knee on the concrete floor and behind her a huge stack of detritus: a nose-less surfboard, a wooden toolbox, tent poles. He realized what was happening.

'We're leaving, aren't we?' he said, standing in front of her. 'It makes sense if we are. It's probably a good idea for us to leave. I'll get my mum.'

She reached forward and put her hands either side of his cheeks and admired him.

'And we'd *love* to take you with us.'

Her lips were wet. He'd never seen her drinking before.

'Well, I'll go get my stuff then,' Albert said.

She laughed and smiled at him in a way that said she found him endearing. Being thought of as endearing was one of Albert's least favourite things.

'We can't very well take you away from your family,' she said then, with a sideways glance, 'much as you might like us to.'

It was supposed to be a joke of some kind, that last bit, because of the way she'd said it, but Albert had no idea what she was getting at. Isaac had appeared in the doorway behind him, Albert knew, because of the weedy snivelling noise.

Marina's eyes flicked to the doorway and back to Albert. She still had his cheeks between her hands. 'Did Isaac tell you where we're going?'

Albert felt his face go hard. When things were annoying he found his face went hard and sometimes he breathed through his mouth.

'Where are you going?' Albert said.

'Didn't Isaac say? Northumbria. Not so far away.'

Albert heard the sound of Isaac sniffling behind him. Marina had her hands on his shoulders now. The jacket he was wearing had epaulettes and she dusted them off. If she dared call him a little trooper or soldier then he would lose it.

'We'll visit you. You and Eyes can be pen pals.'

'Pen pals,' Albert said.

Somehow those two words felt incompatible with everything he knew about the future of the planet. Either she was treating him like an idiot or she was an idiot herself. Albert's experience of the evening so far had been, broadly, that nobody was his intellectual equal.

'Why can't I come with you?' he said.

'Because you have to stay with your family. They love you and they're the most important thing.'

It was becoming increasingly clear with each answer she gave that she no longer knew what the right priorities were.

'You and Isaac have got a little while to say goodbye to each other. We won't leave until this mist clears.'

'Did you hear our announcement?'

'What's that?'

'We made an announcement about the bad news.'

She looked surprised and then made a face of recognition, but not a convincing one.

'Oh yes, I heard something. I was in here, packing up, but I heard it. I thought it was . . . yes. It was great. It was *excellent*.'

'It wasn't excellent. Nobody listened.'

'But it sounded like everyone really enjoyed it.'

He had a bad feeling that there was literally no one he could think of who wasn't in some very significant way a let-down. At least his own mother had been asleep all this time. There was only limited damage she could do to her reputation while sleeping. He had known people to leave him all through his childhood; his best friends were always leaving. He had a way of dealing with it, which was to stop being friends with them. In the time between hearing the news they were leaving and the time they left, you stopped being friends so that, on the day of their departure, it was a total breeze. For want of anything better he put his arms round Marina. Up close he noticed that her grey hairs had a different texture from the other ones. They looked like the hairs on a horse or a pig. He tried crying but found nothing there.

He said: 'I'd like to say goodbye to Isaac now please.'

After kissing him on the cheek, she carried out a box of prized creations, leaving Albert and Isaac alone. The shelves along one wall were still populated with people's ill-conceived clay models. The pottery shed had been the official safe place, being out of the way and one of the few lockable rooms, so all the stuff cleared out to make way for the party had been stashed here: a red Gibson SG, furred with dust; a portable telly; some French oak planks.

Albert went to the door, shut it, turned the key. The pottery shed was filthy, spattered windows suppressing the first hints of daylight outside. The concrete floor was textured with dried-on blots of clay.

'I'm going to miss you,' Isaac said.

'You didn't tell me you were leaving.'

'I was scared. I'm sorry. I don't want to go.'

'How long have you known?'

Isaac looked befuddled as he tried to count on his fingers. To Albert, Isaac didn't look cute. Albert didn't get cuteness.

'I'm not letting you go,' Albert said.

'Good. 'Cause I don't want to.'

Albert scanned the piles of stuff that obscured the back wall.

'But if I do go then Mum says we can write real letters to each other and you can visit me.'

One of the shelves rattled as the bass glissando'd an octave.

'Just 'cause we're apart dun't mean we can't be friends.'

When Isaac was upset he reverted to babyish language.

'You can't even hardly fucking *read*, Eyes.' Albert picked up one end of a surfboard and dragged it out of the way. He was looking for something. Isaac stared at the ground and started rubbing his eyes. From this far away, the female vocals sounded gagged.

'Come and visit me,' Isaac said, and he took two steps towards Albert's back.

'Lie on the floor.'

'What?'

Albert turned and punched him in the neck. Isaac took two steps back and then sat down. Returning to the mound of stuff, Albert yanked down a plastic box of metal coat hangers, which scattered over the floor.

'What are we doing?' Isaac said.

Crying brought out the puffiness in his face. Albert hauled out a bedside table, then flipped a blue mattress, launching fireworks of dust in the gathering light. Next he got hold of a camping gas stove and dragged it out, making a *ga-ga-ga* juddering noise on the concrete. Behind that he found a plastic case that had the word *Blitz* on it. It was normally kept in the barn, but Albert knew his mother had stashed it here so that none of the revellers would find it.

'Where I'm going in Northumbria,' Isaac said, 'there's a big slide.'

'You're going to be so stupid when you grow up.'

He brought out the hard case and laid it on the floor. Clicking the latches, the case opened, showing a tin of charges, cleaning solution, two brushes and the bolt gun, which looked like a switched-off light saber. Isaac knew what it was because together they had practised putting holes in the Yellow Pages.

The bass-heavy music went through another build-up. Albert

didn't understand how these morons could get excited again and again. Every time, just when it seemed like something really was going to happen, it carried on with the same damp thump.

Albert picked up the gun and unscrewed the cap. He took a charge from the tin, slotted it into the top with ease and put the cap back on. He pulled up the firing pin, which looked like the top of a sports water bottle.

'What's the plan, Alb?'

Along the bottom shelf on one wall were the recently kilned creations. A stoneware goat looked like a square battery on legs. Albert held the base of the bolt pistol to the goat and squeezed the red trigger. The charge exploded and the model shattered in a satisfying way, tiny chits of clay falling on to the floor. It seemed easy now, and he didn't know how he had been so weak with Belona. Isaac laughed, involuntarily. A wisp of smoke moved across the room. The smell was fierce. Albert was already reloading.

'Nice one!' Isaac said, and he stood up and pointed at a delicate milk jug. 'My mum made that one – get it!'

Albert pulled up the pin, aimed and the thing exploded, the noise reverberating in the small room. Isaac asked for a go.

'Shut up, Isaac,' he said, and kicked him in the knee.

Isaac sat again and held his leg with both hands. Albert reloaded and, one handed now, squeezed the trigger and shattered quite a pro-looking hen. It wasn't possible to see the bolt go in and out – it just looked like things were exploding at his command. Albert's shoulder hurt, from the kickback. The smoke on the inside of the room wasn't yet as thick as the mist on the outside.

'What are you doing in there?' Marina's voice from outside. She tried the handle on the door. 'Let me in.'

'Do this one,' Isaac said, standing up again and pointing at a miniature punk rocker sitting in an armchair. Albert reloaded and held the gun to the man's head, managing to knock it clean off without damaging the body. The noise was loud, but they were used to loud noise. 'You're great, Albert.'

'Open this door now,' Marina said. Her voice sounded different from every other time Albert had heard her.

'You're my best friend,' Isaac said.

'You'll believe anything. We're not friends any more.'

'Alb.' Isaac put his hand on Albert's shoulder. 'It stinks in here!'

'Do you trust me?'

'Yes.'

'Open up *this minute!*' Marina said.

'Lie down then.'

'Okay.'

'Eyes and Albert! Enough messing around!' Her fist banging the door.

Isaac lay down on the concrete, legs together, arms at his side, coffin-ready. Albert put another cartridge in the gun, which was hot now. The light coming through the window was brightening and Albert had a shadow as he knelt at Isaac's feet.

More banging. She rattled the door handle again, harder. The shape of a head appeared at the grid of small windows set into the door which were too dirty to see through. A hand wiped the glass but couldn't clear it.

'I'm scared.'

Albert held the bolt gun with two hands. The last time he had held this gun, he had been unable to follow things through and he hated himself for that.

'Will you do everything I tell you to?'

'Yes.'

'Say "I'm a fucking idiot."'

'I am a fucking idiot.'

'Say "I dunno who my dada is."'

The tears were rolling out the sides of Isaac's eyes and down into his ears.

'I dunno who my dada is.'

'What are you *doing*?' Marina yelled.

He hovered the bolt gun at the sole of Isaac's left shoe. From where he was he could see inside Isaac's nostrils. Outside, Marina was calling for help.

Albert shuffled round on his knees. He had his hands one above the other and moved the base of the gun over the end of Isaac's toes, along the top of his foot, then followed his left shin to the kneecap, where he let it hover. He thought of the game with the electrified wire and the hoop and if you touch the wire you're dead.

'Let me in or I'll break this door down,' Marina said, and to Albert it didn't sound threatening. She wasn't believable any more.

'Tell me how it's going to end,' Albert said.

'I don't know.'

'Tell me.'

The witching hour used to be midnight but nowadays, Varghese said, you have to run a party to four in the morning before it can take on a mythic quality. It was 4.48 a.m., and if it weren't for the mist, it would have been full daylight, this time of year. Don was standing near the biofuel generator, ready to pull the plug. It was running on vegetable oil from Paco's Diner and the smell held the memory of a thousand glistening breakfasts. It was lucky that Don still didn't really like any music, because whatever this was, it was terrible. He was the oldest person he could see. Scattered across the yard were piles of shiny metal shells that he had learned were the by-product of nitrous, a drug he'd never heard of. Nearby, a couple were hard snogging on the ground, the boy's hand unselfconsciously cranked up her gore-soaked wedding gown. The mist made everywhere seem private. Varghese was wandering about filming people. He only seemed interested in the casualties, like the girl he was speaking to now, wearing animal slippers and a high-visibility jacket. Someone was yelling help and running through the mist, and Varghese immediately filmed the figure approaching. Don waited for the person to say 'Help, help, I'll die if I don't find a king-size Rizla' or whatever, but she didn't and it was Marina. Varghese tracked her. She grabbed Don's hand.

When they got there, there was the sound of Isaac's wailing, high like a kettle. Don couldn't see through the window. He wiped it with his sleeve, but the dirt was on the inside. Hunching slightly, he spoke to the rusty lock of the door.

'Albert, it's your father here. Are you and Isaac okay?'

There was a pause. When Albert finally spoke, his voice was quiet.

'I'm not okay.'

The key wasn't in the lock. Don peered through the keyhole. There was a wait as he listened to a throaty noise that, he realized, must have been Isaac. He knew he needed to say something but doubted that, after what had happened this morning, his son would want to listen to him. All Don could offer was that, on this occasion, he would remain present. 'Albert, your father's here for you.' That was all. His physical self. He put his ear to the keyhole as Albert spoke.

'Turns out Marina has no idea what's going to happen. Turns out she is actually an *idiot*, just like you always said.'

Marina stayed silent and just crouched down, her ear to the slatted wood. She showed no reaction. Don had to concede she achieved dignity.

'Dad?'

'I'm here.'

'I'm upset.'

Don could hardly hear his son's voice. 'I know you are.'

'What are you doing?' Albert said, with a note of distrust.

'What would you like me to do?'

'I don't know. Maybe something big.'

'Okay, good,' Don said, and he knew that, whatever he did, it ought to be something his son could see and hear, something permanent.

'Albert, how about I put my hand through one of these small windows?'

There was no sound for a long time, then an affirmative noise. Don stood back from the door, stepped forward without hesitation and put his fist through one of the twelve opaque beermat-sized windows. He went for the one just above the lock. He scraped the back of his knuckles and drew blood. The sound of glass on the concrete floor was pretty. He retracted his hand and peeked through the shattered mouth. The second time in one evening that punching seemed like the best option. The smell in the room was fierce. The key, he saw, was down on the floor next to Albert, who was holding the bolt gun, which was touching a boy's left temple, and the boy was Isaac, who was trying to stay perfectly still and quiet. Albert's eyes flicked across to his father at the window, and it was clear to Don that more was expected of him; he put his mouth to the broken window.

'Albert.'

'What?'

'I love you.'

'*I know.*'

'I realized I was wrong about not wanting you to go to school. You should go to school.'

Don had no nuance and was glad of it. Again there was a wait. It was probable that Albert kept expecting his father to say more, but he didn't.

'Why?' Albert said.

'You will have a great time and they will absolutely fucking love you.'

'Don't swear, please.'

Don was in some pain with his hand. It actually helped him concentrate.

'Those boys will be your friends. I think they were here tonight.'

'Which boys?'

'The quad-bike boys.'

'I didn't see them.'

'They came to see you. They'll come again.'

'Oh.'

Don paused, then said: 'And you'll be getting your own quad bike, is the other thing.'

Don's thinking mind, which he ignored, had a few things to say about the financial realities of this. A very long wait.

'I know what you're doing. You're buying my love.'

'Absolutely right. It's expensive.'

'Okay.'

Don focused on the bleeding hand.

'While you're at school, it'll be best for you to live in Mumbles with Uncle Patrick.'

'What does that mean?'

'It means you stay at his place during term-time.' He clenched and unclenched the hand. 'Those lads will be your friends. You will be ten minutes' walk or three minutes by quad from school.'

'Dad, what will you do?'

'I'm going to stay here and turn the big house into a youth hostel.'

It was a surprise to himself. It sounded okay. Marina was squinting at him.

'What about you and Mum?'

'She's going with you.'

'You should get divorced.'

'We will. I love you.'

'I know.'

Albert was now standing back by the shelves, grinding his eye socket with one fist and holding the bolt gun in the other. Isaac, still flat on his back, stretched his hand across and picked up the key, then crawled towards the door, army-style.

Marina listened for the key turning, and once it clicked she pulled back the door, swooped in and grabbed her son, picked him up at the armpits and, without a word, disappeared into the greyness with her boy silent in her arms. Don stepped into the pottery shed and closed the door before Varghese, who, he only now noticed, had followed them, could come in.

The floor was scattered with severed heads, legs, bits of architecture. Don walked up to the shelves and stood next to his son, who was now pointing the bolt gun at the Eiffel Tower.

'Will everything keep going for ever?'

'I believe so,' Don said.

At the far end of the shelf, there was a whole family of clay people that was supposed to be the Rileys. Some unremembered guest had made them as gifts, totems, voodoo dolls. Freya perversely obese, Kate with an ape's posture and Albert with massive biceps. Terrible likenesses.

'This is us,' Don said, and he pointed, dripping spots of blood on the concrete.

The model of his father was from the days when he had a beard. The artist had made it look as though the beard was just an extension of Don's skull.

Varghese filmed them through the broken window.

Albert took aim.

Kate was searching through the mist, checking the bodies in the grass here and there to see if they were her brother. Up until a few moments ago, she had been in the porch of a stranger's tent, finding that spliffs kept going out in her hand because she talked so much. She had been cheerily describing her parents' break-up to the strangers, and it had felt totally healthy and normal. The Hulk had been there too, getting off with a tall girl dressed as a peacock, and every time they really went for it, the girl lost one of her feathers. Eventually they'd snuck off together – and Kate was fine with that.

But then, someone else had talked about the amazing performance art that had taken place, earlier in the night: the little boy, up on the roof, who gave a hilarious speech about how the world was going to end, which was all choreographed to coincide with the mist and that song by Prince, and how fucking great it was, and now Kate was outside, looking for him.

In the live music yurt, a man was either doing a very downbeat, a cappella, unplugged version of 'Help!' by The Beatles or he was genuinely asking for assistance. She had to sidestep the stumbling shapes that emerged from the grey. She found the remaining heavy drinkers still going, swaying riskily next to the fire.

Father and son were in bed now, propped up against the headboard. Albert was fully clothed and staring at the mist pressing its face against the window. Somehow he didn't feel tired. Don had his foot up on two pillows.

'Isaac's going to leave as soon as the mist clears. I don't want him to.'

At the bottom of the bed, the duvet was ickily warm from the previous residents, a couple who his father had kicked out but were still audible in Kate's room. They heard the woman make encouraging noises – 'That's it, come on, that's it' – as though running alongside a dog. The music was still physically loud, removed of all melody by the walls of the house, just the bottom end pushing through.

'Is the mist clearing?' Albert said. 'It looks like it's clearing.'

He felt his father's hand on his shoulder.

'Albert, I wanted to tell you how proud I am of you about Belona – you did what I couldn't.'

Albert slowly shook his head and watched the window. 'I didn't do it.' It took Don a little while to realize what he meant.

'Well, in that case, I'm even prouder of you. For your humanity. I know I've said it a few times now, but I love you very much.'

That didn't cheer Albert up. The bass hit the right frequencies for the roof beams and dust snowed on them.

'I think you'll feel better after a sleep.'

Don took a single sheet of toilet paper off the roll on the bedside table. A little plume rose as the perforations tore. He folded the sheet five times, spat on it, squidged it down with his fingers until it was about the size and shape of a thirteen-amp fuse. Then, turning his body and holding the top of Albert's head with one hand, he squeezed the now grey-looking plug into Albert's ear. The ear was filthy, as was the rest of him, and the plug had to displace some grit on the way in.

Albert's mouth tightened. Don tamped another bit of paper into shape and let a glob of spit fall. He held Albert's head the same way a hairdresser does, turned it and dabbed the block inside. Don gave him the *Are you okay?* hand signal the way deep-sea divers do. Because he knew it was what his father needed to see, Albert made the signal back at him.

The earplugs meant he could hear his own heart. It was keeping pace with the kick drum.

Up at the yard, Kate found Varghese organizing a survivors' photograph, herding drunks and wreckheads to stand in front of the house. The only person still dancing to the DJ was the DJ. The sun was beginning to burn off the mist.

Kit Lintel, who she only now saw for the first time, was practising the art of movement up on the flat roof in the first rays of dawn. He was sizing up a jump from the lip of the stand-alone bath, though she couldn't see where he was planning to land.

In the house, she searched the schoolroom and kitchen, but still no sign of Albert. Upstairs, his room was empty. In hers there was a couple going at it on her bed, the slick hairs on the man's back reminiscent of seaweed when the tide's out.

She finally found her brother in her father's room, awake, sitting up with pillows behind his back, knees pulled up. He had earplugs that stuck out like little cartoon explosions. He was still in his naval jacket, staring at the clearing mist. Next to him was her father, also propped up but without the earplugs and asleep, head slumped forward, eyes fractionally open, in close imitation of a man who has been shot.

Albert watched a small patch of blue sky that was just visible through the top-right window. Outside there was the noise of old-skool jungle being rewound and rewound and rewound.

Looking round, Kate saw her father had left deliberately odd-looking gaps where her mother's pictures had been – untanned rectangles of wall – and the bookcase without her novels had a bar-code quality to it. Finally, someone managed to get the music off, and from outside she heard cheers and wolf-whistles and just one disappointed-sounding person. The quiet seemed to help Albert, who looked at her for the first time. She sat on the side of the bed and tried to think what they could do.

She remembered something and got on her stomach to crawl across the duvet. They used to do this. Going over her father's shins, but not waking him, she slid off the side of the bed, landed loudly on the floor, then came crawling back underneath it, kicking with her legs, before appearing head-first on Albert's side and sitting back beside him. 'Remember that game? Sandworms!'

'You're trying to cheer me up.'

'That's right.'

'Please don't.'

She brought out her tickling mandibles.

'Clack clack,' she said.

He shook his head. She stopped. She tried to think what else there was. Her mind was not agile.

'Tick.' She wasn't expecting to say it.

'Don't. Not now.' He went back to watching the window, his gaze now fixed, as if he had decided which direction he wanted his eyes to point and was happy to stick with that for ever.

'Tick,' she said.

He had gone for a slightly raised angle, one you might use to read a departures board.

'Tick,' she said, and she held out her hand.

In the communal bathroom, weak sunlight came through the misted glass. There were gels, travel-portion shampoos and 2-in-1s on the window ledge. Albert leaned back against the door, staring across the room at the window's textured glass.

'I can't do this,' he said.

She switched on the shower and it sizzled. '*We have* water pressure.'

It wasn't clear to her if this was the right thing to do, but it would be worse to back down now.

'I'm racing you,' she said and, hopping, took off her plimsoles. 'I'm winning.'

She caught sight of herself in the mirror and realized that she no longer resembled a panda. Her pupils were sinkholes and her face paint was cracking along previously unnoticed wrinkle lines. Her panda had smudged to a ghoul. She went to her brother and undid the gold buttons down the front of the weird naval jacket he'd been wearing. *We're kids*, she thought. *This is fine.* Pushing the coat over his shoulders, she tugged it down his arms and let it drop on the floor. He watched tentacles of steam creep out of the cubicle, frothing around the edges of the shower curtain. She got down and untied his shoes. He rolled the back of his head against the door. She lifted each of his feet in turn and yanked his shoes off. His striped socks were like second skin; she peeled them off, thinking nothing of the smell. There were motes of sock fluff all over his feet and ankles.

'Come on. Do you want to lose?' she said, not sounding convincing.

'I'm too old for this.'

Tiny particles moving around each other started to fill the room. She sat on the bench and pulled off her tights. He watched steam lit by spotlights.

'We'll say that this is the magic portal,' she said, signalling to the cubicle, 'and once we step inside, then we've been chosen, you and I, and when we step out, the world will be brand new, and we're linked for ever, no matter what happens, we're the survivors, and everyone else, even if they don't realize it, they're dead, and there's you and me together, alive, in a world of zombies, and I'm sorry but Mum and Dad will have to die too because once we step in the chamber it's just me and you and that's it, okay?'

'I'm too old.'

His teeth were chattering, though it wasn't cold.

'Put your hands in the air, motherfucker,' she said.

He shook his head but put his hands up anyway.

'Come on, the portal's almost ready.'

She pulled his jumper and T-shirt up over his head in one. He was textured with bumps and she could see the shadows of his ribs through his skin.

'You'd better hurry up,' she said, and pulled her own T-shirt off.

Albert slid to the floor and pulled his knees up to his chest as she started to unbutton her black skirt. Her arms were painted black like sleeves, but her shoulders were bare and the paint made a V down her chest. Albert watched her and was glad that her face paint made her unrecognizable. Just a pair of weird eyes floating in a grey-black mess. He pushed himself into the corner of the room.

They were blurred, becoming smudges.

'We go in together, you and I – the world switches off and on, returns to factory settings, and when we come out we pretend everything's normal despite the bodies everywhere.'

He watched her hands work at her bra clip, which was at the front, in the middle of her chest.

'Prepare for doom,' she said.

He put his head down against his kneecaps and covered his ears.

'This is it,' she said. 'You can put an end to everything by stepping inside. It's like *Stars in Their Eyes* but tonight, Matthew, we're going to be the last two humans on earth in a world of corpses, cyborgs and the brain-dead.'

'I think you should stop. That would be for the best.'

'The por-tal is clo-sing,' she said, and she turned away from him.

He saw a bra drop to the floor but told himself it was not his sister's because this person was not his sister. A name floated back to him: Sheila La Fanu.

'I'm absolutely fine and need no more help,' he said.

Out the window, proper sunlight was coming through. He saw her feet turn to face him. Water particles had reached every corner of the room. They started to dissolve. She was tugging at him, pulling at his armpits, trying to get him up.

'Come on,' she said.

He didn't want to. He didn't want to. He looked. The gaze of her nipples, their slightly raised stare, the same raised angle as his father's jaw whenever he was about to say something important.

'I'm too old,' he said, and he put his head back down again between his knees, squeezing the side of his skull as hard as he could. He didn't like what was happening to him.

'I'm about to win,' she said, 'and then you'll be dead, you'll be a zombie like the rest of them. Do you want to be a zombie?'

She charged into the cubicle, yelling 'The change! The change!' as she did so. Throwing her head back, she spun in circles; the water running off her was the colour of late-stage dishwater. Taking the shower head off its hook, she fired it at him, where he was sitting. She kept firing and making machine-gun noises.

'Come on, wuss bag!' she said, stepping out of the cubicle with a bottle of shampoo. She squirted contraband on to his head.

The water was hot enough to be painful. Hot water meant that the photovoltaic cells were working, which meant that the sun was shining, which meant that there was no mist, which meant that Isaac had gone.

'Welcome to the land of the living,' she said, and more shampoo landed on him. She stood above him, using the shower head as a watering can. 'We made it and I love you more than anything.'

'You've taken drugs,' he said.

His eyes stung but he felt awake. He rubbed his face hard. After a while, he achieved a lather. The water was running under the door and out into the hall.

'You're changing colour,' she said.

'I know.'

Stretching the lead taut, she handed him the shower head and he fired it at the centre of his own face, from close range.

Barefooted, they stepped out of the bathroom and into the hall where water had run partly down the stairs, only halted by the slumped dead body of a man on the landing. He was painted to look like a full English breakfast. Next to him was a dead girl, her body turned blue. Albert was beyond tiredness and into the place that follows, the place that feels like you are watching a film of yourself. His sister had a towel round her waist and a T-shirt on and remnants of black paint along her jawline like a fashionable beard.

'Check for survivors,' she said.

Albert's jeans dripped four tracks on the carpet as he walked to Janet's room and pushed back the door. The curtains were closed but glowing at the edges. Two bodies were on the bed, arranged in crime-scene outline poses. He couldn't make out their faces. He tried the light switch, then a stand-up lamp, but the power in the whole house was gone. Going closer, he saw that it was Janet and Patrick who had passed away, fully clothed. Albert observed that his hand had been under her shirt when they died.

He turned to look back down the corridor and mouthed the word *dead* at his sister. She checked in Don's room and confirmed, by miming her own throat being cut, that he was a goner too.

They both checked their own bedrooms. Whatever Kate saw in hers, she didn't like. In Albert's room, there was a familiar-looking boy whose flesh was putrid green and, beneath the duvet, it was clear that some animal was eating him; the sounds he made as he died were horrendous. There were various long feathers on the floor next to the bed, which must have been torn off the animal during the struggle.

Light was coming in a tractor beam through the round window above the stairs. They carefully stepped over the bodies on the landing and went down to the hallway. In the schoolroom there was a jigsaw of corpses, laid out amateurishly, some in half-open body bags, some loose on the sofas with their hands dragging on the floor. Children's clothes were tangled in the teeth of the loom. The smell was what Albert expected mass death to smell like.

In the kitchen there was blood on the chopping board and evidence of someone having decomposed, right there and then, into a pool of pungent sludge, half in the sink and half running down the cupboard door. The fridge was open and had been ransacked by scavengers. Also, something was cooking in the oven, but Albert did not dare look.

Out in the yard, the light felt thick. On the bench there was a wedding dress stained with red. Three bodies were top-tailed in the shade of the tarpaulin. On the gravel, one of the zombies had written I CUT MYSELF QUITE BA in blood but had died before it could finish the message. Near the workshop someone had drawn a cock and balls using vegetarian sausages. Scattered in piles here and there were shiny metal shells – used ammunition, most likely, it seemed to Albert. The slanted light gave the henge of Portaloos long shadows. One of them had been pushed over on to its door. They would stay like that for millennia. An empty pan had been tipped up next to the apple tree, staining the soil with blood, into which armies of ants and worms were amassing. The static of a burgeoning fly population. Apples rotting on the ground.

'Just you and me then, Albert.'

Kate went to the decks and held up the last ever record. Its label was blank, white, and Albert thought that if the world's ending had wiped all human music, then in all honesty, after tonight, he wasn't bothered to see it go. Just then the hens made a noise and it was good to know that at least the animals had survived. Somewhere, far off, the guttural yell of other beasts, unknown. Thin clouds filtered the sunlight and there was a bonfire smell. He and Kate stood shoulder to shoulder in the middle of the yard, waiting, with the sun on their closed eyelids. Eventually, they heard footsteps on the gravel behind them. They turned around to see their mother – or what looked like their mother – puffy and newly arisen, carrying a glass pint of orange juice and wearing men's shorts and an unfamiliar jumper.

'Stay where you are, bro,' Kate said. 'I know what this looks like, but it's not really her. It is not even a *her*. Sometimes the body keeps moving after death.'

Kate walked slowly forward, then sidestepped round, coming behind the figure who resembled their mother and covering its eyes with her hands.

'Remember, we can't be sentimental,' Kate said, then she leaned in close to its ear and said a few things that Albert couldn't hear – presumably last rites – before letting go and taking a step back. 'It'll die down any second now. The last few spasms.'

She was right. The body immediately fell down on one knee. The glass bottle dropped from its hand but didn't smash. Its mouth dropped slightly and the body keeled, falling sideways, silently mouthing 'ow' as its head hit the ground. The body jerked a bit, its feet knocking the pint bottle, which rolled further away, and it kind of nuzzled the gravel, its mouth ajar, close to a cigarette butt, little bits of dirt sticking to the side of its face and then one more jolt and it stopped, eyes still open.

'Sorry you had to see that.' Kate stood astride the body and spoke up to the sky. 'Our parents are gone and we are orphans in a barren and ruined world.'

Albert came to look down at the body. He waited for it to move or twitch or for a little smile at the side of the mouth.

'It's over,' Kate said. 'Just you and me and one pretty major clear-up operation. Corpses for compost.'

The body's mud-covered hands looked like they had been dead for centuries.

'I'm sad,' Albert said.

'Me too.'

'*You're* not sad. You're loving this. I'm *actually* sad.'

'Would our parents have wanted their passing to be a miserable affair or a celebration?'

'A miserable affair.'

'Do you want to close its eyes?'

The body had not blinked or visibly breathed and it was impressive.

'Not really,' Albert said, but he knelt down anyway. 'Why do they close the eyes?'

'To show who's living and who's not.'

He reached forward with his thumbs and softly shut them.

Kate picked up the body's arm then let go and it slapped on the ground as it landed, deadweight. Albert took hold of its wrist and felt around for a pulse but couldn't find one. The body actually hadn't moved or done anything apart from looking sincerely dead for some time, and this was no longer fun.

Albert put his ear to its mouth and listened for breathing.

'We don't have time for your soppy bullshit, Albert. Take the legs.'

'Okay, stop now please, Mum.'

'You'll feel better once it's on the pyre,' Kate said, taking both arms, preparing to drag the body.

'Very good. Joke's over.'

His sister waited for him.

'You can stop now,' he said.

The body stayed still. Kate stood there waiting. Albert shook his head and looked around. Then he took hold of both legs and the body opened her eyes.

Acknowledgements

Thanks: Matt Cape, Laura Emmerson, Ally Gipps, Gregg Morgan, Jeane Mowatt and Amhurst Community; Agnes, Emma, Julian and Reuben Orbach, Paul Mitchell, Laura Stobbart and Brithdir Mawr; Francesca Alberry, Simon Brooke, Ahmed Murad, Alastair O'Shea, Dylan O'Shea and Burbage Farm; Tobias Jones, Francesca Lenzi and Pilsdon Community; Savannah Lambis, Emily Kitchin, Rob Kraitt, Yasmin McDonald, Linda Shaughnessy and Donald Winchester at A. P. Watt; Matt Clacher, Anna Kelly, Juliette Mitchell, Anna Ridley and Joe Pickering at Penguin; Ryan Doherty at Random House US; Megan Bradbury, Seth Fishman, Joel Stickley and Caroline Pretty; Tim Clare, Chris Hicks, John Osborne, Ross Sutherland, Luke Wright and Homework; Priya and Nick Thirkell; Mum, Dad, Leah, Anna and Marc Hare. Special thanks: Noah Eaker, Georgia Garrett and Simon Prosser. Special thanks and special apologies: Martha Orbach. Extra special thanks: Maya Thirkell.

JOE DUNTHORNE

SUBMARINE

Meet Oliver Tate. Convinced that his father is depressed and his mother is having an affair with her capoeira teacher, he embarks on a hilariously misguided campaign to bring the family back together. Meanwhile, he is also trying to lose his virginity – before he turns sixteeen – to his pyromaniac girlfriend Jordana. Will Oliver succeed in either aim? Submerge yourself in *Submarine* and find out.

'A richly amusing tale of mock GCSEs, sex, death and challenging vocabulary'
Time Out

'Perfectly pitched . . . Dunthorne can make you laugh like you did during double physics on a wet Wednesday afternoon' *Observer*

'Brilliant, laugh-out-loud enjoyable . . . the sharpest, funniest, rudest account of a periodically troubled teenager's coming-of-age since *The Catcher in the Rye*' *Independent*

SUBMARINE IS NOW AN ACCLAIMED FILM BY RICHARD AYOADE

He just wanted a decent book to read ...

Not too much to ask, is it? It was in 1935 when Allen Lane, Managing Director of Bodley Head Publishers, stood on a platform at Exeter railway station looking for something good to read on his journey back to London. His choice was limited to popular magazines and poor-quality paperbacks – the same choice faced every day by the vast majority of readers, few of whom could afford hardbacks. Lane's disappointment and subsequent anger at the range of books generally available led him to found a company – and change the world.

'We believed in the existence in this country of a vast reading public for intelligent books at a low price, and staked everything on it'
Sir Allen Lane, 1902–1970, founder of Penguin Books

The quality paperback had arrived – and not just in bookshops. Lane was adamant that his Penguins should appear in chain stores and tobacconists, and should cost no more than a packet of cigarettes.

Reading habits (and cigarette prices) have changed since 1935, but Penguin still believes in publishing the best books for everybody to enjoy. We still believe that good design costs no more than bad design, and we still believe that quality books published passionately and responsibly make the world a better place.

So wherever you see the little bird – whether it's on a piece of prize-winning literary fiction or a celebrity autobiography, political tour de force or historical masterpiece, a serial-killer thriller, reference book, world classic or a piece of pure escapism – you can bet that it represents the very best that the genre has to offer.

Whatever you like to read – trust Penguin.